ROSEMARY AND THYME

"And No Birds Sing"

BRIAN EASTMAN
with
REBECCA TOPE

First edition published in Great Britain in 2004 by
Allison & Busby Limited
Bon Marche Centre
241-251 Ferndale Road
London SW9 8BJ
http://www.allisonandbusby.com

A catalogue record for this book is available from
the British Library.

10 9 8 7 6 5 4 3 2 1

ISBN 0 7490 8341 7

Printed and bound in Great Britain by
Bookmarque Ltd, Croydon, Surrey

BRIAN EASTMAN heads one of the UK's leading independent production companies, Carnival Films, and has produced a wide variety of TV programmes and feature films including Agatha Christie's *'Poirot'*, 'Jeeves and Wooster', 'Shadowlands' and 'Traffik'. He created, and produces, 'Rosemary and Thyme' for ITV.

Chapter One

It was a chilly day for gardening, the wind blowing in from the east, bringing heavy clouds that sprinkled drizzle on Laura's head every now and then. But she was not to be deterred. Nothing worked so well as digging out buttercups and putting in the last of the annual bedding plants, when it came to having a good long Think.

Her hands worked automatically, as her mind whirled. And yet, she could not have said precisely what it was that bothered her, what it was she needed to think *about*. She had woken early that morning, to a soaring dawn chorus, and a very nasty sense of foreboding.

Beside her, Nick had grunted and huffed in his heavy not-quite-snoring routine. Nick, who had forgotten their twenty-seventh wedding anniversary the previous week, and seemed to be still trying to appease her for his omission. At least his sickly smiles and heavy sighs were presumably his own odd way of saying sorry. Not that Laura set much store by such rituals. She recalled that they had both forgotten their eighth – or was it ninth? – and they'd laughed about it, blaming the demands of two young children. That now seemed like a very *very* long time ago.

In any case, Nick had gone out that day and bought her a pair of rather sweet turquoise earrings to add to her enormous collection. Laura had a thing about earrings.

But today there was something in the air that she could almost smell and taste, like a gathering storm. Working rhythmically along the front of the big border at the side of the house, she tried to capture the reason for her sense of unease. Something had felt awkward for a few weeks now, although she hadn't liked to admit it to herself. The atmosphere in the house had changed, so that she took every chance she could to get outside amongst the plants.

One reason could be the friction with her daughter Helena, which seemed to have got a lot worse in the past few weeks. Clever creative Helena, who never seemed to be quite relaxed in her mother's company, never able to accept a compliment as it was intended, or advice of any sort. Laura habitually felt as if the ground was strewn with eggshells whenever she tried to talk to her daughter. Her poor head had been metaphorically bitten off more times than she could count. Like any mother, Laura tended to blame herself for this state of affairs – but try as she might, she couldn't think what she'd done to deserve the frosty treatment she'd received last Sunday.

On top of that was the generalised feeling that her life was rushing through her fingers, and she wasn't making the most of it. Other women of her age had gone out and found a job the moment the youngest child started school. They'd taken Open University degrees, or worked up a career ladder through initiative and flair and ended up as Chief Executive of a chain of High Street shops. Although far from being lazy, Laura had given her time to committees and charity coffee mornings. She had been one of those tireless women who keep society going, without recognition or payment, and now she was growing jaded with it all. Her only genuine source of pride was the fact that her garden was the envy of the entire street.

And that, she concluded, was all she had to worry about: the uneasy relationship with Helena and her failure to make a successful career for herself. She sat back on her heels and surveyed her afternoon's work. The border was immaculate. Not a weed to be seen. Other people might use chemicals, or fancy gadgets or a paid gardener. She just squatted down and set to work with bare hands and a small garden fork. Her father would be proud of her, she caught herself thinking.

Stiffly, she went to the shed to tidy away the tools,

and make sure there were no more seedlings waiting to be planted out. In a little while, it would be time to put the casserole in, and catch the news on the radio. Nick would be home in an hour or so. With his job, you could never be quite sure when he'd show up – which had been one big reason why Laura had never felt able to find paid employment for herself, or embark on a course of study. Even when Matthew and Helena had been at the secondary school, she had wanted to be sure that at least one parent was around to check on their homework and enforce rules on bedtime. When Nick was working on an urgent case, doing door-to-door enquiries, or ploughing through hundreds of computer listings, he might easily be out until midnight. And his compensatory time off was never at a moment when he might have come in useful.

Suddenly, she heard the front door bang shut, while she was still putting the fork away in the shed. She looked at her watch in disbelief. Surely it couldn't be Nick home already? He was almost never early. Hurriedly, she went round to the back door, expecting to see him in the kitchen, where he always went on first arriving home. He had his own special chair in there, where he would sit with the evening paper and a mug of tea for a few unwinding minutes.

The kitchen was empty, but she heard a thud from upstairs. 'Nick?' she called. 'Is that you?'

An answering grunt did nothing to explain why he had come back an hour before the usual time, but at least it sounded as if he was alive and well. She spent a few minutes washing her hands, and turning the oven on. She had made the casserole earlier in the day; now it just needed to be heated through. Then she went up to the bedroom to see what was going on. Her mind was a complete blank, as she slowly mounted the stairs. But her stomach was churning, and her hand on the banister was damp. When a husband of twenty-seven years did something completely outside the normal routine, the first reaction was anxiety. She didn't even have any questions to ask him – at least none she could put into words. Her whole self was simply one large question mark.

He was taking clothes out of the wardrobe when she went into the room. Their oldest suitcase was lying open on the bed. She looked at it for a long minute. It still had an airline label on the handle, from when they'd gone to Rome together ten years earlier. They'd spent a week there, and shared the case, filling it with souvenirs and Italian wine when they came home.

'You could use the matching cases Matthew gave us for our Silver Wedding,' she said.

He turned to stare at her. 'What?'

She shook her head. 'Never mind. Where are you going, Nick?'

He concentrated on the three ties he held looped over his fingers. Then he put one of them back on the rail inside the wardrobe door. 'I'm moving out,' he said.

'My goodness.' Laura's insides felt as if some icy waterfall was sluicing through them, drowning liver and lungs and making them numb. But already she could feel a warmer trickle of rage starting from somewhere very deep. 'What brought this on?'

'There's no need to be sarcastic. It isn't easy, you know.'

'No, I can see you're having trouble deciding which ties to take with you. You'd better give it plenty of thought. The others'll be off to Oxfam in the morning.'

'Laura…'

'Yes?'

'I've fallen in love, you see.' His big head drooped forward, and he glanced at her under his eyebrows. He looked for all the world like a dog in disgrace.

'I see. Bully for you.'

'You've every right to be angry.'

'Yes, I know I have.'

'But she's so sweet, so lovely. Clever, as well. I can't pass up this chance of happiness. You'll be all right. You've always been strong. I've been going through hell, these last few weeks, wondering what to do.'

So that was why the nights had felt so odd. She'd been lying next to a man who'd been secretly going through hell. And she had never even glimpsed the truth.

'Why didn't you tell me sooner? What am *I* supposed to do?' The rage had become mixed with a spurt of panic. Without her husband, who would she be?

'I couldn't face you. I thought I might get the packing done while you were downstairs or in the garden.'

'That was rather stupid. And cowardly.'

'I know.'

'What'll the children say?'

'I've told the children. They're being very supportive.'

'Of you? *You* need support, do you?'

'Of us both. Well, Matthew, anyway. He's always going to be there for you.'

'And Helena's taken your side, has she?'

He didn't reply to that, but rummaged at the back of the wardrobe for the cord jacket he never wore.

'Will you at least tell me who she is. I have to hand it to you, I never suspected a thing. At least...' Without warning, some barrier gave way in her mind, and all the little clues that she had so steadfastly refused to notice came to the fore. Phone-calls that Nick seemed to end very abruptly when she came into the room. Changes in work patterns that hadn't had any of the usual explanations. A midweek conference, during which the hotel apparently couldn't locate Nick in his assigned room, when Laura tried to phone him. And a definite falling-off of marital relations in bed.

'She's called Emily. You've never met her.'

'Is she divorced?'

'No. She's never been married.'

'Children?'

'No, no. For heaven's sake.' He shook his head like a cornered bull. 'Stop asking all these questions, will you.'

'Just one more. How old is she, Nick?'

He wouldn't meet her eyes, but she saw the flush spread across his cheeks. He didn't have to answer the question for Laura to get the picture.

'That young? You bloody rotten swine.'

'She's mature for her age. She's always been very advanced.'

'Always? How long have you known her?'

'Well, most of her life. She's Graham Sinclair's daughter.'

Laura thought she was going to be sick. Ghastly inferences were rushing into her mind. Nick hurriedly averted them.

'No, it's not like that. What do you think I am? Look, she's twenty-three. All this started four or five months ago. She came to the Christmas dinner dance. The one you missed because you had that awful cold.'

'I remember her,' Laura said slowly. 'She was at the dinner dance the year before, as well. Thin, with a big mouth.'

'I didn't think you'd remember,' Nick said gloomily.

'Well I do. And you can probably guess what I think about it.' But thinking wasn't the problem. It was the feelings of revulsion, despair, betrayal that were already overwhelming her. When she had time to really think about it, they could only get worse.

'I'll be out of your way in a few minutes.' He left the room, and she realised he'd gone to collect razor and toothbrush from the bathroom. She looked at the suitcase on the bed, still less than half full. What else would he be taking, when he started this new life with a girl the age of their own daughter? Nick had never been much of a reader, never had hobbies or played any sports. His work had been his life, and nobody could deny that he was a good copper. He'd habitually discussed police cases with Laura, treating her like the colleague she had once been, many years before. Between them they had kept abreast of change and weathered countless storms. Over the years, it had been an assumption between them that the horrible things people did to each other were simply part of life's tapestry, and it wasn't worth getting upset about it. Justice was not always done, victims were often damaged forever, and criminals seldom changed their ways. Despite all that, there were frequent satisfactions as well as some laughs.

And there were the intimate friendships. Most police work involved officers going around in pairs, and although the pairings shifted, and were not always harmonious, they could lead to strong feelings of loyalty and mutual support. Graham Sinclair, father of the seductive Emily, had never been paired with Nick. This, at least, was a relief to Laura. Graham was nearing retirement, divorced, with a barely-concealed drink problem. He was like a policeman in a gritty crime novel, dogged and basically decent, but with a morose manner that alienated most people. The only thing he ever seemed to talk about, when Laura had met him at various functions, was his precious daughter. How, she wondered, was he going to react to what had happened?

'Does Graham know about this?' she asked Nick when he came back into the room.

'Not yet. He isn't going to like it.'

'He'll probably smash your head in.' Laura found this idea highly appealing. 'Maybe I'll phone him.'

'I should never have told you who she is.'

'Trust me, Nick – I would have found out. I might be sick of the sight of you, but I do at least want to know the identity of my replacement in your life.'

'Look, Lolo, if I could have made this any easier for you…'

'Don't call me that!' His use of her pet name was like a kick in the gut. Why couldn't he have realised that for himself?

He finished his packing, and lugged the case downstairs. It had been heavy even when empty. Laura followed, fighting to maintain control. She could all too clearly imagine herself clinging to his ankles as he headed for the door, screaming and pleading with him to stay. Letting him go with her own dignity intact was suddenly the only thing that mattered. Fighting for control, she turned to the hall table, fiddling with the things lying on it. One was a letter that had arrived that morning for Helena.

'You'll be seeing Helly, will you?' she said in a dull tone. 'If so, you can give her this.'

He gazed at it blankly. 'What is it?'

'I know the writing – don't you?' She waved it under his face and he shook his head without properly looking at it. 'It's from Sam and Vickie. A birthday card, I expect. They won't have her new address. Knowing Sam, there'll be money in it.'

Nick took the letter, and pushed it into a pocket. 'Right,' he nodded, turning away from her.

'You're going to regret this,' she said to his back, as he opened the front door. 'Believe me, Nick – in the long run you'll regret this far *far* more than I will.'

He did not reply; nor did he turn round for a last look. Laura held her breath. Let him think she didn't care, that she could manage quite well without him, that her contempt had instantly withered any love she might have felt for him. That was surely better than pathetically begging him to change his mind. Already she knew that nothing could ever be the same between them again, even if he did turn back at the last moment. He had killed some vital spark inside her.

He took the car, which was only to be expected, but it felt like a final twist of the knife. Laura wanted to scream after him, to demand how she was supposed to manage, what she was meant to do. Instead she went into the kitchen and sat down, trying to quell the wild beating of her heart. Then she realised that the oven was still on, and got up mechanically to turn it off. She looked out of the window at the back garden, and pointlessly inspected the corners of the room for cobwebs. At last she sat down again. When she reached out for a spoon, just to have something to hold, she noticed her hand was shaking.

It was still not quite six o'clock, still not the time Nick would normally get home. Perhaps that strange man who had just driven away had been an impostor, somebody only pretending to be her husband, and in a minute the real Nick would walk in, whistling and wanting his mug of tea.

But as she sat there, watching the rays of the setting sun stream across the room, highlighting the motes dancing so carelessly in the air, nobody came through the front door. It was almost dark before she got up, and that was only because she had to go to the loo.

The downstairs toilet had nothing of Nick's in it. Even the calendar had been given to Laura by the woman who did her hair. *If I sit in here for the rest of my life, I need never admit he's gone* she thought to herself. And when she came out again, the thought extended to a grim awareness that there were signs of Nick in every other part of the house. The barometer in the hall that he used to tap every morning; the pressure cooker in the kitchen that he used every time he cooked anything; the numerous items of his clothing sitting in the washing basket, ready to go back into the drawers upstairs.

The bedroom was entirely unbearable, so she crawled fully clothed into the spare bed, at nine o'clock, and lay awake until two in the morning. She thought about Nick as he had been when she first met him. She thought about how kind he had been when she had the babies, and every time she'd been ill since then. She lingered over the moments when he had been a thoughtful and attentive partner, going beyond what most women might have expected. She clung to the knowledge that it had been a good marriage for at least twenty-six of the twenty-seven years. She refused to fall into the trap of rewriting history, retrospectively turning everything to dust and ashes. If it had collapsed now, then that was terrible, and she was as frightened as she was hurt and angry, but it did not reduce her whole life to rubble. And she did not blame herself. If her sin had been to gain some weight and become rather too fond of her garden, then she couldn't find any real cause for self-reproach in that. She had never looked at another man, never nagged or criticised, never wasted money or taken to drink. All she had done was to get older, and it clearly wasn't fair to blame her for that.

Just before she fell asleep, her churning thoughts turned to her son and daughter. What must they be thinking? Had Nick expressly told them not to speak to her until he'd given her the news? Would they be on the doorstep first thing in the morning, offering – what? Matthew would be concerned, affectionate, rueful. Matthew was the easy one, her firstborn and her favourite. Helena was much more complicated. It had felt, at times, as if there was no space for her in the family, with her exhausting noise and energy. Nick had made a much better job of loving her than Laura had. He had been so happy to have a daughter, while Laura had to admit to herself that she was quite content to settle for a son. Helena had always been competitive, judgemental and volatile. Nobody could work out where the creative streak came from, or what the best channel for it might be, but eventually she had settled for an Expressive Arts course at a Northern university, much to Laura's relief, and was now working as a sculptor in wood, making remarkable objects that Laura found both disturbing and uplifting.

If Helena were to turn up, she'd probably launch into a tirade starting, 'What did you do to upset poor old Dad?'

She slept for four hours, and woke feeling hot and crumpled. Everything came flooding back, as soon as she worked out which room she was in, and why she wasn't in her usual pyjamas.

Laura was a morning person, as befitted an enthusiastic gardener. Outside there were birds belting out their dawn mating songs, and the new-risen sun cast a pearly light through the uncurtained window. On the back of the bedroom door hung Nick's old dressing gown, that had been relegated to emergency use by visitors. Had he packed his new one, she wondered. The one she had given him only last Christmas.

She was thirsty, so much so that she had a headache from the dehydration. Nick had always brought her a cup of tea in the morning; she could almost hear the kettle boiling and the mugs clattering as he moved around the kitchen.

But he wasn't there. He was in bed with a thin young tart, lost to Laura forever. With a vivid insight, she understood that she would be having thoughts like these whenever she was in this house that she had shared with him for so long. She would wallow in self-pity and rage and humiliation every time she came across a reminder of him. The solution was therefore obvious. She would have to go somewhere else.

Quickly, she threw all the summer clothes she could find into the two matching suitcases that Matthew had given them for their Silver Wedding anniversary, along with a selection of earrings, shoes,

make-up and toiletries, two or three books and a travelling clock. Then she went for a hot bath. Lying in the
deep scented water, she tried to decide where she
would go to escape the painful memories. The answer
had just come to her when the phone rang.

She almost didn't answer it, but old habit forced
her out of the bath, wrapping herself in a big towel and
going downstairs to the phone in the hall.

'Mum?' came her son's voice. She could hear a
wealth of concern, hesitancy, embarrassment and love
in that single word.

'Matthew,' she said. 'I gather you know what's
going on.'

'He's told you then.'

'Last night. He's packed his bags and gone.'

'It's...I mean, I don't know...'

'That's okay, Matt. I don't expect you to console
me. It was nice of you to phone at all.'

'Come on, Ma. I gave Dad a deadline, actually. Told
him if he hadn't come clean with you by last night, I'd
tell you about it myself.'

'Does everybody know except me? Like the tired
old cliché about the wife being the last to find out.'

'Well...you know how it is. It's a small world in
this job. I could hardly avoid the stories going round,
so I tackled him about it.'

'Brave of you.'

'Not really. So – how are you feeling?'

Laura gave a harsh laugh. 'Very much as you'd
expect, probably. Furious, scared, sick, humiliated.
And quite a lot of other things.'

Matthew made a sound, part groan, part guffaw.
'You'll be okay, Mum. You're going to come out of this
with all flags flying.'

'Possibly. Meanwhile, I can't stay here. It's too full
of memories, associations. I don't need all that grief at
the moment.'

'So where will you go?'

'I think I'll try Sam and Vickie. They're our oldest friends, after all. Sam's so good keeping up with Helena, and he isn't likely to take sides. Vickie's less predictable, but I don't suppose she'll turn me away.'

'But they're *miles* away. I assume Dad took the car? How're you going to get there?'

'Taxi and train, dear. No problem at all. Let me give you the address, and you'll be able to contact me there for the next week or so.'

'Go on, then.'

She dictated the address and thanked him for his support. When she put the phone down, she actually did feel better for a few minutes.

Chapter Two

Rosemary Boxer packed her notes roughly into the battered briefcase. In order to get it closed, she had to ram hard, crushing the worksheets, course reports, personal profiles and memoranda that she always had to carry around with her. It was Friday morning and she had a meeting with three of her colleagues in five minutes' time.

It was a meeting that she had hoped she would never have to go to. For weeks now it had been suggested and resisted, argued and agonised over. But finally she and the others had felt they had little choice but to carry through a plan that had begun as a joke and had now become something more closely resembling a coup.

The four of them were all senior lecturers with a total of well over fifty years at Malmesbury between them. Rosemary herself had clocked up eighteen years. Tom Bishop and Deirdre Fellowes had both been there for twelve, and Fergus Cooke for ten. They had all joined the staff when it had been a plain and simple agricultural college, training young farmers, horticulturalists, florists and rural mechanics. It had known its place and ran on a system of collective responsibility that had worked to everybody's benefit. Rosemary had long been on friendly terms with the other three, sharing their incredulity as the college had turned into something none of them could recognise or approve.

It had applied for university status eight years earlier, and in the ensuing transformation process had managed to change virtually every aspect of its work. This in itself might not have been a bad thing. The world beyond the college was, after all, changing rapidly, and it was obviously important to keep pace. The problem lay in the senior management – specifically in Professor Julian Marchant, currently Principal of the college.

The meeting was to be in a remote wooden hut on the edge of the campus, despite Rosemary's preference for the local pub. 'Far too risky,' Tom Bishop had objected. 'What if somebody overhears us?' Originally the hut had been the office for the dairy farm attached to the college, but when the cows were all sold and the herdsman made redundant, the building fell into disuse. 'Nobody's going to find us there,' said Fergus, who from the start had enjoyed the cloak and dagger aspect of their activities.

Glancing around, Rosemary trotted through the handsome rhododendrons which had been planted to screen some of the more overtly agricultural areas of the college, and down the path towards the one-time dairy. She was last to arrive, which surprised nobody.

'We thought you weren't coming,' said Tom Bishop, a big man with red cheeks and a loud voice. His subject had been meat production and butchering in the early days. By a bizarre educational evolutionary process he now found himself lecturing on retail management and economics, which he hated.

'Nobody saw you, did they?' queried Deirdre, who had been nervous about their conspiracy all along.

'Don't worry,' Rosemary reassured her with a wink. 'I was careful to make sure I wasn't followed.'

Fergus Cooke, a bearded bohemian who belonged to a different place and a different time, laughed. 'You're enjoying this,' he accused her.

'Well, you've got to take your fun where you can find it,' said Rosemary. 'But I'm with you – you know that. We can't go on like this.'

'Okay,' Tom went on, as self-appointed Chairman. 'What are we going to do about it, then?'

After a short silence, Rosemary spoke. 'I can't see any other course of action apart from writing to the Chairman of the Governors. They still retain overall control, in spite of what Julian might think. We'll have to give chapter and verse, listing all Julian's mistakes and bad decisions. We could try and get more people on our side, but we haven't much time. If we're to get what we want, it's all got to be settled by the end of this term.'

'Nobody's going to risk joining us,' said Deirdre. 'Not after Lois Grayling's efforts on Julian's behalf.'

'Lois Grayling!' scoffed Fergus. 'What does she have to do with it?'

Tom answered him. 'She's been going round the staff arguing Julian's case. She's darn good at it, too. Making promises of salary reviews, timetable improvements, reduced class sizes. We might have heard it all before, but most of the others are too new to see through the garbage to how things really are.'

'But – does she know we're plotting against him, then?'

Tom shook his head. 'Not in any detail, no. But I don't think anybody could miss our general disgruntlement. My God – when I think of the mess that idiot's making of this place...'

'Okay, Tom,' Rosemary soothed him. 'Not now.'

Tom subsided, with a few huffs and puffs.

'So we're on our own, thanks to the deplorable Lois,' Rosemary summarised. 'Pity.'

'But we're the four most senior members of staff,' Fergus said. 'We've got more influence than any of the others, and if we act together, the Board's got to take notice of us. I vote we don't pull any punches, either. Julian's been a disaster on every front. Financial, as well as the rest. The place'll go bust if he carries on the way he is.'

'Lois says he's going after business tycoons for endowments,' Deirdre told the others. 'Former students, as well.'

Fergus laughed again. 'Some hope!' he scoffed. 'How many of our former students have any money to give away?'

'One or two, I think,' said Deirdre mildly.

Rosemary tried to keep them to the central point. 'So we're going all out to get rid of him, are we?' She looked from face to face. 'Demand his removal by the Governors, on the grounds of incompetence?'

The others all agreed, and the gang of conspirators spent the rest of the lunch break composing their letter to the Chairman of the Governors of the college. Rosemary agreed to prepare a final draft, and show it to them during the coming week, with a view to posting it by the next Friday.

Pausing to check her pigeonhole before her first lecture of the afternoon, Rosemary found an unexpected letter.

Hello, Rosemary – I wonder if you remember me? I was a mature student of yours about a hundred years ago (I think it's six, actually) – Daniel Kellaway. Though I say so myself, I seem to have done quite well since then, and you might have noticed one or two Kellaway Garden Centres around the place.

Anyway, the reason for this letter is to pick your brains about a difficulty I'm having with an avenue of trees here at Winterbourne Manor. I've got some health problems myself, which is why I can't do much on my own to investigate the cause of the trouble.

It would be great if you could come over sometime. I remember your lectures with great pleasure, even now, and I'd love to see you again. I hope everything's going well for you, and for Malmesbury. It was a fine college, with a wonderful collection of tutors and lecturers.

Give me a ring, and maybe we can arrange a date for your visit.

All best wishes
Daniel.

Rosemary indulged in a few moments of nostalgia, remembering Daniel and his unusual levels of enthusiasm for the subject. As a mature student, he had been notably more committed than most of his fellows, setting them an example that few had taken. He had been especially interested in the propagation of plants, with the breeding of new species the subject of his final year dissertation. He had been focused, friendly and a pleasure to teach.

The afternoon passed slowly, as Friday afternoons so often did, but at last she was packing up and preparing to draw the working week to a close. Unfortunately, she did not feel the sense of release that most of her colleagues doubtless did. It would certainly be good to get away from college for the weekend, with the looming crisis over Julian Marchant and the inevitable clashes arising from the letter she planned to send to the Governors; it would also be good to have a change of scene. But it wasn't going to be a *release*. Not when she was spending the next two days with her mother.

At eighty, Barbara Boxer was at least as fit as her daughter. Her daily routine would have put almost anybody to shame, and it certainly intimidated Rosemary. Up at first light, she would fill every waking moment with a rich mix of socialising, reading, home maintenance and – above all – gardening. She grew everything from seed or took cuttings that never failed to flourish. Her garden had burgeoned over the years, spreading upwards, as well as lengthwise, when the owner of the field at the far end was eventually persuaded to part with a strip of land. There were good-sized trees, most of them festooned with clematis and other climbers, and an ever-diminishing patch of lawn where visitors might sit and admire.

As she got within a few miles of her mother's, Rosemary mentally ran through the news she could safely relate. There really wasn't very much, which was actually a good thing. There'd be less for her mother to analyse with her habitual sharp judgement. Obviously, she would make no mention of the proposed unseating of Julian Marchant. Her mother's reaction to such a rebellion could go in any of several ways – but Rosemary didn't think she'd enjoy hearing any of them.

The forecast for the weekend was fine, fortunately. Sitting out in the glorious garden would go a long way towards ameliorating the slightly scratchy exchanges they generally went in for. On the whole, the garden encouraged much more harmony than did anything else they might find to discuss.

Knowing her mother would detect the Land Rover's engine a good quarter of a mile away, Rosemary fully expected to be greeted at the front gate. She was not disappointed, and braced herself for the ritual inspection of the vehicle that was always Mrs Boxer's first act. 'Going all right, is she?' she demanded.

'Absolutely fine, Mum. She's a queen amongst Land Rovers.'

'I thought I heard a bit of a cough, when you changed down to second.'

'She's never liked low revs. It's nothing new.'

'When did you last change the points and plugs?'

'Five weeks ago. And she's got lovely new oil in her system, too. The battery's holding up brilliantly. The only glitch is she sometimes doesn't start.'

'What?' It was as if Rosemary had announced that a priceless Old Master had developed a fungal infestation. 'What do you mean, won't start?'

'It must be the starter motor. Probably just needs a bit of a service.'

'Let me see.' Before Rosemary could speak or move, her mother had the bonnet open and was fingering a piece of the still-warm engine. 'Give it a try, will you,' she said.

'What – now?'

'Of course now.'

Rosemary obeyed, and the engine fired perfectly. She leaned out and asked if she could turn it off again. Her mother nodded.

'It's probably the pinion. Here, let me show you. Have you got a spanner or something?'

Rosemary fished around for a toolbag under the driver's seat and produced a heavy spanner. Barbara took it, waving at Rosemary to watch what she was doing. 'See? That's the starter motor there. All you do is tap it sharply, just *here*.' She suited her action to the words. 'I bet you anything that'll do the trick. It only takes a moment.'

'Gosh, thanks, Mum. I don't have to get anybody to fix it, then?'

'I wouldn't bother. Mechanics these days often do more harm than good, when they start messing about with anything they don't really understand. Unless you've got a promising rural mechanic at that college of yours?'

Rosemary shook her head. 'We don't offer that course any more.'

'Pity.'

The two women stood side by side, scrutinising the vehicle as if it were a horse or a fine dairy cow. 'I still wish your father hadn't let her go to you,' Mrs Boxer admitted. 'I know it's selfish of me, when you had so much more need of it than we did – but I really do miss her.'

'I know, Mum. But honestly, I love her just as much as you ever did. She's quite safe with me.'

'Well…'

Rosemary sighed. It was the same every time, and she ought to be used to it by now. She understood what a wrench it had been for the old lady to part with her beloved machine, but it had become genuinely useful for her work – not least on the days when she'd managed to take students out on field trips. That happened less and less in recent times, regrettably. She'd enjoyed the boost it gave to her image, as a woman of independence, with a slightly rugged individualistic edge. To start with, she'd worried that it might damage her love life, putting men off with the butchness of driving such a motor, but whatever difficulties she might have had in that department lately, she certainly couldn't blame them on the Land Rover.

'Well, come on in. You'll be hungry, I expect. Pity the light's gone – I wanted to show you the passion flower. It's already got over twenty tiny buds. Can you believe that?'

'I can believe anything, where your garden's concerned,' laughed Rosemary, who had long ago learned that things went much more smoothly if she stuck to lavish praise for her mother's efforts. And she had just about given up hoping for something similar in return. Or so she tried to convince herself. Like any daughter, her need for at least some parental approval never quite seemed to go away.

Her mother babbled on, a stream of news about friends, expressions of opinion about anything that had come her way, long accounts of her latest plans for the garden. Rosemary knew better than to merely feign interest: it had to be the real thing. She was expected to know exactly who everybody was, what the latest world situation might be, and which plants were recent additions. The effort of paying so much attention usually sent her back to college quite worn out.

On Saturday morning, they performed their customary ritual of walking slowly around the garden, with Barbara pointing out her favourite successes, often quite pink with pride. They started with the passion flower, with its impressive number of very tiny buds. Rosemary's admiration for it did much to sweeten the atmosphere. Nothing would induce her to admit to her mother that she thought that particular plant garish and inappropriate for an English village garden.

'Mum, you're a genius,' said Rosemary, brushing her hand against a vigorous frond of lavender that pushed itself out of a raised bed. 'So much work!'

'I'm doing more raised beds, ready for the day when I can't bend so easily. I thought I'd take out all this alchemilla and whatnot, and make a sort of buttress wall for a raised bed. There are plenty of stones from where we dug the pond.'

'Jim still comes to help then, does he?'

'Strictly when I need another pair of hands. He's sulking at the moment because I haven't needed him since last year. He's getting much more decrepit than me, poor chap.'

Jim was a mere seventy-two, semi-retired from a host of odd jobs around the village.

The paths were made of old red brick, set in patterns, and curving between the different areas of the garden. At a fork, two-thirds of the way from the house to the far end, Rosemary began to veer left, as usual.

'No, wait a minute,' he mother said. 'Have a look at the *humulus lupulus*. Its colour is extraordinary, and it has put on a real growing spurt this year.' She pointed up at a golden-leaved hop, thrusting its way through the boughs of a small whitebeam.

'Very nice,' said Rosemary, this time quite sincerely. The foliage of the two plants did indeed work well together. 'But aren't you worried that the whitebeam will take over in another year or two?'

'I can trim it – and there's always more space than you think.'

Without really giving it any conscious thought, Rosemary turned back to her original course, aiming again for the left fork in the path. 'Oh! Um...' he mother said, behind her. 'Why don't we go back for coffee now?'

'But we haven't finished.' Rosemary paused. 'What's the matter?'

'Nothing. It's just taking rather longer than I anticipated.'

'Mum, it's taking as long as it always does. And I definitely want to have a look at those ageratums you put in. How're they doing?'

She headed for the spot where she remembered her mother planting a large bed of flossflowers, a few months earlier. 'I'm always looking for a good splash of blue,' Barbara had said.

'Oh dear.' Rosemary looked down at the plants, and understood why her mother had tried to divert her. 'What's going on here, then?'

'I think they're just slow to get going, that's all. They're perfectly healthy – just a bit small.'

'They shouldn't be like this, and you know it.' She knelt down to examine the plants. 'They're only half the size they ought to be by now. And the flowers aren't right. It's too early, for one thing.' She ran a hand lightly through the leaves and flowers, noticing that a few stems broke off at her touch. 'Hmm, brittle stems, too.' She looked up at her mother, who was standing very stiffly on the path, her chin held high. 'You know what this is, don't you,' Rosemary said.

'They're all right, I tell you. Just a bit confused. It's this global warming. Nothing knows when it's meant to flower any more.'

'That's true, but this is much more than a bit of confusion over the season. You've got a case of chrysanthemum stunt viroid, unless I'm much mistaken.'

'But these aren't chrysanthemums,' Barbara said, superfluously.

'No, but it affects a few other garden flowers sometimes. Especially ageratum. I'll take a sample back to college with me, just to be sure, but I promise you, that's what it is. Premature flowering, stunted size and brittle stems. Classic symptoms.'

'Oh, well, I suppose you've been giving lectures on it only this week.'

'Something like that,' Rosemary smiled. She understood well enough how damaging it was to her mother's pride for her daughter to know better than she did about any aspect of the garden. 'But I'm afraid they'll all have to come out. It shouldn't be a problem for anything else in the garden – but if you're going to try ageratum again, buy them from somewhere else. Preferably somewhere that doesn't have chrysanthemums. That's probably how it originated, you see. It affects commercial florists, and stunts the growth of their cut flowers. It can cause quite some losses.'

'All right, don't lecture me,' sniffed Barbara. 'Poor little things. I hate to pull them all up.'

'I'll do it for you this afternoon,' Rosemary offered.

Her mother accepted this with reasonably good grace, and they finished their tour of inspection in the usual mood of careful amicability. Neither questioned the shared love of plants and gardens, the trouble arose from their very divergent ideas and methods. Barbara favoured the 'architectural' approach, with large dark-leaved shrubs dominating much of her garden, spiced with big bright old-fashioned plants like the passion flower, dahlias and red hot pokers. Rosemary preferred more subtle effects, using feathery foliage and varied textures.

When Rosemary opted to study Botany when she went to university, she hoped it would be interpreted as admiration for her mother's greatest passion in a life full of hobbies and interests. Unfortunately, though not entirely surprisingly, Mrs Boxer saw it more as direct competition. This potential conflict persuaded Rosemary that it would be wise to move into the academic aspects of plants. She specialised in the pathology of trees, concentrating on woodland habitats, making every effort to convince her mother that her supremacy in the cultivation of flowers and vegetables was entirely unchallenged.

Back in the house, Barbara went to heat up a pan of soup. When it came, in thick hand-thrown bowls with crusty granary bread, Rosemary sighed with pleasure. 'Your soups never change, Mum,' she said. 'I can remember having exactly the same when I was eight.'

'Your father taught me how to make it.' Rosemary knew this already, of course. Her mother mentioned it repeatedly, but it was comforting to hear it again. She was always glad to have her father brought into the conversation.

'Mmm,' was all she replied.

'Will you be going to the grave tomorrow? It probably needs a bit of tidying up.'

'I might. Are we doing anything this afternoon?'

'Nothing planned. Why?'

'We could do the grave today, then. I don't like going on a Sunday, with people at services, coming and going.'

Barbara nodded accommodatingly. 'Good idea,' she said.

Both women loved the small churchyard on the side of a hill, where old and new graves were fitted into the odd-shaped ground, and they would now and then visit it for a quiet spell of remembrance. Lawrence Boxer had been a man of many virtues that well suited him to the roles of both husband and father. Patient, attentive, witty – and above all quick to praise. Both his womenfolk had blossomed under his good-humoured approval of all their varied endeavours. When, on rare occasions, one of them did something to offend or annoy him, he would indicate his feelings by silence. Rosemary used to call it his 'frozen face', where the absence of a smile spoke more than any amount of criticism.

The sun was warm on the new stone on Lawrence's

grave. Quietly, mother and daughter cleared away the new spring growth, until Rosemary noticed the vigour of her mother's weeding. 'Hey, steady on!' she said. 'It doesn't have to be a scorched earth exercise. Leave that daisy. It's not doing any harm.'

Barbara paused and inspected her work. Rosemary could see her indecision clear on her face. 'It'll spread, though, if we leave it. In no time, there'll be daisies all over everywhere.'

'No there won't. Sorry, Mum, it's probably sentimental of me, but I think that little flower looks exactly right where it is. Why destroy the poor thing?'

'Oh, have it your way,' Barbara grumbled. 'Seems I can't win today.'

Rosemary laughed lightly. 'Your turn will come, I'm sure.'

Neither of them wanted to argue over the grave, and after a few more minutes they wiped their hands and agreed the job had been satisfactorily accomplished. 'I do miss him,' sighed Barbara. 'Nobody could have asked for a better husband.'

Rosemary linked her arm gently through her mother's. 'That's a nice thing to say. He was a pretty good father, as well. Come on now. Let's go and have a cream tea in the village.'

Despite the constant conversation, with the need to go carefully around sensitive topics, Rosemary found herself relaxing into the weekend. By the middle of Sunday, she was actively enjoying herself, and not at all eager to return to the muddle and rush of college life. This feeling became overwhelming, when Barbara's phone rang, and she called out to Rosemary, 'It's for you.'

In great surprise, Rosemary took the receiver. She couldn't think of anybody who would call her at her mother's on a Sunday. Or, she corrected herself, a split second before hearing the voice at the other end –

only *one* person would have the gall.

'Rosemary?' Her guess was quickly confirmed. 'Sorry to bother you on a Sunday.'

Julian Marchant, no less. She sighed. 'What's the matter, Julian?'

'Well, it's all rather exciting. I've had this letter, you see. From a chap called Daniel Kellaway. I gather he was a favourite of yours, some years back. He's *the* Kellaway. The garden centre chap.'

'Slow down,' she pleaded. 'You're not making any sense. I do remember Daniel. Actually...' She stopped herself just in time. It might not be at all wise to reveal that she too had had a letter from Daniel until she knew what Julian was going to say.

'That's good. Now listen. He wants us to go down there, to talk about an idea he's got for giving us some money. It'll be an endowment, apparently. He says he's seriously ill, and would like to see him as soon as possible. I thought we might make a trip tomorrow.'

'Why me, Julian?'

'Oh – didn't I say? He asks for you, specifically. Something about a tree disease he wants your opinion on. I'm phoning now so you can sort everything out – swop one or two lectures around, that kind of thing.'

His vagueness made her want to scream. 'Short notice, Julian,' she said tightly.

'Yeah, I know. Sorry. But this has come at *exactly* the right time, you see. I don't want to risk it going wrong. And Kellaway sounds as if he's in a hurry.'

'Don't you remember him at all?'

'Um... Remind me.'

'Mature student, quite a bit older than the others. Floppy brown hair. Nice hazel-coloured eyes. Fairly tall.'

Julian snorted. 'If you told me something about his work, I might be more likely to remember.'

'His work was very good,' she said, knowing she

was being unhelpful. 'He was a credit to the college.'

'I expect I'll recognise him when I see him,' Julian said, as if it hardly mattered. 'Can you arrange to leave at about eleven o'clock tomorrow, then? I'll wait for you in the office.'

Recognising an order when she heard it, Rosemary tersely agreed. Only when she had replaced the receiver did she realise the implications. With an inward shudder, she thanked her stars that she had not yet written and posted the trouble-making letter to the Chair of Governors. The potential for confusion and acrimony that would arise from this latest development did not bear thinking about.

With a warm hug, she took leave of her mother in the early evening. It was a two-hour drive back to her campus home, and she had a lot to arrange for the coming day. She also had a lot of thinking to do about the mess she and Fergus and the others might so easily have walked into. The main foundation of their complaints against Julian had been undermined by the Kellaway offer. The rebels would have been left looking exposed and foolish, as Julian blithely waved the endowment cheque at the Governors, and bought himself another few years of secure tenure. It was sickening.

'Thanks, Mum,' she said, from the driving seat of the Land Rover. 'That was a lovely break.'

Her mother gave her a searching look. 'You needed a break, didn't you?' she observed. 'And you haven't told me why.'

Rosemary forced a smile. 'Honestly, there's nothing to tell. No more than the same old moans about targets and league tables and government guidelines. It gets a bit wearing, especially at this time of year.'

'Well, don't give in to them, that's my advice. Stick to your guns. It'll all come right in the end, you see.'

'I expect it will,' Rosemary agreed, while privately

thinking she didn't really have the time or the stamina to wait for things to 'come right'.

The starter motor performed perfectly, and she pulled away, waving cheerily through the open window, wishing for once that she could just stay safe and hidden, in her mother's cottage, enjoying the beautiful garden.

Living on the Malmesbury campus in a hall of residence meant she had no garden of her own. Despite having graduated to the most coveted suite of rooms on the top floor, which she generally found comfortable and convenient, she nonetheless would have liked her own patch of ground to cultivate. It seemed odd, she sometimes thought, for a lecturer in plants not to have any she could call her own.

College that Monday morning was in no more turmoil than usual – and the first person Rosemary encountered was Professor Julian Marchant, standing in the general office, exasperation coming off him like steam. 'Morning, Julian,' Rosemary chirruped, refusing to let him annoy her. 'Are we still on for eleven o'clock?'

It was just the right thing to have said, assuming that embarrassing Julian was the intention. He flushed, and glanced around the office. Billie Jones, the Junior Admin Assistant (or Secretary, as she had originally been entitled) glanced up with a smirk. Lois Grayling, generally regarded as the college airhead, was at the photocopier. Her sharp intake of breath echoed through the room.

'Of course,' said Julian. 'Will you be ready?'

'Certainly I will,' she said. 'I wouldn't dare keep you waiting, Professor.'

After he had swept importantly out of the room, Billie and Rosemary exchanged glances, unseen by Lois. 'Why doesn't he just stay where he belongs, without harassing the rest of us?' Billie wondered. 'Most Principals wouldn't be seen dead in the general office.'

'Julian's a very hands-on Principal,' came Lois's voice.

Rosemary rolled her eyes. 'If you ask me, he misses the knockabout stuff down here at the chalk face,' she said. 'He's lonely there at the top, struggling to keep the place afloat.'

'I think you're wrong.' Lois was dignified in her sycophantic support for her superior.

Rosemary gave her a long look, a smile flickering around her lips. 'Lois, your faith in human nature is magnificent. You make me feel hopelessly middle-aged and cynical. If Julian's to your taste, then good luck to you.'

Lois blushed. 'I didn't say he was to my taste. I just think you undervalue him.'

'You're probably right,' Rosemary shrugged. 'All I can suggest is that you suck it and see.'

Billie giggled. 'Oh, Rosemary, what a thing to say!'

Lois turned away, giving a moist-sounding sniff. Billie rolled her eyes, in a silent message to Rosemary, which more than adequately conveyed that things were not good between Lois and Julian. 'Oh, Lord,' said Rosemary. 'Sorry. Well, all I can say is, you're well out of it.'

Lois gathered up the thick stack of documents and clutched them to her chest. 'You're quite wrong,' she said. 'There was never anything inappropriate between Julian and me. And I still think he's an excellent Principal.'

'And I believe in fairies,' said Rosemary cheerfully.

But she didn't feel very cheerful as she waited in the office a few minutes before eleven o'clock. College politics had always depressed her, and she regretted to some extent her conspiracy with the others. The letter from Daniel Kellaway had reminded her of pleasanter times, before Julian became Principal and things took a nosedive, but it had also shown her that Julian did have his uses. Perhaps he would be able to persuade a number of the college alumni to donate cash in return for some sort of honorary Chair, and improve conditions for the staff in the process.

Julian breezed in at a few seconds before eleven. 'Come on, then,' he ordered her. 'Time to hit the road.'

'In your car?'

'Well…no. If we're looking at trees, we'll need a whole lot of equipment, won't we? Much better if we take your Land Rover.'

Rosemary blinked at this. On the one hand, she much preferred to drive than to be driven, and she genuinely enjoyed taking the Land Rover on a good long run. But with Julian beside her, doubtless complaining at the draughts and the lack of suspension, most of the pleasure would soon evaporate.

'Does he give any clue as to what's wrong with the trees? We might only need a few sample pots. Even your minimalist car would have space for that.'

'It must be something fairly obscure, or he'd have solved it himself. That's assuming he was as good a student as you seem to think he was.'

'He got a decent two-two. But if he's bedridden, he'd have trouble solving anything, wouldn't he?'

Julian took a few impatient steps across the room and back. 'Rosemary, why do you always have to *argue*? I've decided we're going in your vehicle. This is a business trip, on a professional matter. Your skills are being called upon, in accordance with this man's stated request. Because he's planning to donate a large sum of money to the place where we both work, I would have thought it incumbent on us to do everything to keep him happy.'

She gave up, and they went out to the car park. 'How far is it, anyway? I haven't got a lot of fuel.'

'Eighty or ninety miles. We can get some on the way.'

They didn't talk much for the first few miles. Rosemary realised she'd left it too late to reveal that she too had had a letter from Daniel Kellaway, and she hoped he wouldn't give her away by mentioning it.

'What are we going to do for lunch?' she asked. 'What time are they expecting us?'

'We can buy something when you get fuel. Crisps and stuff. I called last night and said we should be there by three.'

'Easily. We've got *far* too much time. Why don't we stop at a pub on the way?'

'Because he lives in a small village, where the roads are narrow and winding, and we might get lost. We daren't risk stopping anywhere. And this vehicle doesn't exactly burn up the miles, does it?'

'Don't insult the Land Rover,' she warned.

He grunted, and fell silent for another ten miles. Then he began to talk about the promised endowment. 'Plant Genetics, I thought,' he said, almost to himself.

Rosemary winced. 'You mean you want to get on the GM bandwagon, and this is your chance.'

'Not necessarily. We still don't know which way that's going to go. But Kellaway doesn't seem to care what we call it. If you ask me, he's just out for whatever bit of immortality he can get.'

'I wonder what's the matter with him? Does he say? Poor Daniel. He can't be much over forty. Did he ever marry – do you know?'

'Apparently, yes. He says…' Julian consulted the letter: '"My wife and I would be happy to see you here at your earliest convenience." But I have no idea what's wrong with him. We'll soon find out, I suppose.'

'It will be nice to see him again,' Rosemary said. 'I hope I can solve his tree problem for him. Otherwise, I'm going to feel a bit in the way, aren't I?'

He didn't reply to that, and Rosemary found herself musing on Lois Grayling and the likely scenario between her and Julian. Chances were he'd flirted with her quite casually to start with, only to increase his attentions to the point where she'd expect something serious to develop between them. The poor girl wouldn't have stood a chance against the amorous Principal. But combined with sympathy, Rosemary felt a certain impatience. Hadn't Julian's reputation warned her that she couldn't hope to extract any kind of commitment from him? And where exactly had the flirtation got to, she wondered. Judging by Lois's manner that morning, she wasn't entirely sure of the answer to that question herself.

Chapter Three

Laura's second earring wouldn't quite go through the hole in her pierced lobe, and when she pushed it harder, the resulting pain made her wince. 'Damn it,' she muttered. It felt like the final straw, on top of everything else. Her earrings always slid in effortlessly, even without looking in a mirror.

Outside, a car was drawing up, and she glanced out of the window to see that the taxi had arrived. A final effort got the earring in place, and she stepped away from the window.

Then the idiot taxi driver hooted, and a renewed surge of rage flooded through her. Were all men like this? Domineering, insensitive, selfish bastards. She strode out to the hall where the suitcases sat waiting. For a moment, her instincts were to heft them manfully and carry them out to the waiting car herself. Then she thought better of it. Why should she when there was a man out there doing nothing? A man she was paying to drive her, and who would expect a gratuity simply for performing that basic service. Let him earn it for once.

She stood unmoving in the hallway for a few moments, ignoring the second hoot of the taxi's horn. He could probably see her through the crinkly glass of the front door, a shadowy figure preparing to leave for the railway station. What would he think when she finally opened the door? Probably nothing. Probably he'd never even notice the bags under her eyes and the pallor of her skin. To him, she'd just be another fare.

As she had known he would, the taxi driver finally came to the door. She waited for him to ring the bell, and then she threw the door open without a word.

He was a man past his best, grey-haired and round-shouldered. Only a few days earlier, Laura would have taken pity on him, apologised for keeping him waiting. But now she could not afford to be kind or encouraging. She just needed to get away from this house and the pain it was suddenly causing her.

'Didn't you hear my horn?' the man asked.

Laura ignored him, merely tilting her chin at the suitcases, and leaving him to work out what was required. With a hard-done-by sigh, the man lugged the cases down the garden path, and opened the boot of his car. Instead of following behind him, Laura turned to look back at the house. It was a grim moment, which she wanted to mark in some way.

Casting her eyes over the well-tended garden, she moved towards the rockery. She had taken special pride in this feature, planting it with alpines and heathers, and installing a small trickling waterway next to it. Deliberately, she bent down and selected a good-sized pebble from the pool. Weighing it in her hand, she slowly spun on her heel, at the same time raising her arm and hurling the stone as hard as she could at the front window of the house.

The sound of smashing glass rang loud in the quiet empty street. The taxi driver looked up from his car boot in alarm. Laura felt a surge of strength and satisfaction, which lasted for several seconds. Then, as she began to walk down to the road, the phone started to ring inside the house.

She scarcely paused. Much too late to go back now. *It'll be Helena*, she told herself. *Finally decided to see how I'm doing.* She should go back and answer it, she knew. She had never been able to understand those people who cheerfully chose to let a call go unanswered. But now things were different. Laura was a changed person, and she did not have to respond to summons from husbands or daughters or *anybody*.

Eyeing her nervously, the driver opened the car door, and watched her settle stiffly onto the worn plush. Then he got into the driving seat and looked at her in the rear-view mirror. 'The station, wasn't it?' he asked, and then added 'Madam?'

She stared straight ahead, not meeting his eye, her expression stony. There was a long pause, before she agreed, 'The station.'

Julian was showing obvious signs of impatience, as Rosemary took her time paying for fuel and stocking up with two packets of crisps, which was all they seemed likely to get for their lunch. Irritably she pushed her wallet into the back pocket of her jeans, deliberately avoiding her boss's eye as he sat glowering in the passenger seat. What on earth did he have to sulk about, she wondered. They'd made reasonable time so far, despite heavy goods traffic, and she'd been careful not to say anything to annoy him. All she could do was adopt her usual cheerful manner, hoping to avert whatever mean-minded remark he was on the brink of making.

She knew he wasn't finding the Land Rover a very appropriate means of transport – but since he had insisted on their taking it, he could hardly complain now. This, she supposed, was the most likely source of his irritation, and when the engine failed to respond to the key turning in the ignition, Rosemary had to fight an urge to apologise.

'We're going to be late,' Julian warned her.

'No, I don't think we are. In any case, Daniel won't mind. Punctuality was never his strong point.'

Calmly she reached under her seat, extracted the large spanner her mother had advised her to keep handy, and climbed out of the vehicle. Daniel was still talking. Inwardly excited and slightly apprehensive, Rosemary tapped the starter motor exactly as Barbara had shown her. What if it didn't work? She'd have to suffer Julian's scorn – and they really might be late for the Winterbourne appointment.

Julian watched her with incomprehension, but he was not diverted from the subject of Daniel.

'I wonder if we'll get all the papers signed this

afternoon. I think there's a business partner who's likely to have some say in the whole thing. If Kellaway really is dying, the other chap probably takes over the whole caboodle.'

'I can't believe Daniel's dying. He always had so much energy and zest for life.'

She replaced the spanner under her seat and turned the key in the ignition. The engine roared. Inwardly, she gave a jubilant cheer and a silent thanks to her mother.

'The starter pinion gets jammed,' she explained to Julian. 'But for all that, she's a good old wagon.' She gave the steering wheel a friendly pat, doing her best to ignore her passenger's so-help-me glance at the sky. 'Still in plenty of time,' she added. 'Which crisps do you want – salt 'n' vinegar or roast chicken?'

'I'm not too keen on either,' he grumbled. 'But I'd prefer the chicken.'

They'd finished their meagre snack before she sensed him gazing at her. A rapid glance confirmed her suspicions, and she looked away determinedly, eyes on the road ahead.

'Rosemary.' The tone was ingratiating, conciliatory.

She tried once more to sidestep whatever might be coming. 'Listen to her,' she said.

'What?'

'The motor. When she's in top gear, somewhere between three and three-and-a-half thousand revs, you get this lovely satisfied hum. Can't you hear it?'

'Very gratifying. Rosemary, I've been thinking.'

Oh, God, she thought. *What now*? She threw him a flippant smile. 'Get away! I thought that was forbidden for college principals.'

'I was thinking about *us*,' he pressed on.

'Oh, help. Surely not. Not after all this time.'

'We were good together, weren't we?' His lapse into appealing-little-boy mode was nauseating. Nobody was less like an appealing little boy than

Julian Marchant. Rosemary thought she'd convinced him of that months ago. She couldn't see any choice but to sustain her flippant arm's-length manner.

'Do you mean when we were…?'

'Yes, of course I do.'

'You have to be kidding. We were hell on wheels.'

'Nonsense. We had some really good times.' He reached out a hand and rested it on her leg.

She pushed it away. 'I can't think of any.' She wanted to remind him of the countless times he'd been late for a date; the offensive way he'd tried to conceal their affair from all their colleagues; the final callous note in which he'd informed her that he believed it would be best if they restricted themselves to purely professional contact from then on. It had been by sheer accident that she'd discovered he'd dumped her for wretched Lois Grayling. Suddenly she made the connection. Having grown tired of Lois, he was hoping he might be taken back by Rosemary. The man was a disgrace, a shameless exploitative pig, and she wished she had the gumption to tell him so.

But she held her tongue. None of that would do any good now, and she very badly did not want to hear whatever lying excuses he might try to come up with so late in the day. Not that she could pretend to have missed his attentions, once he'd transferred them to Lois. Escaping from a liaison with Julian had been like emerging from a cave into a bright sunny day. Besides, she had felt she was getting a fitting revenge on him in her conspiracies with Tom and the others. Whatever her personal feelings towards Julian might be, the fact remained that he was a lousy Principal. She had known that, even when she was involved with him.

But annoyingly, he wasn't yet ready to abandon his efforts to seduce her all over again. 'Well, be that as it may, why don't we give it another go?' He stared fixedly at her, trying to make her turn her head and meet his eye.

She kept her own gaze firmly on the road ahead, listening to another few seconds of the Land Rover's musical rhythms before replying. Julian was, after all, her boss. She had to keep this light. 'Because the go went, Julian. After eight months with you, I decided I would never again get romantically entangled with a man who pronounced both the r's in February. Sorry, but there it is.' She smiled as he silently mouthed the word two or three times.

'I see,' he lied. 'Well, all right, then. I just thought…' and he said not another word all the way to Winterbourne Manor.

Rosemary forgot all about her mildly embarrassing exchange with Julian as they drove through the imposing gates of Winterbourne Manor. 'Wow!' she breathed. 'What a beautiful house!'

'Mmm,' said Julian. 'At least we're not late.'

He was out of the Land Rover almost before it stopped, and Rosemary caught up with him as he was ringing the doorbell. Then she turned her back on the house to examine the gardens. It was almost more than she could take in. From extreme formality in the foreground, with a parterre in full sunshine and an ornamental lake of rigorous symmetry, the landscaping widened into lawns, then much less formal areas of woodland and hedgerows. It was a classic example of garden design and it made her heart soar just to see it. Fields and hills beyond were drawn into the picture, blurring the boundaries and creating long vistas of delight. An avenue of mature trees stretched away to the left, presumably leading to another entrance.

Daniel broke the spell with a loud tutting sound. 'Where the devil are they?' he said. Rosemary realised they'd been standing there for quite a few minutes.

'Try again,' she advised unnecessarily.

This time, it was only a few seconds before the door was opened by an apparition that seemed all the more ludicrous for its contrast with the perfection of the gardens. The woman standing there seemed to be about sixty, and was dressed in an ill-assorted collection of brightly-printed cottons, covered with a shapeless knitted cardigan and topped off with an impossible crocheted beret. Except that 'beret' was too generous a term for it. It was large and saggy, placed lopsidedly on the back of the woman's head, so that it seemed on the verge of falling off. It attracted the eye irresistibly, magnetically, as one waited for gravity to work its way, or for the wearer to jerk it straight.

'Yes?' said the woman, with astonishing aggression.

Julian ventured a smile. 'We'd like to see Mr Kellaway please?'

'What for?' The question seemed to arise from a genuine bewilderment as to why anyone would come to the house and make such a request.

Rosemary made a quick diagnosis of insanity, possibly early Alzheimer's Disease. 'Who are you?' she asked, with some gentleness.

'That's not the question,' flashed the woman, amply confirming Rosemary's suspicions, and increasing her sense of helplessness.

Fortunately, rescue was at hand. 'That's all right, Mrs Potts,' came a sweet voice from inside the house.

The elderly woman turned round slowly. 'They was ringing the bell.'

'I'll take care of it,' said the newcomer calmly, as she appeared in sight. She was tall and slim, in her late thirties and oozing firm competence. 'I'm Alicia Kellaway,' she told the visitors. 'And you must be Professor Marchant and Miss Boxer?'

Relieved, Julian and Rosemary shook hands with her, before following her into the house.

On the train, Laura struggled not to think about anything that had happened. Instead she stared out of the window, counting trees, gateways, clouds, willing herself to stay calm. It had worked in the taxi, focusing first on the back of the driver's head and the way his hair thinned on the crown, and then on the strange habit lampposts seemed to have of rushing at you as the car sped along.

Now she only had to keep hold of herself for two more stops before alighting at the small station which served Devenish, where she hoped she might find sanctuary. It had come as yet another unpleasant shock to realise how few friends she possessed; how difficult it would be to find someone with a shoulder to rest her head on for a few consoling moments.

Another taxi took her the final miles to a house in the centre of Devenish village. This time the driver loaded and unloaded her bags without demur and was tipped accordingly. With violently beating heart, Laura knocked on the front door. This was a big mistake, she was sure of it. She ought at least to have phoned in advance. What if there was nobody in?

But there was. The door opened briskly, and Vickie Trent stood there. And stood there, her expression blank with incomprehension, for another full minute. Laura stared at her, lost for words. Finally Vickie spoke. 'Oh, gosh, it's...' She frowned. Laura was appalled.

'Laura,' she supplied, with a touch of indignation. The woman was supposed to be her *friend*, for heaven's sake. So what if they hadn't actually seen each other for nearly two years? Friends were supposed to pick up where they'd left off, regardless of any intervening years.

'Yes, yes. Of course. You look...different. I'm so sorry, Laura, I was busy with something important. My head's full of spreadsheets. Well, you'd better come in.' At the sight of the two large suitcases, she blinked. Laura picked them up and marched into the hall, fighting to maintain her dignity.

'Go on into the lounge,' Vickie invited, with

another wary glance at the cases. Laura went ahead and threw herself down on the sofa, realising as she did so that she was nearing the end of her self-control. Shortage of sleep, acute emotional upheaval, rage, worry and shock were all beginning to take their toll.

'He's left me,' she said, as soon as Vickie followed her into the room.

'Oh.' The woman's inadequacy seemed to be deepening by the minute. Was she never going to pull herself together and offer tea, sympathy and lots of good advice?

'For a twenty-three-year-old tart,' Laura added, with venom.

'Oh dear,' murmured Vickie uselessly. 'Well, Sam will be home later. He'll know what to do.' She paused, apparently listening to a voice inside her head. 'Sam and Nick were best friends,' she said faintly. 'And your Helena's his god-daughter.'

'That's right,' Laura confirmed. 'And I did rather think that you and I were more than just the wives of best friends.'

'Yes, yes. I *am* sorry, Laura. You looked so... well, standing there with those cases. You were out of context, I suppose. And I have been so very worried... Isn't it odd the way everything always happens at once?'

Laura closed her eyes for a few seconds. Any other time, she would have been more than willing to listen to Vickie's worries. As it was...

'Do you think you could make me some tea?' she asked. 'I haven't had anything since early this morning, and I'm parched.'

'Oh! Yes. Yes, of course.' And Vickie disappeared to the kitchen, leaving Laura to brush away a few tears.

Alicia Kellaway took her visitors directly to Daniel's room on the second floor, making it seem uncomfortably full of people. Rosemary looked at them one by one, trying to work out what it was she and Julian had just walked into.

The man in the bed could only be Daniel, but she would never have recognised him. The skin on his face, neck, arms and hands was covered with yellowish blisters, some the size of a tenpence piece. Between the sores were purple scars. He glistened with an application of what she assumed must be ointment. He looked monstrous and pathetic and revolting. She had to tear her horrified gaze away, taking the opportunity, with some relief, to attend to the others in the room.

A broad-shouldered man was standing beside the open window. He nodded to her and Julian when Alicia made the introductions. 'This is Sam Trent,' she said. 'He's Daniel's business partner. Sam, this is Miss Boxer and Professor Marchant.' Nobody attempted to shake hands. Probably, thought Rosemary, because it would be impossible to touch Daniel, so there's an unspoken agreement to leave it out altogether.

'And this is Doctor Whittaker. Bob. He comes every few days to give Daniel a check-up.' The doctor was a slimmer, younger man than Sam Trent. He smiled tentatively and fiddled with the catch of his bag.

'I'd better be off now, I suppose,' he said, looking at Alicia with an expression that reminded Rosemary of a banished dog. She observed a flicker of something pass between the doctor and Daniel's wife, which she immediately forgot. The doctor made no move to leave; instead he addressed his patient, as if there were no one else in the room. 'Daniel, your skin really isn't responding as well as it should be. Are you sure you're putting plenty of the cream on?'

Daniel gave a snort, half humorous, half annoyed. 'Alicia keeps me covered in the stuff,' he said. 'She's just finished another session.' He tipped his head towards a table next to the bed, where a pair of surgical gloves lay on top of an unlabelled plastic tub. The gloves had smears of white cream on them. 'I don't know how she copes with it.'

'I expect she's got used to it by now,' said the doctor.

Daniel frowned. 'Yes, I expect she has. It's been nearly a year now, after all, and everybody's still keeping up the pretence that I'm going to get better. Well, quite honestly, I'm sick to death of it. As soon as one section starts to heal, I break out in another. And the scars! Look at me! I'm disgusting, even to myself. I don't understand how any of you can abide to be in the same room as me.'

His wife stepped closer to the bed, a hand held up to quieten him. 'Hush, darling,' she soothed, as if to a young child. 'Not now.'

The doctor stood at her elbow, nodding inanely, plainly embarrassed. Rosemary supposed it would be disconcerting to have your patient so very obviously failing to get better. If this was how Daniel looked *after* the doctor's ministrations, it was tempting to wonder whether he'd be better off leaving whatever-it-was to nature.

Daniel fell back onto his pillows. 'No, you're right. I'm sorry.' He looked at Rosemary. 'Hello, Miss Boxer. Nice to see you again.'

'Hey!' Rosemary protested. 'What's with the "Miss Boxer"?'

He smiled crookedly. 'Just teasing. But really, I hate you to see me like this. I'm not a pretty sight, am I?'

'Don't worry about it. We're mates, remember.' She hesitated, and then plunged in with the question she was burning to ask. 'What exactly is it? That's wrong with your skin, I mean?'

Daniel met her gaze, looking as if he was more than happy to explain. 'It began about a year ago. I had an acute case of urticaria —'

'Pardon?'

'It's the smart word for nettle rash, actually. I

turned out to be allergic to aspirin. But somehow it just never went away. It got so bad that I couldn't bear to have clothes against my skin. And the damage started to break down the tissue in some places, which makes me vulnerable to infections. I'm a mess, basically.'

Alicia moved towards him, saying, 'But it has been better lately. There have been some spells of remission.'

Daniel closed his eyes for a moment. 'Every time we think it's finally been beaten, it comes back again. It's like hiding from an invisible enemy. I never know when it's going to leap out at me again. It's exhausting.'

'I can imagine,' Rosemary sympathised. 'What an awful business.'

Tired of taking a back seat, Julian came forward. Unable to shake hands, he stood at a loss for a moment, glancing around at the others in the room for guidance. Grudgingly, Rosemary came to his rescue.

'Daniel, you remember Professor Marchant, don't you? He's been promoted since your time, of course. College Principal, no less.'

'Of course I remember him,' said Daniel. He looked towards the window. 'Sam, will you come over here and help us with the business stuff?'

The burly business partner did not move. Rosemary watched his face, and realised he had reservations about Daniel's decision. *Oops*, she thought. *Trouble brewing here, I shouldn't wonder.*

'Um,' she said out loud. 'Should I get out of the way?'

'No need,' said Sam Trent. 'This is all Daniel's baby. Nothing to do with me. I might as well tell you I'm not in agreement with this endowment idea. I think there are better uses for the spare cash that Daniel believes is sloshing around. I'm here because I hoped to talk him out of it, before you arrived.'

'But you failed,' said Daniel gently. 'I'm sorry, Sam, but my mind's made up. And I've assured you, time and again, that you won't lose out by it.' He glanced at Julian and Rosemary, and then at his wife. 'There's no harm in telling you that I've left my entire share in the business to Sam, after the money for the endowment is deducted. That's no small legacy, Sam, now is it? Not to mention the minor detail that you've got a half ownership of this place.'

Sam wriggled uncomfortably. 'Don't talk like that,' he pleaded. 'You're not going anywhere, so why the talk of leaving anything to me?'

Daniel sighed. 'Don't pretend,' he said. 'I'm not a fool. There's only so much a body can put up with, and we all know I'm lucky to have lasted this long. I should have sorted this business out with the college weeks ago.'

'Well,' said Alicia. 'I think I'd better let you get on with it. I'll ask Mrs Potts to bring us some tea in a quarter of an hour or so, shall I?'

Only the doctor replied. 'I really must be going,' he said again, with a visible effort. 'Don't bother to show me out.'

'Oh, hang on, Bob,' said Sam, finally stepping away from his post at the window. 'Before you go, would you write me up for some more Digoxin?'

The doctor transferred his attention to Sam's face for a long moment. 'You're not overdoing it, are you?'

'Of course I'm not.' Sam's defensiveness clouded the air in the room, causing everybody to look at him. Daniel gave a sigh, and Rosemary wondered whether he was feeling guilty at the way he was treating his partner. Sam did not look too well, either, she observed. There was a clamminess to his skin and his breath seemed to be rather laboured. If she had to give this Doctor Whittaker marks out of ten, he'd have been lucky to earn a score of three, if these patients were anything to go by.

'Okay, okay,' soothed the doctor. 'It's only that digitalis is dodgy stuff. Stick strictly to the dosage I told you, all right?'

'Just write the prescription,' growled Sam, and Doctor Whittaker obliged. After the doctor and Alicia had both left the room, Sam seemed to relax slightly. 'Don't look so worried,' he told Daniel. 'I'm fine.'

Daniel met Rosemary's eye. 'Sam had rheumatic fever as a child, you see. His heart's never been a hundred per cent since then. Now I'm laid up, all the work's fallen to him, and I know he's been doing too much. Vickie, his wife, is quite exercised about it, and who can blame her?'

'Shut up,' said Sam affectionately. 'I only do what I want to do. Vickie makes a lot of fuss about very little.'

Rosemary began to revise her impression of Sam Trent. Initially he had struck her as rather hostile, but now she saw him as a kindly man, concerned for his partner and probably feeling under a lot of pressure.

'Do you live here as well?' she asked him, remembering Daniel's reference to the house.

'No, no,' he shook his head. 'It's really just on paper. It was convenient for the tax situation, when we first set the business up. To all intents and purposes, this is Daniel and Alicia's house. They know that.' He gave Daniel a straight look. 'I don't even know why you brought it up.'

'Only because I want you to understand that your own position is perfectly secure,' said Daniel. 'Whatever happens to me.'

Julian was getting restless. He swung his arms, as if limbering up for something, and cleared his throat. 'We really do appreciate what you're doing for the university, you know,' he told Daniel.

The sick man responded immediately. 'Well, pass me that blue folder, and we can get on with it,' he said.

Julian picked up the folder from a table beside the

door and took it to the bedside, leaning over Rosemary to do so. She understood that he regarded himself as the main player in the coming transaction, and that she was there merely to smooth the way. For a moment she considered digging a sharp elbow in his ribs to keep him back, but then thought better of it. He was, after all, senior to her. So she edged her chair aside, to give Julian space. She even made a point of examining the room, to show that she had no interest in the tedious subject of money.

The room was large, but gloomy. The broad casement window opened onto a balcony, with overhanging eaves immediately above it. A quick automatic glance at the sky revealed that it faced north, so there would never be any direct sunlight. Besides the bed, there were two small tables, both covered with medical apparatus, two comfortable chairs and a chest of drawers. A curtain was drawn across what was probably an alcove, between the bed and the chest of drawers. More medical equipment stored away there, she supposed. Poor old Daniel! What a state to be in.

Daniel took a contract from his folder, his hands working clumsily, and flipped through it. 'It's all in here,' he said, attempting to pass the document to Rosemary.

Decisively, she backed away, waving a hand towards Julian. 'Professor Marchant deals with all this grown-up stuff,' she said.

Completely missing her tone, Julian began to read. '"A Proposal for the Endowment of the Kellaway Chair at the University of Malmesbury." Are we going to sign it here and now?'

There was a brief stir from Sam Trent but he didn't speak.

'Better not rush it,' said Daniel. 'Just have your legal people go over it, first, and then I'll sign whatever's needed to set everything up properly.'

Then, as if at a signal, the door opened again, and

Mrs Potts appeared with a tray laden with tea things, followed by Alicia. Rosemary was impressed by the realisation that the elderly woman must have climbed up two flights of stairs with her precarious load. Perhaps she wasn't quite as unstable as she had first appeared. Her forearms looked muscular and her step was quite steady.

'Tea,' she said, superfluously.

'Put it on the table, will you?' said Alicia. There was a bustle as space was cleared on the larger of the two tables and cups arranged. The tray contained a teapot complete with cosy, but one cup was already filled.

'That one's for Mr Trent,' said Mrs Potts. 'He has his own special herbal tea, without caffeine. I think it's still nice and hot.'

'Thanks,' said Sam, mournfully. He took the tea and drank it down in a few gulps, working his mouth afterwards as if the taste had not been to his liking.

Alicia took over from the older woman, and poured strong tea for everyone present. Rosemary, who would have greatly preferred coffee, even in mid-afternoon, sipped at the cooling stuff without enthusiasm, trying in vain to catch Sam Trent's eye. It seemed a pity that he wasn't more wholeheartedly in favour of Daniel's donation to the University.

Julian clearly felt there was more gushing to be done. 'I absolutely can't tell you how grateful we are, Mr Kellaway.'

Daniel waved a hand, dismissing the gratitude, but Julian wouldn't stop. 'I understand you've got a problem in the garden, that we should look at?'

Rosemary strolled over to the window and craned her neck for a better view. 'There's not much wrong with that garden as far as I can see. It's utterly beautiful.'

'It's made Rosemary's day, I can tell you,' Julian laughed. 'Seeing what one of her pupils can do.'

Daniel shook his head. 'I can't take any credit for it. The gardens are the creation of the previous owner. He was a Malaysian with one of their big electronic companies. He must have spent a fortune, putting in mature trees and landscaping on such a scale.'

'Wasn't it the trees you were worried about?'

'That's right. In the avenue. They've been losing their bark.' He smiled grimly. 'Like me.'

Rosemary forced a chuckle. 'Perhaps you've caught it off them. The first human case of Dutch Elm Disease.'

It was a poor joke, and nobody laughed. Julian threw her a withering look and carefully slid the draft contract back into the blue folder. 'Come on, then,' he said to her. 'Let's go and have a look.'

Sam Trent began to take his leave, the moment the two university people had left the room. 'That's that, then,' he snapped, more to Alicia than Daniel. 'Say goodbye to three years' profits.'

Before his wife could reply, Daniel struggled to sit up and respond. 'It isn't like that Sam, and you know it. The business can well afford it, and the publicity alone will compensate. The university is sure to come to us for all its supplies, for a start. And the goodwill is priceless. Trust me, man. I might be a physical wreck, but I've still got my head for good business. This way, everybody wins. I get my little bit of immortality, the college gets a leg up into another educational league, and you're going to do very nicely. There really isn't any need to grumble.'

Despite himself, Sam was mollified. Left to himself, he would have relied on Daniel to ensure that all was well with the business, anyway. It was only thanks to Vickie, with her obsessive discontented calculations, that his trust had been undermined. And Vickie did not understand abstracts such as 'goodwill'.

'Well, time will tell,' he muttered. 'Thanks for the tea, Alicia. Look after yourself, Dan.' And he was gone.

The Kellaways, alone together at last, did not look at each other. Alicia fussed over the flower arrangement on the table holding most of the medical supplies and Daniel allowed himself to sink back into his pillows, closing his eyes. 'Poor old Sam,' he said. 'He does seem in a state.'

'Don't worry yourself over him,' advised his wife. 'You just concentrate on yourself.'

'I'd much rather not. I get more and more depressed when I do that.'

'Those people seem nice. Especially the woman. You've never really mentioned her before. She seems to know you pretty well.'

Daniel's eyes opened, and he examined the back of Alicia's head, the sweep of her neck as she bent over the flowers. The hint of jealousy amused and touched him. It was a miracle that she could continue to love him as she did. He chose to tease her a little.

'Rosemary is a remarkable woman. Extremely clever, as well as being enormous fun. Her lectures were priceless. She'd somehow manage to get us to remember about twenty long Latin names every time, simply by making us laugh. I can still remember every word, just about. But she never really earned recognition from the admin people. You know how it is – all they ever cared about was targets and bums on seats and endless idiotic inspections. And that Julian was never one of my favourites. Humourless bloke.'

'Is he married?'

'What? I have no idea. Probably.'

'So they're not an item, then?'

'Rosemary and Julian? I wouldn't think so. She's worth twenty of him. Though she does like men.'

'Yes. I noticed that.'

'Don't worry, darling. My flirting days are long over.'

'Don't say that, Daniel. Please make an effort – for my sake.'

Daniel did his best to stifle the long sigh that escaped his lips.

Laura was wishing she'd found another – *any* other – friend to throw herself on. Vickie was hardly even trying to make her feel welcome or cared for, and after her initial revelation, Laura had not felt encouraged to say more. The cases remained in the hall and Vickie fidgeted restlessly once the tea was finished.

'Look, Laura,' she burst out, 'this will sound very rude, but I really am in the middle of something. Sam's got himself in a right old muddle over the finances, and it's all down to me to straighten everything out. I can't leave anything to him, quite honestly. Not the paperwork, anyway. He's great when it comes to dealing with the personnel at the garden centres and being charming to the customers. But now the business has got so big, he's quite out of his depth. Mind you, I'm a bit tired of being an unpaid accountant. It's only because it's in my own interests…' She tailed off.

Laura did her best to listen intelligently. 'Surely there's a proper accountant attached to the business?' she queried.

'Oh, yes, of course there is. But that's for the business as a whole, do you see? I'm talking about what's specific to Sam – and Daniel.' She pulled a face, expressing a strange mix of pity, revulsion and exasperation at the name.

'Daniel?'

'Kellaway, of course. The Great Man himself. Sam worships him, always has. Says he's indebted to him for everything we've got. Now the bloody fool's giving away half the profits to the footling little university where he did his degree.'

'Sam is?' Laura was lost.

'No!' Vickie almost shouted. '*Daniel*, of course. He thinks he's dying, or something, and wants to endow a Chair, whatever that means. I've sent Sam to try to talk him out of it, but there's no real hope he'll succeed.'

'Well, don't mind me,' Laura said, abandoning all attempts to follow this tangled tale. 'I'll just sit here quietly with a magazine, and you get on. I'm sorry I turned up the way I did.' She took a deep calming breath. 'It's just that I couldn't think of anywhere else to go.' The admission was humiliating. She felt another prickle of tears, but wrestled them back where they came from. All she had to do was let time pass, let the world surge on in its own good way, and she'd eventually feel better.

Vickie took her at her word, and disappeared. Well, Laura thought, trying to be charitable, other people have their problems besides me. I can't reasonably expect her to drop everything and let me soak her shoulder with self-pitying tears. Except, of course, that was exactly what Laura had done for Vickie, seven or eight years ago, when she'd been rushed into hospital with a second ectopic pregnancy, sealing her fate as a childless woman once and for all. It had been with a vague sense of a favour owed, a balancing of needs, that she had sought out Vickie in the first place. Evidently, life didn't work quite like that.

Sam himself sounded harassed and overloaded, from what Vickie had said. And yet, Laura reminded herself, he had remembered Helena's birthday, and gone to the trouble to get a card and post it. Not many men of his generation were as thoughtful as that. Especially as the Trents and the Thymes had been drifting apart for some years now. Nick and Sam had met for occasional drinks, maybe once or twice a year, exchanging news of their jobs and commenting on the world at large, but there had been none of the rackety foursomes, eating and drinking late into the night, the men recalling their days at school and the women doing their best to find common ground, that they'd enjoyed in the early years. The strongest bond now was between Sam and Helena – with him behaving more like a fond uncle than a formal godfather. Laura didn't think he had once forgotten the girl's birthday, in twenty-two years.

She heard Sam's car draw up outside, his key in the lock, the muted slam of the door closing behind him. She heard Vickie's whispered explanation of the bags in the hall, her voice rising as she tried to convey her feelings. 'She can't stay here, Sam. You'll have to go and tell her.' The words were at normal volume, impossible not to overhear. Laura shrank even further into herself, wondering what came next, where she could possibly lay her head for the coming nights.

Almost immediately, he came into the room to find her. She had forgotten how broad his chest was, how kind his eyes. She jumped up and threw herself at him. Sam had been in the Sixth Form with Nick, more than thirty years ago. Sam had been Nick's best man when he married Laura, and had been chosen without hesitation as the ideal godfather for Helena. Somehow Sam had always been there, on call, when friendship was required.

'Oh, Sam,' she mumbled, before finally letting the tears flow.

Rosemary and Julian went out into the garden, following Alicia's directions to the affected trees. They proceeded slowly because Rosemary repeatedly dived off to one side or the other to examine and admire the many impressive plants. 'That Malaysian certainly went to town,' she said. 'Look at what he's done here – germander and *hamamelis mollis* tucked in together, with the best Jackman's Blue I've ever seen! Fabulous!'

Julian, who had always preferred his plants sliced up on laboratory slides, or in regimented experimental rows in polytunnels, was less than impressed. 'Very nice,' he muttered. 'Probably had a top professional designer to do it all for him.'

'Even so. I wonder who's maintaining it now. It could do with a bit of TLC, actually. Look at this bindweed. It'll strangle the witch hazel if they don't stop it.' She pulled sharply at the weed, unable to let it continue its destructive progress.

'Hey! Don't do that. You're not the gardener.' Julian glanced worriedly back towards the house.

'Julian – nobody likes bindweed. I've just doing what anybody would do.'

There was no reply, and Rosemary headed excitedly for a clump of feathery fennel. The positioning of it was inspired, softening a corner where two hedges met.

It took her some minutes to notice that Julian had opened the blue folder that Daniel had given him, and was reading it with complete absorption. 'Julian...' she began.

He ignored her, and with some irritation, she turned her attention to the diseased trees in the grand avenue. There was a red sap oozing down the trunks, in addition to a rapid shedding of bark. The impression was of a sort of canker or fungus, but she had never seen the condition before. 'This doesn't look very good at all,' she muttered. 'I'll need to do quite a bit of research to work out what's going on.'

'Well, I know I can leave it in your capable hands,' said Julian, absently. 'Look, I'd better get back. I've ordered a taxi for four-thirty.'

'What?' Rosemary was bemused. 'Aren't we meant to be tackling this together?'

'Don't be silly. I can't just abandon my college duties. Besides, you're more than capable of sorting it out without me.'

'Wait,' she insisted. 'How long am I meant to stay here? What about my lectures? I've got a third year Pathology group tomorrow at nine-thirty.'

'Oh, I'll get Frank Peterson to take that for you. No, you'll have to stay here until this tree thing is fixed. We owe it to Kellaway after everything he's doing for us. This really is a very generous endowment, you know. It's come at precisely the right moment, too. I must admit I was beginning to let the financial side of things worry me a bit.'

Rosemary tried to meet his eye, in vain. 'Julian, I get the feeling I've been kept in the dark about this. I thought we'd have a look at the trees together, take some samples, and then both get back this evening. I hadn't expected to be dumped here for an unspecified stay. I haven't even got my toothbrush!'

'Well, you should have paid more attention,' he said, reminding her yet again of just how impossible he was, and always had been. 'Obviously one of us has to put some serious time into this. There's a nice-looking pub-cum-hotel place in that village we came through, a few miles away. Dowminster, or something. You can stay there.'

'And who's paying?'

His toe dug a groove in the woodchip path. 'Well, you can claim for a night or two on the college budget. After that, you'd better bill Kellaway direct.'

And he was gone, in that curious way he had of vanishing before things got nasty. Rosemary was left fuming, promising herself that one of these days she really would get back at him. With immaculate timing, she heard the toot of a car horn as he disappeared. It had to be his taxi.

As she often did, she sought solace in the plants. Slowly moving down the avenue of well-positioned mature trees, she peered at one after the other. Many of them had the mysterious ailment, the scarlet sap like blood weeping from fissures in the peeling bark. Already her mind was sifting everything she knew about the species in question and all the diseases it was heir to. When nothing seemed to fit, she began to assess the sources she would have to consult to find the solution. For Rosemary Boxer, plant pathologist, was perfectly certain she would eventually find whatever it was that afflicted the trees. Hadn't she diagnosed her mother's suffering ageratums? And Julian was right in one respect: it was the least they could do for poor Daniel, lying up there with his ruined skin.

Sam gently pushed Laura back onto the sofa, and sat down beside her, waiting for the tears to subside.

'Oh, Sam – I don't know what I'm going to do,' she wept.

'Has he barred you from the house?'

She shook her head. 'Oh no. But I can't bear to be there on my own. Everything reminds me of him, all the lies and betrayals. I had to get away. I'll make him agree to selling it, as soon as I pull myself together.' She heaved a shuddering sigh. 'If I ever do.'

'You will, of course you will. But you need to think it over seriously before you make any rash decisions.'

She pulled away and gave him a penetrating look. 'Did you know about all this?'

'Not until Vickie told me just now. How can you ask? I didn't know a thing.'

'What did she say?'

'That Nick's left you. Is there another woman?'

'Didn't Vickie tell you that part? Or have you truly not had it from Nick? You are his friend, after all. I'm not sure I can believe you.'

'Laura, I'm *your* friend as much as Nick's. And after what you've told me, you have to believe my loyalty is to *you*. Come on, love, trust me. All the same, it's a big shock, I don't mind telling you. I'd have said Nick was the very last person to do something like this.'

Laura's lips quivered. 'That just makes it worse. He spends twenty-seven years pretending to be a decent human being, only to turn out just like the rest of you.'

Sam grunted at this, half laughing, half outraged. 'Steady on!' he said.

'Sorry, but that's how I feel. And I gather Vickie doesn't want me staying here. What am I going to do?'

He patted her back, like a small child. 'There, there,' he soothed. 'Vickie's right, I'm afraid. We've stripped the spare room, because it had to be replastered. We got rid of the bed that was in there, in the process. And she's taken over the third bedroom as an office. So there genuinely isn't anywhere for a visitor to sleep at the moment. Give us a few days to sort it out, and you'll be very welcome to come back. Look, there's a splendid little hotel in Dowminster, called the White Hart. I'll phone them now and see if they can have you.'

'Thanks,' she mumbled, feeling anything but grateful.

A few minutes later he was back. 'Is there anything I can get you? Did Vickie give you some tea?'

Laura nodded. 'Yes, she did. I'm fine thanks. Unless you're having some.'

He shook his head. 'I'm not supposed to have it, by rights. We'll have a proper drink in a bit.'

'Why can't you have tea? What's the matter with you?'

'Oh, nothing new. Irregular heartbeat or something. Caffeine isn't recommended, but I don't have to be fanatical about it. I hate those awful herbal teas everybody gives me instead.'

She gave him a searching look. 'You do seem a bit peaky, now I come to think about it. Pale and drawn. Not overdoing it, are you?'

'Probably. My partner's been ill for the best part of a year. He does manage some of the paperwork, but effectively it's all on my shoulders these days.'

'Vickie said something about that. She seems quite bothered.'

'Yes, well, it's a stressful time. These things happen.'

Laura nodded in wholehearted agreement. 'What did the White Hart say?'

'Oh, sorry. Yes, it's fine. They've got three rooms free tonight, so you're spoilt for choice. It's a nice place. You'll be quite comfortable there.'

Rosemary took her leave of Winterbourne Manor without speaking to either of the Kellaways again. Unsure of her exact position there, she preferred to leave all the discussion and negotiation until the following day. By then, with any luck, her rage might have subsided.

Julian had done this to her before, or variations of it, and it always came as a shock. However hard she tried, she could never get him to explain the whole story when they were providing their advisory services to garden owners. There had been one time when he'd airily told her they were taking a few students on a field trip, herded everybody onto a minibus and driven them nearly a hundred miles to Gatcombe Park, home of the Princess Royal. Rosemary had been wearing muddy jeans and a sweatshirt with a hole under one arm. Despite not meeting anybody remotely regal, the whole experience had been breathtakingly annoying. The fact that she had effortlessly diagnosed and cured the problem with the Gatcombe lilies had earned her the applause of the students, but not a word from Julian. And it had not made her feel any better about the whole expedition.

What was the matter with the man, anyway, that everything had to be kept so close to his chest? Secretive should be his middle name. Knowing she wouldn't be able to shake off these dark thoughts only made her angrier. Julian was not worthy of so much emotion, especially as she was liable to crack the enamel on her teeth if she carried on in the same vein.

The Land Rover started obediently, and she retraced the route back to Downminster, forcing herself to pay attention to the surrounding countryside. It was late May, when the wild flowers as well as the gardens were in full glory. Everywhere there were drifts of colour: pink campions in the hedgerows and azaleas in the cultivated gardens. The blue of wild *anchusa* which was Rosemary's favourite of all the wild flowers seemed especially vivid in the slanting late afternoon light.

The White Hart was easily located, at one end of the village. Mullioned windows, hanging baskets and predictable half-timbering all drew attention to it as a typical English hostelry. Inside it smelt pleasantly of furniture polish and toast. A man was writing on a pad behind the small reception desk, and he looked up the instant he heard her come through the door. *So far, so good*, thought Rosemary, accustomed to receptionists steadfastly *not* looking up until the regulation ninety seconds had elapsed. In her fantasy life as a ruthless chainsaw killer, the world was littered with slaughtered receptionists from doctors' surgeries to tax offices, and a hundred others in between.

'Good afternoon,' he said, in a mellow tone spiced with a hint of Wiltshire, if she was not mistaken. He had very nice eyebrows, she noted, with her reliable instinct for a likely-looking man.

'Oh, hello. Is there any chance of a room for a couple of nights? Possibly more.'

'Of course. No problem at all. On your own, are you?'

'Sadly, yes,' she smiled. 'It's a business trip.'

He refrained from making the obvious remark that people generally booked their accommodation in advance when on business trips. *Hmmm, discreet as well*, Rosemary approved.

He left his post, glanced rapidly around for any luggage, and then led her up to the allotted room. The absence of luggage was only just occurring to Rosemary as a problem. No toothbrush, no pyjamas, no clean pants. In her shoulder bag she did have a hairbrush and some make-up, luckily, but very little else that would come in useful. And by now it was too late to call and ask someone to come to the rescue. The only candidate was Billie at college, and she would have gone home an hour ago. And any shops that Dowminster might possess would already have closed.

'Dinner starts in a few minutes, and goes on until nine,' the man told her. 'Will you be having it?'

'Oh, yes, I'm starving,' she said. 'But I'll need a little while to settle down first. Then I'll probably pay a quick visit to the bar. Let's say I'll be ready to eat at about eight, if that's okay?'

'No problem at all,' he said again. It was a catch-phrase she had noticed was catching on everywhere.

Sam and Vickie both seemed slightly more relaxed as they sat with Laura on the patio at the back of the house, watching the setting sun. Laura herself was every bit as strung up as she had been that morning, however. She remembered throwing the stone through the window, trying in vain to recapture that moment of satisfaction as the glass had smashed.

'What a day!' she sighed, as she ran a critical eye over the Trents' garden. Considering that Sam worked with plants, it was not a very impressive show.

'When... I mean, well, *when* did it all happen?' Vickie was awkwardly fumbling towards sympathy, or so Laura supposed.

'Do you mean when did he first start shagging his tart, or when did I find out? Or even when did he tell me he was leaving me for her?'

Vickie spread her hands, in a gesture that said, *At least I'm making an effort. Give me a break.*

'Well, I don't know the exact timetable of events, but he says it got started at the Christmas party. Her father works with him, and brought the girl along instead of a wife.'

'And you didn't go.'

Laura shook her head. 'I'm trying not to kick myself about that. I did have a streaming cold at the time.'

Sam gave her a consoling pat on the arm. 'Don't start blaming yourself,' he said.

'No, I'm not.' She ground her teeth. 'I most definitely am not.'

'Good.'

'And you never suspected anything?' Vickie asked.

Laura pulled a face, screwing up her eyes. 'I did and

I didn't,' she said. 'It's hard to explain. Deep down, I knew things weren't wonderful between us. I wasn't getting my – um – conjugal rights, for one thing.'

Vickie flinched, but Sam gave a chuckle. 'Conjugal rights, eh?' he echoed. 'Once a copper, always a copper, isn't that what they say? Only the police use words like "conjugal".'

'Do they?' Laura was momentarily diverted. 'What about lawyers, and marriage guidance counsellors? And people in Ann Summers shops?'

'Laura! You haven't!' Vickie gasped again.

Laura shook her head, with some regret. 'No, I haven't. And come to think of it, they probably name names with absolutely no inhibitions. Sam's right. Conjugal is a very plodding sort of word. But the fact remains that I have had no nookie, hanky-panky, how's your father or sexual intercourse, for rather more than three months.'

Having got that moan off her chest, she felt a bit better. The stunned faces of both Trents added to the feeling that she was rallying slightly. Talking about sex was definitely a liberation that was long overdue. She sat there, quietly considering the subject for a few minutes. The truth was not exactly as she had just implied. With an honesty that came quite naturally, she admitted to herself that she had not really missed Nick's attentions in bed. This, however, did nothing at all to assuage the fury she felt towards him – if anything it only made it fiercer – but it did push her into a wider analysis of just what had gone wrong in her marriage.

Regrettably, Sam and Vickie were not the people to share this revelation. Vickie had quickly started bustling about with the garden furniture, staring theatrically at the sky and predicting rain. 'We'd better go in,' she ordered. 'And, actually Laura, if you're ready, I think it might be time for Sam to drive you to Dowminster.'

The fact that Vickie had not so much as offered to feed her rankled quite sorely. Some half-baked story about having nothing in the house worth eating, and being so bowed down with spreadsheets had sounded quite embarrassingly unconvincing. With a great effort, Laura tried to be charitable. Other people had troubles as well as her, and she had apparently walked into something that was deeply worrying to her friends. Sam had done his best to be kind, but it was obvious that his mind was on something else.

'Right, then,' she agreed. 'I hope my cases will fit in your car boot.'

Rosemary had eaten her rather pleasing lamb casserole with local vegetables and a half bottle of surprisingly good red wine. Drinking red wine always made her feel young, for some odd reason. It was almost invariably her first choice, with just about any meal.

She had then indulged in apple crumble with cream, feeling slightly relieved that there were no other diners to observe her gluttony. She had just ordered coffee when two people appeared at the reception desk. Rosemary had a perfect view of the scene, through the open archway between the foyer and the dining room. And her curiosity was increased when she recognised Sam Trent from that afternoon. The partner in the Kellaway business, who had hovered by the window with a disapproving air.

The landlord, whose name, she had discovered, was Robin, once again did his ten-out-of-ten greeting, despite not having been at his post when the couple first arrived. By some miracle of sensitivity, he was there in seconds, smiling and nodding and seeming to know just what was required. 'Oh yes, you phoned. Mrs Thyme, I've put you in Room Three. I think you'll be comfortable there. Are these your bags?'

Rosemary examined the woman with Sam Trent. Superficially they looked rather alike. Same broad shoulders, and self-assured tilt to the chin. Brother and sister, she wondered.

'Will you be having dinner?' Robin asked the woman. 'We stop serving at nine.'

Before she could reply, Sam glanced quickly at his watch, pressing a tiny button on the side of it. Rosemary had heard nothing, but it seemed it must have beeped at him.

'What's that for?' the woman asked him.

'Time for another pill. I can never remember to take them if I don't set the alarm.'

'Pills as well? Sam...'

He interrupted her with a quick wave of his hand. 'Don't fuss, Laura. They do the job, keeping the old pump in service. I'm just glad this stuff exists.'

The woman was diverted from the subject by Robin hefting her suitcases and heading for the staircase. 'Well, Sam, you can be excused now,' she told him.

He took her in a sudden hug, saying, 'I'm so sorry we couldn't put you up. It must seem very ungracious. It's just rather bad timing.'

'Don't worry about it. I'll see you tomorrow, then. As long as you're sure it won't put you out.'

'I'll be here to collect you at half past eight. Have a good night.'

She grimaced at that. 'I'll try. Thanks for everything.'

'Bye, then.'

'Bye bye, Sam.'

Rosemary lingered over her coffee, with nothing else to do but return to her room and have a ridiculously early night, or watch depressing news reports on the television. It had looked as if the new guest was going to want a late dinner, and Rosemary felt she might like to have company in the rather gloomy dining room.

When she eventually did come back, it was quarter

to nine, and the waitress's impatience was palpable. Thrusting a menu at Laura, she hovered for a moment, hoping for a quick decision. But there clearly wasn't going to be one, so she marched back to the kitchen, presumably to commiserate with the cook, who would also be wanting to get off home.

As Rosemary sat trying to catch the woman's eye, she could not help but observe a growing distress in her fellow guest. The menu fluttered in her hand, as she stared at it, obviously not giving any attention to the words before her. What could be the matter? She looked healthy, well-dressed, nicely made-up, with pretty earrings and well-kept hands with a tight-looking wedding ring. It could, of course, be any one of a thousand things. Family, probably. Maybe she'd come here for a funeral. That seemed highly likely, except that the clothes didn't look right. Well, there had been two large suitcases, no doubt containing a dark suit for an early morning cremation. And perhaps one of them had been empty, ready to collect goodies from the dead person's house, after the funeral.

Satisfied with her own cleverness, Rosemary drained her coffee. Perhaps she would speak to this Laura – what had he said the surname was? Time? Sounded a bit odd. Anyway, she could use her acquaintance with Sam Trent as an opening for conversation. It would be nice to have somebody to talk to. They could sit in the lounge for a bit...

The chair made a loud clatter as Laura pushed it back from the table, over the wooden flooring. With a definite sob, and unmistakable tears on her face, she dashed out of the room and up the stairs. Rosemary sagged with amazement and concern. That poor woman – she'd seemed absolutely desperate in those few seconds before she disappeared. Rosemary gazed at the empty table, where the menu was on the floor and the white napkin crumpled in front of where Laura had been sitting.

The waitress came back, and directed an accusing look at Rosemary. 'Where did she go?'

'Up to her room, I think. It doesn't look as if she'll be having dinner after all.'

When Rosemary plodded back to her own room, feeling the return of much of her earlier frustration towards Julian, she had to pass Room Three. Through the stout oak door she heard the unambiguous sounds of weeping. Plain human decency suggested to her that she should knock and offer condolences. She curled her forefinger preparatory to rapping gently on the door. And then she changed her mind. People often wanted a good cry uninterrupted by well-meaning strangers. Sometimes they even booked into small country pubs for that very purpose. Besides, there was always tomorrow morning, when Rosemary had every intention of coinciding with the woman over breakfast.

Chapter Five

Rosemary's plan worked in part. Rather than sidling up to Laura over a full English breakfast, thanks to a shameful lie-in until well past eight-thirty, she encountered her fellow guest in the hotel lobby, when she went to make a phone-call.

In truth, Rosemary's primary concern was with her lack of clean clothes. All she had was the things she'd arrived in, and wearing yesterday's pants was something she hadn't done for years. Contacting Billie was a matter of real urgency, so when she realised the payphone was already in use, she gritted her teeth in frustration.

Fortunately, Laura Time, or whatever her name was, had not got through. Rosemary found her listening to an unresponsive receiver, almost shaking it in disbelief. Eventually, she put it back on its rest, and only then noticed Rosemary.

'Oh, sorry. Are you waiting to use it?'

'That's okay.'

Laura said nothing further, but went to the front door and looked out into the street, checking her watch, and showing clear signs of impatience. Rosemary only half registered the growing signs of anxiety.

To her great relief, Billie was at her post in the college office, and more than willing to drive out into the wilds with a bag of Rosemary's essential needs. 'Oh, yes, and my laptop and *Exotic Dendrology*, if you can find it,' she added to the list. 'I'll have to go out for a bit, but I'll be back at lunchtime. Aim for about one, if that's all right.'

Replacing the receiver, she turned to the other woman. 'Problems?' she asked lightly. This seemed enough to cover the tears of the night before as well as the obvious anxiety this morning.

Laura turned a blank face towards her. 'I don't

understand it,' she said. 'Sam promised he'd be here at
eight-thirty, and he's never late. Now there's no reply
at the house. It's only a five-minute drive. It doesn't
make sense.'

'It's Sam Trent, isn't it?'

'That's right. Do you know him?'

'I met him yesterday for the first time. He lives
near here then?'

'Devenish. He and his wife are old friends of mine.
I thought I could stay with them, but they're replas-
tering the spare room. It's quite nice here, though,
isn't it.' Her gaze returned to the street, the worried
frown deepening. 'Oh, I wish I knew what had happened to him.'

'Well, let's go and find out, shall we? I'm going
back to Winterbourne this morning, and Devenish is
on the way. I'll give you a lift.'

'Thanks.' With only the slightest of raised eyebrows, Laura accepted the ride in the Land Rover –
which once again started at the first turn of the key.

Despite her concern for Sam, Laura's thoughts
were chiefly on her own situation. Almost before they
were clear of the village, she had responded to
Rosemary's friendly manner, and was pouring her
heart out.

'We were married for twenty-seven years. Two
lovely kids, everything rosy as far as I could tell. Well
– looking back I suppose you could say there were a
few cracks, but isn't that true for everybody? And it's
such a horrible cliché, middle-aged husband running
off with a girl half his wife's age. *Less* than half, if I'm
honest. She's blonde, thin as a rail and a humiliating
twenty-three years old. That's only a year older than
my daughter. Isn't that terrible!'

'How did he meet her?'

'At work. He's in the police. That's where we met,
when I was a WPC. I gave it all up when the children
arrived. Now what have I got?' She thumped the dash-

board hard.

'Careful! You'll hurt your hand.'

'I don't care. Why should I care!'

'He'll come back, when she gets bored with him.' Rosemary tried to sound convincing.

'You're joking! I wouldn't have him back now if he crawled over broken glass.'

'Atta girl!' They smiled at each other, and then laughed.

'Oh, but I do *hate* men,' Laura added. 'Nasty disloyal creatures, the lot of them. Oops – should I say that? Are you married?'

'No, not me. Been on the brink a couple of times, but the best ones got away. Besides, I think I like men too much to tie myself down to just one. If that makes any sense.'

'It makes perfect sense,' said Laura gloomily.

'Hey! What's going on here?' Rosemary slowed the Land Rover to a crawl, in response to a vigorous wave from a policeman at the junction ahead. 'Gosh – there's been an accident, look.'

Laura stared at a blue car lying on its side in a ditch, the whole of the visible flank battered and buckled. A breakdown truck had just begun to lift it free, and as the two women watched, the rear end was raised high enough for the number plate to be legible.

'Oh my God!' Laura gasped. 'That's Sam's car.'

'Are you sure? I wouldn't think it's recognisable, the poor thing.'

'Yes, I know the number. One of those silly police habits that never fades. It's definitely his.' She was already scrambling out of the Land Rover and trotting towards the policeman.

'What happened?' she demanded. 'Where's Sam?'

The man looked at her through narrowed eyes. 'And who might you be, madam?'

'Laura Thyme. I'm a friend of his. I saw him last night. Where is he?' Wildly she looked around, at the trees and hedges and fields beyond, as if expecting Sam to come strolling towards her.

'Well, I'm very sorry to inform you, madam, that there was a fatality here last night. Preliminary examinations suggest that this car failed to stop at the junction, and was in collision with an oncoming vehicle. A very large vehicle, unfortunately. We have the driver as witness to the events. Meanwhile, if you would kindly carry on your way, we can proceed with our investigations.' Then he seemed to have a new thought. 'Did you say you saw him last night, madam?'

'Yes. Oh, heavens! I might have been the last person to see him before this happened.'

'Would you be good enough to let me have your details, then? Just in case we need to get in touch with you.'

'Yes, of course. Laura gave her name, and home address, without thinking. She couldn't take her eyes off the wreckage of Sam's car, trying to absorb this ghastly new turn of events. She spoke, almost to herself. 'But I *know* Sam. He would never drive in front of a lorry. Especially at night. He'd have seen its headlights in plenty of time.' She scanned the junction, trying to imagine what must have happened. Visibility was good, the weather had been clear and dry.

'That's as may be, madam,' said the policeman repressively.

Giving up, Laura walked slowly back to the Land Rover, where Rosemary was standing in the road waiting for her. 'Did I hear that right?' she asked. 'The car driver died?'

'So it seems. I can't believe it. Sam can't be dead. He was always such a careful driver.' She turned her ravaged face to Rosemary. 'And it's all my fault. He was must have been coming back from delivering me to the White Hart.'

'Don't be silly.' Rosemary was brisk. 'That's just nonsense talk, and you know it.'

'Well, I bet you Vickie thinks the same. She's never going to forgive me.'

'That's up to her. Your job is to forgive yourself. Or rather, to convince yourself there's nothing *to* forgive. For heaven's sake, people drive about all the time, they get careless, cars go wrong – that's the way it is. You can't go round looking for somebody to blame. It doesn't change anything, after all.'

Laura looked at her new friend with interest. 'Quite a philosopher, aren't you,' she muttered, with a mixture of impatience and respect.

'No, I'm a college lecturer,' Rosemary chuckled. 'Now come on, they want us out of here.'

They got back into the vehicle, and Rosemary turned the ignition. Nothing happened. 'Blast!' she hissed. 'She always does this at the most inconvenient moments.'

'What? Are we stuck?'

'No,' Rosemary sighed, before repeating her familiar routine with the spanner and the starting motor. She ignored the patronising looks coming from the policeman at the junction, and the guffaws from the men belonging to the breakdown lorry.

'Where to?' she asked Laura, once they were moving. 'Will you still go to the Trents' house?'

'Good God, no. I can't possibly intrude on Vickie now.' Ruefully she imagined the scene if she did. Always volatile, Vickie would either scream accusations of murder at her, or fling herself sobbing onto Laura's bosom and cling for days. Neither prospect was endurable, in present circumstances. After all, Laura had problems of her own to deal with.

'You can come with me to Winterbourne, then. I'll be glad of the company.'

'Are you sure? I really don't know where to go, or what to do. It's a very strange sensation.'

'You'll get used to it. And something's sure to turn up. It always does.'

There were several cars parked on the gravel sweep in front of the manor house, and a cluster of people had gathered beside an old stone wall covered in climbing roses. Rosemary quickly identified them for Laura.

'The slim woman in the pink cashmere is Alicia Kellaway, and the man beside her is the doctor who attends Daniel – her husband. I assume the other woman is your Vickie Trent. And it looks as if the policeman is leaving.'

'Why's Vickie here, I wonder? Gosh, doesn't she look dreadful!'

Laura jumped down from the Land Rover and approached her friend, one arm outstretched as if to grab Vickie's hand. Vickie turned towards her, but made no responding gesture. Laura let her arm fall, wary of the extreme emotions on all sides.

Vickie took a step towards Laura, babbling almost hysterically. 'They came to tell me just before midnight, and rushed me to the hospital. But it was too late. He died in the car, you see. Oh, Laura – he was only going to be gone twenty minutes. I never even said goodbye to him. I was all taken up with you.'

Laura flinched, but there didn't seem to be any reproach in Vickie's voice. The story continued.

'I stayed there for a while, and then that policeman took me to the station for a cup of hot chocolate, and I couldn't face going home in the small hours. And there didn't seem to be anybody else I could call so late at night, so I just stayed there until morning. Then he brought me here.' She looked at the young officer, who was in his car. 'Thanks again!' she called after him. 'He's been wonderfully kind, you see.'

'Vickie, we're all so dreadfully sorry.' Laura turned to examine the speaker – Mrs Kellaway. Her face was soft with sympathy. A pretty face, Laura noted dispassionately.

'Alicia, I'd be lost without you. But —' she turned

back to Laura. 'Why are *you* here? You don't know the Kellaways, surely? You would have said.' She sighed miserably. 'Doesn't yesterday seem ages ago, now. Like far distant history.'

'I know just what you mean,' said Laura. But for her, ancient history dated from two days earlier than it did for Vickie. 'I came with Rosemary. We're both at the White Hart, and she kindly gave me a lift when Sam didn't show up.' Vickie's moan informed her that this had been a thoughtless thing to say. 'Oh, Vick, I am terribly sorry. Sam was such a fine man. A wonderful man. It's a wicked loss.'

'They think he might have had a heart attack,' Vickie wept. 'And he was being so good, taking the pills and avoiding caffeine and other things. He was sure he'd got it all under control.'

At which point the doctor joined in. 'His heart was giving some cause for concern,' he said. 'But there was no reason to think… well, this has come as a complete shock to me, I must say.'

'Daniel's dreadfully upset, too, of course,' said Alicia. 'In fact, I must go to him. He'll be feeling very left out.' She glanced up at a high window, behind a balcony, with eaves just above it. 'Although he can probably hear most of what we're saying.'

Everybody paused, as if waiting for confirmation from above their heads. When nothing was heard, the group began to disperse.

'I must have another look at those trees,' said Rosemary. 'You can come with me, Laura.'

'And I'm late for my appointments,' said the doctor, taking a hesitant step towards the cars.

'I'll have to go home, I suppose,' said Vickie. 'But I haven't got my car.'

'I'll take you,' said the doctor. 'Go and get in. It's the red one. I haven't locked it.'

Laura began to walk down the formal garden path, beside the ornamental pond, while Rosemary went to fetch tools from the back of the Land Rover, parked to one side of the house, not far from Daniel's window. Glancing towards the house, Rosemary caught a moment of intimacy between Alicia Kellaway and the doctor. He was apparently giving her a lingering farewell before driving Vickie home. No more than a touch of hands, and a meeting of eyes, but it spoke volumes.

'Hmmm,' said Rosemary to herself.

The two women had the garden to themselves, and were glad to get away from the grief-stricken household. Laura couldn't stop talking. 'There'll have to be a post-mortem, of course. It'll be obvious whether he did have a heart attack or not. What do you make of that doctor, by the way?'

Rosemary chewed her bottom lip for a thoughtful moment. 'He seems to spend a lot of time here, for one thing. After what I just saw, I'd be tempted to think he's got something going with that Mrs Kellaway, even if she does seem devoted to Daniel. Can't really blame her, I suppose. He's obviously not a lot of use as a husband.'

'What a thing to say!' Laura was genuinely angry. 'There's more to marriage than sex, you know.'

'Oops. Yes, I'm sure there is. Of course. But Alicia's young and pretty, and the doctor's not a bad specimen. They'll have been thrown together over the sickbed, sort of thing. Isn't that a classic situation?'

Despite herself, Laura gave a little giggle. 'I wouldn't know,' she admitted. 'Gosh, you do have a knack for cheering people up, don't you. Doesn't anything ever depress you?'

'Loads of things. My boss, for example. Shall I tell you the long sad story of bloody Julian, Principal of Malmesbury University?'

'Oh, yes. That sounds just the thing. Gosh, these verbascums are good, aren't they! Don't you love the texture of them.'

Rosemary aborted the flow of invective against Julian, to stare at Laura. 'You're a gardener, are you?'

'Depends what you mean. I like gardening, and I know a lot of plants. I'm quite good with colour, though I say so myself.'

'Well fancy that. We ought to make a good team, then.'

'Why? Are you here to do the garden? I get the feeling I've lost the plot in the last few minutes. There's me moaning on about Nick and not giving you a chance to say anything.'

'Plenty of time. Which reminds me, what *is* your surname?'

'Thyme. T.H.Y.M.E. Nick's family always pronounced it like it's spelt, presumably to avoid confusion, but I rather like being named after a herb. It was one of the things I was so happy about when I married him.'

'Definitely,' Rosemary approved briskly. 'Anyway, the reason I'm here, specifically, is to try to find a cure for those poor trees.' She pointed ahead to the avenue, which they had been approaching at a snail's pace. 'It's something I've never seen before.'

'Right. You're a plant doctor.'

'Not exactly. I'm a plant pathologist, and I lecture in plant diseases among other things. We're a very hands-on outfit, doing a lot in real gardens. It's surprising, actually, that I haven't got a gaggle of students in tow. It's only that it's rather a long way from the college, and they've got their year end coursework to do. Most of them are late with it, needless to say.'

Laura began to look all round, in an agitated fashion. 'What's the matter?' Rosemary asked her.

'I'm desperate for the loo. Do you think I could go behind that yew hedge?'

'I think it might be risky. We don't know who's about. Go back to the house. It's nearly coffee time, anyway. Maybe they'll offer us some. Give me a shout if so.'

'All right, then. But I do feel like an interloper. I've got no reason at all to be here, let's face it.'

'Quite honestly, they'll be in too much of a lather to care. Watch out for the madwoman though.'

'Pardon?'

'They've got a woman – a sort of general factotum. She makes tea and answers the door. And wears a hat like a tea cosy. I think she really is a bit demented, poor thing.'

'Thanks for the warning. If I'm not back in ten minutes, come and search for me.'

Laura approached the house by a different path, thinking it looked more direct. The garden was sheer delight, with boldly positioned plants offering an impression of opulent plenty. 'Must be good soil,' she muttered to herself enviously. She had never managed to get peonies to flourish like the lovely mass there was here.

But the urgency with which she needed the loo outweighed the appeal of the garden, and she almost trotted up to the front door. It was half open, and she tapped tentatively, while at the same time pushing it wider.

'Hello?' she called. 'Can I come in?'

There was no response, so she ventured into the hall. Most houses of any size had a downstairs cloakroom not too far inside the front door. Maybe she could quickly make use of it and go again without being noticed.

The first door she opened turned out to be a small sunny sitting room, with large television and an untidy scattering of garments, magazines, knitting and crockery. It looked like a young person's bedsit, except that there wasn't a bed.

She struck lucky with the second door, much to her relief. Coming out again, she could not resist a swift exploration. Other people's houses were always interesting, and this one, with its odd additions and crooked angles was more so than most. A door stood open at the end of the hall, to the left of the handsome staircase. Telling herself that she could truthfully claim to be looking for Alicia, she went to peer round it.

The contrast with the first room she'd seen was almost ludicrous. This one could easily have come from the pages of *Homes and Gardens,* with the expensive wallpaper, lavish antique furniture and gorgeous Chinese carpet. It was spotlessly clean, and quite devoid of any sign of human use.

Feeling slightly repelled, Laura withdrew, and started back towards the door. Not much prospect of any coffee, she concluded. Alicia must be upstairs with the invalid husband, and the factotum was probably preparing lunch.

'What are you doing here?' came a rough voice from behind her.

Before Laura could reply, another voice came from the top of the stairs. 'That's all right, Mrs Potts. This lady is with Miss Boxer. They're doing something in the garden.'

Alicia floated into sight, her face a bland mask of serenity. 'Can I help you?'

'Oh, no, it's all right, thanks. I just popped in to use your loo. I hope you don't mind. I did call, but nobody heard me.'

'Her weren't in the lavvy, her were in't lounge,' announced the person now emerging from a door beyond the staircase. 'I saw 'er.'

'That's quite all right, Mrs Potts. I feel sure you must have been mistaken.'

Laura experienced a brief pang of conscience. 'No, she's right,' she owned up. 'I was trying to find you, you see. And might I say what a very beautiful room it is. Exquisite taste.'

Alicia seemed not to have heard the accolade. 'Oh? And why were you trying to find me?'

'Well...' It obviously wasn't going to be possible to demand coffee, under the circumstances. She invented wildly. 'Rosemary wanted me to tell you she's on the case.'

'I'm sorry. I don't understand.' Alicia's voice was sweet, with careful enunciation. She spoke as she moved, with complete control. The housekeeper seemed to be retreating back to her own domain, much to Laura's relief.

'The sick trees,' she explained. 'Rosemary's giving them a thorough examination.'

'Oh, trees.' The contempt was unmistakable. 'That's Daniel's department. She'll have to talk to him about them.'

'Right. I'll tell her. I expect we'll work for another hour or so, and then go off for some lunch. Is that all right.'

'Do what you like,' said the lady of the house, suddenly weary or bored or distracted by higher thoughts. Whichever it was, Laura thought she was being dismissed rather rudely. This feeling was reinforced by a scornful cackle from the older woman, now standing at the further end of the hall.

Before she left, Laura gave the woman a closer look. The hat was not so much like a tea cosy as a sporran, she decided. Or maybe the bag part of bag-pipes, the way it sagged so heavily, as if waiting to be inflated by a good pair of lungs. But the woman's face was even more compelling. Heart-shaped, with wide-set eyes and a straight nose. Laura's memory banks stirred for a fleeting moment, before she turned away and went back to the garden.

Rosemary was where she'd left her, taking samples of the red sap, and tapping her teeth with a spatula as she stood lost in thought.

'Don't do that,' Laura admonished her. 'That stuff might be toxic.'

'Mmmm? Oh, no I don't think it is. Anyway, I used the other end. It's surprising, actually, how few plants are truly poisonous, statistically.'

'Really? What about laburnum, yew, belladonna, about a thousand types of toadstools – and that's just off the top of my head.'

'Right. And those are the ones everybody knows because they really do kill you if you eat enough of them. And usually it does have to be quite a lot. Most of the others just give you a nasty tummy upset or localised reaction. We've all evolved together, you see. We're mutually interdependent. Plants use us, and we use them. Then there's insects, and birds.'

'Stop!' Laura pleaded. 'You're not in college now.'

'Sorry.' Rosemary laughed. 'I do get carried away, I know. It's a fascinating subject. Any luck with the coffee?'

'Total failure, I'm afraid. I saw the madwoman, though.'

'And?'

'Well, let's just say she wasn't very gracious. But I had a very odd feeling when I had a chance to look at her properly. The word "Withersedge" popped into my head. Isn't that peculiar.'

'Very. Is it a name?'

'I've no idea what it is.'

'The sedge is wither'd from the lake.
  And no birds sing.'

'What's that?'

'Keats. *La Belle Dame Sans Merci.*'

'Ah.'

Rosemary continued her meticulous work of collecting samples from all the diseased trees, as well as examining the ground around the roots, and peering up into the leafy canopy overhead. Laura concluded that she wasn't needed, and went for a further inspection of the garden in the wilder area furthest from the house. Her head was full of the day's events, and half an hour's solitude amongst the plants was just what she needed. The sudden loss of Sam was dragging at her, like heavy damp clothes. It seemed so arbitrary, so unfair and unreasonable. Sam had always been there, a friendly presence, sharing so much of Nick's past, as well as being such a reliable godfather to Helena. Nick! Suddenly she thought of how Sam's death would affect her husband, and what that might imply for her own interactions with him. How would he hear the news? Through work, almost casually included on today's list of sudden deaths? Or on the local television broadcasts, just a brief name and place as one of the minor items? Either way, it would cause him shock and pain. Laura squashed her instinctive urge to phone him and break it to him gently. He had forfeited any right to such consideration from her. It was no longer her place to ease his grief. And somehow that realisation made everything feel much worse.

Fiercely, she resisted the threatening tears. There would be time enough for that in the hours of darkness, safe in her hotel room. For now, she was going to focus on daytime things, like gardens and batty old housekeepers and the refreshingly cheery Rosemary Boxer.

She took a little stroll down a narrow path, forcing herself to notice the plants. When she returned to Rosemary, she had something to report. 'I've got another one,' she said. 'Giant hogweed. There's some down there, by the field hedge.'

'Really? Let's see.' Laura led her new friend along the path.

'There! Rather glorious, isn't it.'

The plants were seven or eight feet tall, with the huge umbrels still not fully formed, so early in the summer. 'Surely they must have been the model for John Wyndham's triffids,' Laura said.

'Phytophototoxic, the same as rue,' said Rosemary.
'What?'

'The sap reacts to light. It's a nasty thing. Don't go near it.'

Laura sighed. 'You're probably right, but I still think it's beautiful.'

'The Victorians agreed with you. They imported it as an architectural garden plant. *Heracleum mantegazzianum*. Lovely name, horrid plant. We've been trying to eradicate it ever since.'

'Which must be why it's tucked away down here, where nobody can find it. Well, good luck to it, I say.'

'Looks as if somebody's been trying to cut it down,' Rosemary observed, pointing to a cluster of hacked-off stems. 'Clumsy way of doing it. Wonder why they didn't finish the job.'

'Probably because somebody like me stopped them, and told them to leave the poor thing alone. It's not doing anybody any harm down here, now is it?'

Rosemary sighed. 'I suppose you stick up for ragwort, too.'

'What?'

'Pretty yellow flowers, quite tall, grows on roadsides. Now that really is a killer.'

'Oh?'

'Yes, it poisons horse and cattle. They die rather slowly, unfortunately.'

'More fool them for eating it,' said Laura. 'What price evolution there, then?'

Rosemary gave her a mock slap on the arm. 'You're just arguing for the sake of it,' she accused. 'Now let's get back to work.'

They returned to the avenue, and Rosemary gathered up her sample pots and other equipment.

'I don't know about you, but I'm getting thirsty, and hungry. Why don't we cut and run? We can go back to the White Hart for some lunch. I have to be there for one, anyway. I've got a girl coming from college with my toothbrush.'

'Anything you say. I'm entirely at your disposal.'

'Come on then. It'll be gone twelve when we get there at this rate. I can't wait to get out of these clothes. I didn't expect it would get so warm.'

Laura looked at the blue sky. 'It is a lovely day,' she remarked. 'Makes it all the more awful about Sam, somehow. People shouldn't die when the sun's shining.'

They reverted to the subject of Sam on the drive back to Dowminster. Laura spoke slowly, thinking hard. 'It's odd, don't you think, that he took a heart pill only a few minutes before he must have collapsed.'

'I saw him take it – I was watching you both from the dining room. Pills don't work miracles, you know.'

'I know, but even so. What if somebody had tampered with them?'

Rosemary turned to give a long sceptical stare. 'What gives you that idea?'

'Watch the road, will you. We're nearly at the place where it happened.'

'Okay. Listen, you're jumping to some very odd conclusions, aren't you? It all sounds quite straightforward to me, even though it's a dreadful thing to happen.'

'He was bothered about something, though.'

'What about that wife of his? It sounds awful, but isn't it very often the spouse behind iffy things like this?'

Laura choked for a moment on the implication, but nonetheless gave the idea some consideration. 'Well, Vickie had been doing a lot of financial analysis on her computer when I arrived, trying to work out where they stood with the Kellaway business. She was so distracted by it, she didn't even recognise me when I arrived on the doorstep. She and Sam both told me about Daniel's illness and the pressures and strains they were under. But I hardly think she'd have any reason for wanting Sam out of the way.'

'I'm sure you're right. It was crass of me to suggest

it. After all, she is your friend.'

'Not so much so as Sam. I've never been quite sure that she likes me, to be honest.'

The village was in sight, nestling in a hollow between two pleasantly rolling hills, a river meandering in a loop just beyond the main settlement. Rosemary slowed the Land Rover. 'I haven't told you about the money Daniel's giving my college, have I?' she said, and proceeded to outline the endowment, and Sam's apparent resistance to it.

Laura gave this some thought. 'I can't see how that's relevant, to be honest. It's probably all perfectly above board, anyway. He did have a weak heart, after all, and he was looking off colour yesterday. I have this awful habit of thinking the worst when there's a sudden death.'

'Mind you, there's the doctor,' said Rosemary darkly. 'I wouldn't trust him. And presumably he prescribed Sam's pills.'

'That's a thought,' Laura agreed. 'And I've just had another one.'

'Oh?'

'Well – what if your Principal chap found a way to poison Sam? Wouldn't that help with his endowment money?'

Rosemary chewed her lip for a minute before replying. 'You know something? There's nothing I wouldn't put past Julian Marchant.'

'This is a sweet little village, isn't it,' Laura changed the subject as they entered the centre of Dowminster. 'Still kept a few of its old shops, as well.'

They scanned the High Street appreciatively. 'Even a proper butcher, look,' said Rosemary. 'And a chemist. Just like the good old days.'

'Long may they last,' Laura agreed. 'Oh, my goodness!'

'What?'

'That woman, coming out of the chemist. It's the

mad housekeeper. Nobody could mistake that hat.'

'So it is. What's that she's carrying?'

Laura peered unselfconsciously through the wind-screen, as Rosemary slowed the Land Rover's pace. 'Industrial quantities of cream for Daniel, is my guess,' said Laura. 'From what you say, he must use an awful lot of it. They probably keep a standing order for him.'

'Maybe that's why they're still in business,' giggled Rosemary. 'Has she noticed us?'

'I don't think so. It's all she can do to stagger along with that great tub of stuff.'

Mrs Potts was clutching a canister to her chest, heading across the street towards the small town car park. Her distinctive hat, as before, seemed to have a life of its own. 'Poor old thing,' murmured Rosemary.

'She seems happy enough to me,' Laura said. 'And I didn't like the way she accosted me in the house this morning. It's one thing to be batty and another to be outright aggressive.'

'Oh, well, she's probably had a sad life,' said Rosemary.

Laura laughed loudly at that. 'You sound just like my mother when you say that. She always gave that excuse for people.'

'And why not? I expect it's true.'

'I expect it is,' said Laura.

Billie arrived before they'd finished lunch, and Rosemary urged her to join them. Making the intro-ductions, she left Laura and Billie to exchange pleas-antries, while she eagerly ran up to her room with the bag of clothes and other essentials. Five minutes later, she felt restored to her usual comfort, having changed into a much lighter top, and clean pants.

'Well, then,' she smiled, going back to the dining room, 'what's the gossip?'

Billie's face seemed strained, and Rosemary wondered whether Laura had said something to annoy her.

'Er, Rosemary…' Billie began.

Rosemary's attention was diverted by the arrival of three coffees. 'Ah, coffee. At last! I've been gasping for this. Amazing what a difference a change of clothes can make. I owe you, love, for bringing them all this way.'

'No problem. Actually, Rosemary…'

'You should have seen the garden we've been working on. Absolutely marvellous. About three acres, altogether, brilliantly designed. Hedges, avenues, wild areas, and an outrageous ornamental pond, right in front of the house. I've almost forgiven Julian for dumping me here without any notice. Especially with the weather so lovely as well.' Then she remembered Laura and the tragic Sam. 'Although, it hasn't be entirely happy, of course.'

'Rosemary,' Billie interrupted desperately. 'I've got a letter for you. From Julian.'

Rosemary took it readily. 'What's this? More instructions from on high, I suppose. Sending me off to some other part of the country to look at leaf scab on somebody's laurel?'

'I think not. Three others in the faculty have had them.'

Rosemary opened the envelope and read the letter, mouthing some of the words to herself, as if that might render them more intelligible. 'This has to be a joke,' she said at last.

'I think not,' said Billie again.

'But he's given me the bloody sack. With effect from the end of this term. Surely that's not legal?'

'It's the same for the others.'

'Which others?'

'Deirdre Fellowes, Tom Bishop and Fergus Cooke. I'm not sure of the whole story, but I gather Lois found a notepad that Deirdre left in one of the lecture rooms, with some sort of draft letter in it.'

Rosemary's hand flew to her mouth. 'No!' she breathed.

Billie cocked her head. 'It's true then – you were conspiring with Deirdre against Julian.'

'That makes it sound awfully underhand. The four of us had genuine grievances, and we were planning to approach the Governors about them.' Rosemary tried hard to retain her dignity, while the ground seemed to be crumbling beneath her feet. 'But we have been trying for ages to make Julian listen to us. It was a last resort.'

'Well, he doesn't like it.'

'So it would seem,' said Rosemary.

'And he's got the backing of the Governors. One hundred per cent.' Billie was rueful. 'I am sorry,' she added, sincerely.

Rosemary saw the whole thing – or she thought she did. Was it possible that Julian had already decided to ditch the four of them, last week? Had Lois's discovery only served to clinch his decision? Whatever the exact sequence of events, her reaction was the same. 'That treacherous, cowardly, vile little bastard! Why couldn't he tell me to my face?'

'I don't know. It's not going to be the same without you. You four have been the backbone of the place ever since I've worked there.'

Rosemary tossed the letter onto the table in front of her. 'Well, you can tell Professor Shifty Double-Dealing Marchant that I'm not coming back. If he thinks I'm going to carry on until the end of term, after this, then he's kidding himself. I'll finish what I've started here, purely because Daniel's a friend, and he didn't know his generosity would lead to me losing my job. But after that, I'm off. Julian will be hearing from my solicitor about the way he's ignored just about every piece of employment legislation in the book – but I very much hope I'll never have to see the swine again.'

Rosemary continued to rage and stamp for the rest of the afternoon. 'Eighteen years I was in that job. The best years of my life. And he casually gets Billie to bring me a letter like that.' They had not returned to Winterbourne, but instead gone for a walk through Downminster and along a footpath leading to a river-bank. The weather continued to be as fine as an English May could manage – which was very fine indeed.

'He can't get away with it,' Laura tried to reassure her. 'You'll get a whopping redundancy pay-out after all that time.'

Rosemary snorted, far from ready to listen to soothing words. She only just caught Laura's muttered afterthought. 'Which is more than I'll get.'

'What are you talking about?'

'Well, I'm redundant as well, aren't I? No longer needed as a wife or mother. And I'll be lucky to end up with half the value of our house. Just about enough to buy a small shed, I imagine.'

'Yes, we're both in the mire, aren't we. What star sign are you – if there's anything in astrology, we must be both going through a bad patch.'

'Leo.'

'That just shows it's rubbish, then. I'm Capricorn.'

'Rosemary, I do think it's outrageous, the way you've been treated, and I know it's too early to say this, but I really think that once you calm down, you might even be thanking your Professor Whatisname.'

'Oh? And are you thanking your faithless husband?'

Laura picked up a stone and threw it overarm into the river. The action reminded her of something. 'I smashed a front window before I left,' she said. 'If it rains, the telly will probably get wet. It's just under that window.'

'Won't the burglars get in?'

'I doubt it. It was only one small pane.'

'Even so. You can't just leave it, can you. All your worldly goods must be in that house.'

'I know. I'll go and see a solicitor one day this week, and try to work out where I go from here. I just hope I never have to see Nick again.'

'You know you will. What about when your daughter gets married? When there are grandchildren to visit? You can't just refuse to see him.'

'I can, you know. I'm a very stubborn person.'

'And didn't you say Sam Trent was his best friend? What about the funeral?'

Laura looked at her in horror. 'I didn't think of that. I know he'll be awfully upset – I was tempted to phone him and try to break the news before he hears it on the grapevine. But the *funeral* never entered my mind.'

Rosemary waited for the implications to stop swarming around Laura's head. She lay back on the grassy bank, and closed her eyes. It really was a beautiful day. Maybe this was better than trying to force some facts about plant pathology into the heads of a roomful of dim-witted students. Maybe Laura was right that one day she'd be thankful that change had been forced onto her.

'If I was still speaking to him, I could see what he thinks about those heart pills,' Laura was saying. 'He could get the results of the post-mortem, with the toxicology report, and I could tell him how Sam was a few minutes earlier. We often used to talk things through like that, even after I gave up the job to have the kids. He was never one of those coppers who won't bring the work home with them. He'd sit down with me and pick my brains, many a time.'

'Sounds nice.'

'It was,' said Laura wistfully. 'I s'pose I should hang onto the good parts, and not rubbish the whole marriage.' Then she scowled fiercely. 'But I don't expect you'd be too shocked if I said it might well have been better if Nick had died under that lorry, and not poor old Sam.'

Rosemary shrugged gently. 'If you must lose him, then it'd be easier to have a nice clean emotion like grief, rather than the rage and humiliation that comes from being rejected. I've heard people say that before. There can't be very much consolation in your situation, having him swan off like that with a bright young thing.'

'All right, don't rub my nose in it. Let's stick to the point, shall we?'

'Which is?'

'Sam's funeral. I really ought to go and see Vickie, or at least phone her, to see what's happening. The Coroner's Officer will probably contact her today to say they've released the body.'

'You make it sound awfully cold blooded.'

'Do I? Oddly enough, I quite like funerals. And the more I think about it, the more sure I am that Nick's going to want to be there. Just so long as he doesn't bring the Tart.'

'He wouldn't do that, surely.'

'I really don't know what he's capable of now. It's a very strange feeling, you know. Thinking you can predict another person's every move, only to find they're somebody else entirely. It shakes you up.'

'So does suddenly finding yourself without a secure job. I'd envisaged doing it for another ten years and then retiring on their not-very-generous pension. Now I've got no idea where I'll be next week.'

Laura got to her feet. 'Come on. This is getting maudlin. You've got to solve the mystery of the oozing tree trunks, and I've got to do my duty by poor Vickie.'

Rosemary bounced up from the riverbank, brushing at the grass stains on her jeans. 'Quite right. No

point in looking back. Live for the day – that's what
my Dad used to tell me.'

'Good old Dad. Mine was a farmer, and he was
always predicting doom and gloom. On a day like
today, he'd talk about the glass dropping and the lull
before the storm. If it rained on his new-mown hay he
used to shake his fist at the sky and curse terribly.'

'He probably felt much better for it,' chuckled
Rosemary.

'No, I don't think he did.' At that, Rosemary burst
into full-blown laughter, forcing Laura to join in.

Vickie had some disconcerting news when Laura
phoned her from the pub. 'They've found something
anomalous in Sam's bloodstream,' she said, clearly
quoting verbatim the words of the Coroner's Officer.
'They want to run more tests, and that means I can't
go ahead with arranging the funeral. They don't know
how long it's all going to take.'

Laura trod carefully. 'Did they say anything else?
Any hint as to what they think they've found?'

'Nothing at all. But they want me to make myself
available for interview, during the next day or two,
whatever that means. It's not as if I'd be going anywhere, anyway.'

'No.' Laura's mind was working fast. If the police
were planning to interview Vickie, then it was highly
likely that they'd want to speak to her, Laura, as well.
She had been the last person to see Sam alive, after all.
In fact, the more she thought about it, the more she
wondered whether she ought already to have told them
about the pill he'd taken just before getting into his car.
And they'd also be well advised to question that doctor, if they hadn't already done so. She said some of
this to Vickie, not sure whether she was being insensitive again. Vickie seemed to be only half listening.

'Laura, I'll have to go now. Alicia's coming over in a
little while. She's been very kind. I never realised what a
sweet person she is, until now. And she has so much on

her plate, with that enormous house and garden, and Daniel so poorly. She makes me feel very feeble.'

'Yes, she does seem nice,' said Laura inadequately, thinking she'd like to meet Daniel Kellaway. Tucked away in his upstairs sickroom, he was beginning to seem like a mythical creature. A rather *rich* mythical creature, she supposed, as presumably he would now be sole proprietor of Kellaway Garden Centres. Unless of course Sam had left his share entirely to Vickie. It was a pity, she thought, that she couldn't just ask outright – but such a question would be impossibly insensitive at a moment like this.

'Well, bye then. Thanks for calling. I'll keep you posted about the funeral. Oh – and Laura – do you think Nick will want to come?'

Laura sighed. 'Yes, Vickie, I think he very probably will.'

That evening, sitting in the lounge of the White Hart, Laura and Rosemary tried to make some plans.

'First, I've got to sort those trees out,' Rosemary repeated, for the fourth or fifth time. 'It's niggling me that there might be a disease I've never seen before.'

'And I'm going to have to bite the bullet and see where I stand,' Laura said. 'I'll have to consult a solicitor, I suppose.'

'Haven't you got one already?'

'Oddly enough, no, not really. We moved into that house twenty-one years ago. I can't even remember who did the conveyancing. My mother had old Mr Frogley, who handled her will and everything when she died. But he's miles away, and I doubt if I could face him, anyway.'

'Did your mum leave you anything?'

'A rather good grandfather clock, a lot of yellow-jacketed Gollancz first editions and eighteen hundred pounds.'

'No house?'

'Sadly, no. She'd sold it three years before she died, and most of the proceeds went to the nursing home.'

'Well, you'll have to go to Fairchester, then, and see if you can find somebody.'

'It seems awfully random, somehow. Wouldn't I have to make an appointment first?'

'I have no idea, to be honest. It must be worth a try. Don't they have stickers in the window telling you what their specialities are?'

'Do they? I've never noticed.'

Rosemary was restless, tapping her teeth and frowning at a patch on the carpet. 'I *hate* not being able to diagnose things,' she grumbled.

'Look, why don't you go up to your room, and have another session with your textbooks? You don't have to stay with me all the time. I've got plenty to do. For a start, I'll need to make some lists.'

'Lists?'

Laura checked them off on her fingers. 'Things to collect from the house. People to telephone, who'll be wondering where I am. What to say to a solicitor. Reasons to be bothered about Sam Trent. And what to do with the rest of my life.'

'Oh, right. I see,' laughed Rosemary, as she got up to go to her room.

Next morning, Rosemary took the Land Rover back to Winterbourne Manor, leaving Laura waiting for the once-a-day bus into Fairchester. 'If I get too bored, I'll come back in a taxi,' she said. 'Otherwise, I'll be on the six-thirty bus this evening. Have fun with your wretched trees.'

'I'll try,' said Rosemary.

The bus ride was a pleasant novelty, after many years of exclusive car use. 'I'd better get used to it,' she told herself. 'Don't suppose I'll ever be able to afford a car again now.'

Fairchester was not a town she knew well, but she

remembered the basic landmarks from a visit she had made many years earlier with Vickie. Handsome Town Hall, positioned at the junction where the two main streets crossed; the big old mansion dating back to the 1700s, housing the Museum and Library; and the gothic church, standing proudly on a slight elevation to the north of the main shopping area – all offered plenty of interest. There was also a bookshop, several charity shops and a delightfully antiquated hardware-cum-garden store, which Laura just knew would make Rosemary's day if she could see it.

There were also four estate agents, two banks, an insurance office and two solicitors' chambers.

The first of these was called Gilbert and Partners, which quite failed to inspire her. There was a sticker in the window announcing membership of the Law Association, and nothing else. Definitely stuffy, Laura decided. The next, which was situated in the part of town which included the charity shops and a place where everything cost a pound, was a lot more inviting. Through a large plate-glass window, a reception area with plants and a busy-looking young woman were clearly visible. There was a youth sitting close to a plant, with a child in a pushchair beside him. 'This is more like it,' Laura muttered, diving in before she could lose her nerve.

The girl at the desk smiled welcomingly, and cocked her head, ready for whatever Laura might say.

'I'm afraid I haven't got an appointment, but if possible, I'd like to talk to a solicitor,' she said, all in a rush.

'That's fine. You haven't been here before, have you?'

Laura shook her head.

'Well, could I ask what it's about. Just generally, I mean.'

'Divorce,' said Laura, surprised at how a simple word could deliver such a kick to the stomach.

'Oh, you'd better see Mandy, then. She'll probably be free in about twenty minutes. Do you want to wait?'

'I think I will, if that's all right.'

'We've got a little bookshop through there, look,' said the girl, pointing with her pen. 'Leaflets and things. You might want to have a browse.'

'Okay.' Feeling as if she'd stepped into some strange new world where solicitors were called Mandy and actually provided useful things like leaflets, she went for a look.

The range of material for sale was impressive. Various kinds of law spelt out for the ordinary person, including a useful-looking book starkly entitled *Divorce*, were displayed along one wall. Laura took the book tentatively, wondering how it was that she had never for a moment expected to need such a thing. Friends and relations had bad marriages, serial relationships, broken hearts and financial struggles. Laura and Nick had been rock solid, with their wonderful children and handsome house. Nobody was immune, it seemed, and she felt foolish for her past complacency.

Mandy turned out to be in her early thirties, with long curly dark hair and deep blue eyes, set rather close together. Her wide mouth smiled welcomingly.

'Hi!' she said. 'Grab a seat.' The accent wasn't American, but the relaxed sense of equality and friendship was. 'Now, tell me all about it.'

Laura hesitated, unsure just where to begin. This was, after all, a consultation about legal matters, not a counselling session. 'Um, well, I suppose I ought to ask how much you're going to charge me, first,' she said.

'Oh, didn't Steph tell you that? You get half an hour for free, and after that I should have a good idea what's required and what you'll have to pay. I'm afraid there isn't much hope of Legal Aid these days, but there are other things you might think about. Like mediation.'

Laura smiled weakly. 'I don't think there's much hope of my husband coming to anything like that.'

'Oh, it doesn't mean what it sounds like. It's a service that looks at all the finances and negotiates an agreement that's fair for you both. It's a great set-up, believe me. Not enough people know about it.'

'Okay. Does that mean you want me to do that before coming to you?'

'Not necessarily. Look, let's go through the basics.' Skilfully, she extracted the information from Laura, nodding encouragingly every few minutes, and noting most of it down. Laura was grateful for the no-nonsense approach, the absence of excessive sympathy. A different approach would certainly have had her in tears.

'Well, that's all quite straightforward,' said Mandy, eventually. 'You can sue him for adultery now, or wait two years for an amicable no-faults divorce. If he doesn't co-operate, and you don't want to raise the issue of adultery, you'll have to wait five years. All your joint assets will be pooled, and probably simply divided down the middle. To be quite frank with you, you might well not need someone like me at all, if you go for mediation.'

Laura found her thoughts wandering back to a week ago when life had seemed so ordered and predictable.

'And are you still in the marital home?'

Laura shook her head. 'It's standing empty. I couldn't bear to be there on my own. It was too full of reminders, you see.'

'Ah, well, you'll have to be careful about that. For a start, some home insurance policies won't cover an empty house. Is there any danger of your husband moving in with his new girlfriend?'

Again, she shrugged. 'It's possible, I suppose. Why – would that matter?'

'It depends how hostile things get between you. It's sad, but true, that people in your situation can do a lot to make life difficult for each other.'

Laura thought of Rosemary and how their lives seemed to be running parallel. 'I haven't considered anything like that yet. It only happened a few days ago.'

Mandy smiled understandingly. 'I know. But it's amazing how quickly people adapt to a new situation.'

'Even at my age?'

'Even at your age,' Mandy laughed. 'Listen – I had a woman of seventy-four in here yesterday. She'd decided she couldn't tolerate her selfish beast of a husband any longer, and wanted to sue him for divorce on the grounds of unreasonable behaviour. She wants to go round the world for a year, spending all their savings. She'll do it, too.'

'Good for her,' said Laura, feeling spineless and pathetic by comparison.

'Well, I hope I've given you enough to take you through the next few steps. Make a decision about the house, suggest the mediation service to your husband, and pop along to the Job Centre.'

'Right. Thanks.' Laura stood up. 'I'll be in touch, then.'

'I'm here if you need me,' Mandy smiled, holding out her hand for a firm friendly handshake.

Laura went to a small café for some lunch, flipping through the divorce handbook, trying to keep its cover out of sight. Knowing it was silly, she nonetheless felt ashamed at having got to such a point. The law seemed pretty fair, she concluded, as she had done at several points in her life. Once a police officer, always an upholder of the laws of the land, she supposed.

On the pavement outside, people strolled by in the sunshine. Two good days in a row was something worth celebrating. Suddenly there was a familiar figure walking past. A woman with bowed head, accompanied by a man Laura didn't know. Vickie! Almost, she got up to run out and greet her friend, before stopping herself. She must have come into town to see an undertaker, or perhaps to meet the Coroner's Officer. In either case, she'd be distracted and busy.

Only then did Laura observe that Vickie's left hand was held tightly in that of the man with her.

Daniel was desperate to keep abreast of events. Alicia seemed to want to shield him from the full truth, and he repeatedly tried to convince her that this was not a kindness. 'But Sam was my friend as well as my partner. I'll have to go to the funeral. You should have brought Vickie up here to talk to me. She must be devastated, poor woman.'

'You can't possibly go to the funeral,' his wife told him. 'You simply haven't the strength.'

'You know,' he said, looking her full in the face, 'I've been wondering whether I'd feel a lot better if I could go outside. On a beautiful afternoon like this, surely I could sit in the sun, in a corner of the garden. It would be such a tonic.'

'Oh, darling, if only you could.' Alicia took his hand, careful to avoid pressure on the blisters. 'But how would we get you downstairs? We might be able to move you closer to the window, where you can get some sunshine. And don't forget we've got the lamp. That's better than nothing, isn't it?'

'Not much. It smells horrible, and is not a bit pretty to look at. Alicia, I am a horticulturalist. I make my living from gardens. Plants are my greatest delight. If I'm shut up in here much longer, I'll go raving mad. Call Bob Whittaker and see what he says. Please! I really don't understand why I can't go out. We could find somebody to carry me downstairs.'

'Yes, all right. I will phone him. But you know he says your whole system has been compromised by the skin condition. You're at serious risk of infection, remember. And it's affected your lungs, which puts a strain on your heart. After what's happened to Sam...'

'What do you mean? I thought it was a simple car accident.' He stared wildly at her. 'What are you saying?'

She dropped his hand, and turned away, biting her lip. 'Oh dear! We were hoping to keep it from you. Vickie phoned a little while ago, saying the pathologist has found some signs that he might have died before the accident. You know his heart wasn't as robust as it might be.'

'Yes, of course. But he was taking medication for it.'

Alicia frowned. 'That's true. Bob insists he was keeping it under control. And you heard Sam ask for another prescription, only yesterday. So he must have been confident that it was working.'

'He might have run out of pills. There wouldn't have been time to get the prescription filled.'

'No, that Laura Whatnot told Vickie that she saw Sam take a pill, only a few minutes before he must have died.'

'Who's Laura Whatnot?'

'I told you. She came with the Boxer woman, from the university. She knows Vickie. Sam had just taken her to Dowminster, when he had the accident.'

'Oh yes. I heard a strange voice.' He looked towards the window. 'I just wish I could see as much as I can hear.'

'Darling, I *will* ask Bob if it would be all right for you to sit in the garden for a bit. It does seem awful, shutting you away up here. And poor old Mrs Potts would be delighted not to have to climb all those stairs with your tray, I'm sure. Now, no more talk. I'll come up again if I hear any more news.'

'Thank you.' He leaned back and stared at the ceiling. 'This means the end of Kellaways, you know,' he mumbled. 'Without Sam, the whole business will go to pot.'

He could hear her fighting to control her voice as she replied, 'It's a bit too soon to talk like that. We can fight this thing, Daniel, and you'll be back at the helm before you know it. Don't you think you owe it to Sam?'

He looked at her, his face puffy and discoloured with the skin complaint. 'What do you mean?'

'Just that you own the whole outfit now, lock, stock and barrel, don't you? Sam's share all comes to you.'

He shook his head irritably. 'Yes, of course it does. So what? I could sell the whole thing tomorrow. Or give it away,' he added gloomily.

Alicia laughed, a quick artificial trill. 'Don't you dare!' she said lightly. 'You'd miss it when you got better.'

With gritted teeth, he closed his eyes, and let her leave the room without any further comment.

Half an hour later, she was back, mobile phone in her hand. 'Daniel, I'm terribly sorry, but I've just spoken to Bob, and he thinks it would be too big a strain for you to go outside. He doesn't think you're well enough to go to Sam's funeral, either. I know that'll be a terrible disappointment, sweetheart, but I suppose we'd better obey doctor's orders, don't you?'

Daniel experienced defeat like a great black wave washing over him. 'Thanks for telling me,' he muttered. 'Look, could you just rub a damp cloth over my face? It's damned hot in here, right under the roof.'

She put down the phone and went to the adjacent bathroom, quickly coming back with a cool facecloth.

'Thanks,' murmured Daniel, as she did as he asked.

They were both suddenly aware of the arrival of a car on the gravel below the window. 'I wonder who that can be,' said Alicia. 'After the way Mrs Potts behaved yesterday, I suppose I should go and intercept her before she says something awful.'

'That woman is a liability,' Daniel said. 'I don't know why we keep her.'

'Because she's loyal, and we'd never find anybody else.'

'And she's cheap,' added Daniel. 'And I should warn you, we're going to have to watch the cashflow from now on, if I'm to keep the business. I'll have to employ a manager to replace Sam.'

Alicia made no reply to that. When she'd gone, Daniel noticed she'd forgotten her telephone.

From below his window, he soon heard the sound of voices, identifying the newcomer as Cynthia Battson, from Calendula Cottage, half a mile away. Before she could get to the front door, Alicia must have emerged and Daniel heard her warm greeting. 'How nice to see you!' she gushed. 'Isn't it a lovely day.'

'Alicia, I don't know how you manage to stay so cheerful, I really don't. Look, don't let me interrupt anything. I was just passing, and I thought perhaps Daniel would like a few fresh eggs. My girls are laying magnificently at the moment, and I can hardly bear another omelette. They're completely organic, you know. Quite honestly, I can't help wondering whether Daniel would be better on a much more natural diet. He's obviously allergic to something. You should consult a naturopath, or perhaps a homeopath would be better.'

'Well...' Alicia attempted to reply.

'I know, it must be so difficult. You poor thing. So depressing for you both. And the *business*. It can't be easy keeping it all going. Actually, I'm going to the garden centre on Sunday with my sister. It's always a good day out there. But now, with Sam Trent so tragically killed – I just don't know how you can keep going, I really don't.'

'You heard about Sam then?'

'Of course! It was on the local news last night. What a disaster!'

'Yes.'

'Look, Alicia, can I do anything? Let me at least take the eggs in for you. I know you've got that…housekeeper, but I can perhaps lend her a hand. I don't like to stand gossiping out here when there must be so much work to be done.'

'Everything's under control,' said Alicia coolly. 'Thanks all the same.'

'And Daniel? How is he *really*?'

'It's sweet of you, Cynthia, to be so concerned for Daniel. We're battling on, and that's all I can say. Of course, we give him the freshest food we can buy. Mrs Potts is a wonderful cook, you know. She's amazing, the things she can come up with. And she's very clever with herbs and old country remedies. But the eggs are just the thing. We're ever so grateful.'

Cynthia would not be stopped – not that Alicia had sounded as if she particular wanted to stop her. 'It must be so *depressing* for the poor man, stuck up there on a day like this,' she repeated. 'Is there any sign at all of improvement?'

'Well, I like to think so. There are some days that are better than others, you know.'

'It all sounds ghastly.' The woman's voice rose high and shrill, echoing across the lawns. Upstairs, Daniel winced at every mention of his name. The smooth-flowing pity spilling from the neighbour's mouth was worse than humiliating. She had started by talking about him as if he was a subhuman nuisance and gone on to imply that with a bit more common sense and willpower, he could get himself better.

Alicia made no audible reply, and Daniel pictured her shrugging, or possibly even belatedly remembering that he could hear every word, and putting a finger to her lips.

The crunch of gravel suggested that Cynthia was

going back to her car. 'Well, you have all my sympathy,
my dear,' she said, her voice slightly more distant now.
'Please do be sure to let me know whenever there's
something I can do to help.'

'You really are wonderfully kind,' Alicia called, as
the car engine started and the vehicle swept around the
driveway to leave via the grand avenue and the rear
exit.

Upstairs, the sick man thrashed his head from side
to side, not caring that this aggravated the blisters on
his cheeks and neck. He even banged his hands down
on the bedcovers, in agonised frustration.

And then he reached for Alicia's forgotten telephone.

Arriving at Winterbourne a little before ten,
Rosemary set to work without announcing her presence. Alicia would doubtless see the vehicle and draw
the appropriate conclusions. It was fairly obvious,
anyway, that the mistress of the house was much less
interested in the outdoors than in maintaining her elegant abode, with its antique furniture and luscious car-
pets. Laura had given a graphic description of the fabulous lounge, as well as the much less refined smaller
sitting room.

'Must be where the madwoman hangs out,' said
Rosemary.

'Lucky she didn't catch me, then. She'd probably
have screamed blue murder, accusing me of burgling
her.'

'You just can't get good help these days.'

'Not legally, anyway,' Laura had agreed. 'But at
least Alicia doesn't have to worry about the help
seducing her husband.'

Rosemary sighed. 'Poor Daniel,' she said, not for
the first time.

Now, thinking there might be some sort of infestation at the root of the affected trees, she started by

scraping carefully away at the soil around one of them. It was slow work, with the ground very dry and tightly-packed. Like an archaeologist, she removed the soil little by little, wary of spreading any plant viruses, or damaging the roots. Every few minutes, she put a trowelful of earth onto a white plastic tray and jiggled it, looking for anything sinister. Some of it she bagged up to examine under a microscope when she got the chance.

As she worked, she grumbled to herself in a long internal monologue.

My trouble is, I got too successful, and too expensive. Too well qualified for a piddling place like Malmesbury, that's what it was. Plus bloody Julian not wanting me cramping his style, showing him up for the plonker he really is. But I'll show him. I'll have them for wrongful dismissal, make sure they buy me off with a really good package. Let them think I'm going quietly, and then dump it on them from a great height. Except for that darn letter. Why didn't we wait a few days? That's not going to help our case at all, now. Maybe I should have gone to see a solicitor as well as Laura.

Hello. Wonder what she's up to!

This last thought was prompted by the sight of Mrs Potts walking through a patch of long grass where the spring bulbs were dying back, carrying a black plastic binliner and a large kitchen knife. The knitted hat bobbed along as if it had a life of its own, visible even when the woman turned sharply and began to follow the course of the narrow path that Laura had led Rosemary down on their first day.

'Must be a herb garden down there somewhere,' Rosemary concluded, while already doubting that this was likely. Herb gardens were normally positioned right outside the kitchen door. Perhaps she knew where there was an elder in flower, and wanted to gather the fragrant flowerheads for cordial or wine. It seemed reasonable to assume that Mrs Potts did the cooking for the Kellaways, and that the garden provided at least some of the ingredients. Rhubarb, possibly, or some very early wild strawberries.

Her flights of fancy led her to the subject of plant-lore, following on from her chat with Laura two days earlier. It had been a major part of her studies at one time, before she'd diverged into plant pathology. Interesting bits of trivia stuck in her mind, such as the best time to pick rhubarb was at night, when the stalks contained more sugar after a day in the sunlight. No doubt Mrs Potts was of a generation of country-women who understood many of these secrets, and would put them to good use in her kitchen.

Half tempted to follow her, just to see exactly what she was gathering, Rosemary took a few quiet steps towards the long grass and the little path. But before she could get any further, she was frozen in place by a blood-curdling scream from the house behind her.

Chapter Seven

By the time she came in sight of the house, Rosemary had concluded that the scream she had heard could only have come from Daniel. Running up the gravel walkway towards the ornamental lake, she could see that her fears were confirmed. In a twisted heap, the body of a man lay motionless under the window of Daniel's sickroom. Horrified, she stopped, afraid to go closer, already sure that Daniel was beyond help. For a few seconds everything was perfectly still. Even the birds seemed to have stopped singing. Then there was the sound of footsteps on gravel, and a shout of 'Alicia!' Rosemary did a full turn, trying to work out where the voice was coming from, but the garden was such a maze of hedges and paths, the house itself flanked by barns and sheds, that it could have been from any of three or four directions.

The front door of the house opened and Alicia Kellaway came out, standing there, gazing round just as Rosemary had done. It was too far to see her features clearly, but she gave the impression of someone emerging blinking into bright light. When Rosemary looked back at Daniel, Doctor Whittaker was miraculously kneeling over him, calling again: 'Alicia!'

Rosemary stayed where she was, observing, but not an active player in the drama. Although not actually hiding, she was in the lee of a hedge and didn't think either the doctor or Alicia had noticed her. She debated with herself whether to follow natural instinct and join them in their efforts to revive Daniel, or to stay at a distance, knowing herself to be more likely to hinder than to help.

'Here! Alicia!' The doctor waved at her with one hand, while holding a mobile phone to his ear with the other. 'Ambulance please!' he said. 'Right. I'm a doctor. We have a casualty at Winterbourne Manor, Devenish. Right. Thank you.' He returned the phone to his pocket, and bent over the patient. Dressed in pyjamas, the red blistered skin looking like awful wounds out in the light of day, he seemed horribly dead to Rosemary. Her fears were strengthened by the sight of one leg buckled at an impossible angle, and not the faintest sign of movement.

'Before you say anything, run in and fetch a blanket, will you? He needs to be kept warm.'

Alicia was gone barely a minute, returning with a large woollen blanket which the doctor tucked carefully around the lifeless form.

'But, what on earth happened to him?' Alicia stood wringing her hands, looking down at her husband. 'I was on the phone. I never heard a thing until you shouted. What are you doing here, anyway?'

'Daniel called me. He said he was at the end of his tether, and if I didn't come instantly, he wasn't sure he could bear to carry on. I came as fast as I could.' He gave her a long miserable stare. 'But not fast enough.'

'He's not dead, then?'

Watching, Rosemary thought it odd that Alicia didn't throw herself across the prostrated form of her husband, or at least kneel beside him and take his hand. Instead she jittered from one foot to the other, and clasped her hands together. A number of thoughts flickered through Rosemary's mind, including a pang of shameful satisfaction that if he was dead, Daniel's bequest to the University might well be rendered void. At the very least it would be a lot more complicated. Uncharitable it might be, but anything that got up Julian Marchant's nose was a bonus, as far as Rosemary was concerned.

But she really didn't want Daniel to be dead. He was a pleasant enough chap, with plenty to live for if only his medical problems could be sorted out. If he had been depressed enough to throw himself out of the upstairs window, then shouldn't his doctor have done something about that? There were several things about this Doctor Whittaker that didn't stack up.

'No, he's not dead,' came the reply, after a gentle examination of the artery in Daniel's neck. 'His pulse is actually quite strong. Good God, Alicia – he must have jumped out of the window minutes after he phoned me.'

'He has been very miserable lately,' she said. 'I couldn't talk him out of it, like I used to be able to. He absolutely hates being the object of people's pity. Oh, poor Dan. What a thing to do. I never *dreamed* it would come to this.'

'Where's Mrs Potts?'

'I've no idea. Why?'

'I just wondered. I mean, the police are going to be involved here, and it would help if we knew where you both were when he fell.' He gave her another of his adoring spaniel looks. 'Do you understand?'

At that, Rosemary felt she couldn't hover on the edges any longer. She walked forward, her feet crunching noisily on the gravel. 'Actually, I saw Mrs Potts a few minutes ago, at the far end of the garden,' she said.

'Oh?' The doctor's reaction was oddly frosty. 'And where exactly were *you*?'

'Over there.' Rosemary kept her face bland, despite the fevered thoughts going on behind it. 'In the avenue.'

'And I suppose there'll be phone records to prove I was on the landline,' said Alicia. 'Although I'm not sure what you're trying to suggest, Bob. It isn't really your responsibility, is it?'

'What's 'appening 'ere, then?' came a harsh voice. 'Who's dead this time?'

'Mrs Potts, something terrible's happened,' Alicia went towards the older woman. 'Daniel's fallen out of the window. But Bob says his pulse is strong, and the ambulance will be here in a little while.'

'Tried to do away with 'isself, then. Can't say I'm surprised.'

'Be quiet,' Alicia ordered. 'Don't say things like that.'

'Sorry, my lady, I'm sure,' came the sarcastic response. 'I'll just get back to the kitchen then.'

For the first time, Rosemary noticed that Mrs Potts was no longer carrying the black plastic bag. Nor had she appeared from the direction of the wild end of the garden. Instead she had come around the other side of the house from where they were all standing. The side which had a collection of outbuildings and a small area which must once have been stables and the stable yard.

Mindful of his duties, the doctor was crouching over Daniel, assessing his vital signs, probing the buckled leg, and – oddly, to Rosemary's eyes – examining his fingertips. 'He seems fairly stable,' he announced. 'But the sooner the ambulance arrives, the happier I'll be.'

As if on cue, the sound of an engine could be heard at the end of the drive. 'No siren?' Alicia commented.

'No need on these quiet lanes,' said the doctor. 'I'm sure he'll be all right now. Just so long as he hasn't broken his back, and I don't think he has. Although, of course, we don't know how deep the concussion is, or what trauma there might be to the brain.'

'Oh, God,' Alicia moaned. 'You're not doing much to reassure me.'

'Hang on, darling. We'll soon have him in the best possible hands.'

Rosemary noted the *darling* with interest. Some people did use sloppy endearments to just about everybody they met – but very rarely did male doctors go in for such language. On the contrary, it sounded as if it had popped out unconsciously, in the stress of the moment. She watched Alicia's reaction closely.

Daniel's wife behaved as if nothing at all unusual had happened. As if, indeed, she hadn't even heard him. Instead she went to meet the ambulance, waving them theatrically to the little tableau under the window. A man and a woman got out, and started their professional routine with great assurance. When they finally got Daniel strapped to a stretcher and into the ambulance, Alicia went with him. Rosemary returned thoughtfully to her suffering trees, wishing that Laura were there to help her make sense of everything that had just taken place.

It was over a rather delayed dinner at the White Hart that the two women finally met up again. Laura's bus had delivered her almost to the door very punctually, and Rosemary had felt in need of a quiet spell in her room after the dramatic events of the day. Both started talking, the moment they saw each other, full of their news.

Rosemary managed to get herself heard first, and stemmed Laura's flow by the stark words, 'Daniel Kellaway threw himself out of his window this morning, and had to be rushed to hospital.'

'What?'

'It's true. I heard him scream, and then saw everything that happened next.'

'Wait, wait.' Laura held up a hand. 'This is incredible. What's going on at that place, for heaven's sake?'

'Let me tell you the whole story, and then we can try and make sense of it all.' And Rosemary proceeded to give a detailed account of the incident. Laura listened intently.

'Do you think he was pushed?' she asked when Rosemary had finished.

'I don't see how he can have been. Everybody had an alibi.'

'Unless there was somebody else in the house. What about the doctor? Where was he? It sounds as if he appeared by magic.'

Rosemary tapped her front teeth with a fingernail.

'He said Daniel phoned him and he rushed over right away.'

'And we believe that, do we?'

Rosemary frowned. 'I did at the time. He seemed in quite a state.'

'Doesn't it strike you that he spends an awful lot of time at Winterbourne?'

'Daniel's probably his most chronic case. He'll need to keep a close eye on him.'

Laura gave her a stern look. 'I thought you said that Daniel's been in bad shape for a year or so now. That's been plenty of time for Alicia and the doctor to get very close to each other – if you know what I mean. You said yourself it looked that way. Don't you think it looks very strange, him being on the spot when this happens?'

Rosemary nodded in agreement. 'It does,' she said. 'It really does.'

'Anyway, what happened next?' Laura pressed on. 'Did the police arrive?'

'They did, actually. But Daniel was off in the ambulance by then, so they just asked for names and addresses and went away again.'

'And what did you do after that?'

'Went over to Bitterton with some soil and bark samples. There's a lab there, and they'll do a preliminary test for viruses. Then I came here.'

Laura was deep in thought. 'It's all very suspicious, isn't it? I mean, after Sam, you can't help thinking something must be going on.'

'Except Daniel *was* very depressed.'

'How about this? Maybe Alicia wasn't *really* on the phone. She could have left it connected, and gone upstairs to do the foul deed.'

'Laura, I think you're letting your imagination run away with you. She really did seem very shocked by it all. And I'm really not convinced that either of these accidents is suspicious. They could both have perfectly natural explanations.'

'I don't think so. There are too many peculiar ele-
ments at play. Daniel's illness, Sam's financial mud-
dles, the doctor carrying on with Alicia Kellaway. And
Vickie. Oh yes – listen to this. I saw her in Fairchester,
holding hands with a man. Walking along the street as
bold as brass.'

'You're joking! Did she see you?'

'No, luckily. I mean, her husband's only just died,
and she's shamelessly out with some other bloke.
What's the world coming to?'

'Well, at least that means she's got an alibi for
Daniel.' Rosemary laughed unconvincingly.

'For Daniel maybe,' said Laura darkly. 'I'm not sure
she's in the clear as far as Sam's concerned.'

'Laura,' said Rosemary firmly, 'I really *really* do
think that Daniel was trying to kill himself. You never
met him, you don't understand how depressed he
was.'

'So why did he scream?'

'Pardon?'

'If he deliberately threw himself off the balcony –
why did he scream?'

'Ah.' Rosemary gave this some serious thought.
'Well, maybe when the reality finally strikes you, as
you're sailing through the air, you *do* scream, even if
you've done it on purpose.' It sounded feeble, even in
her own ears.

'Well, we might get the answer from the horse's
mouth, if he recovers,' Laura said. 'I wonder if we
could go and visit him in hospital?'

'Why would we want to do that?'

'To *ask* him, of course. You're a friend of his. I
don't see why you shouldn't go to see him.'

'We'll talk about that tomorrow,' Rosemary
decreed. 'For all we know, he's still in a coma, and
could be for weeks.'

'So can I tell you about my visit to the solicitor

now?'

'Course you can. I'm all ears.'

Laura's story lasted until it was time to adjourn to the bar for a post-prandial drink. They were there for another hour, still talking, but with the conversation diverted to stories from their youth. As part of the process of cementing a firm friendship, they described their schooldays, their first boyfriends, and favourite travel experiences.

Then Rosemary asked, 'But what *are* you going to do next?'

Laura blinked. 'Well… I don't know. First of all I suppose I'll have to grit my teeth and contact Nick and see what he thinks about this mediation business. If he'll co-operate, I might manage to get some cash out of him.'

Rosemary cocked her head thoughtfully. 'You know, I can't recall a single instance amongst my friends where a man with a new girlfriend has been generous to his wife.'

'Come on – don't they suffer agonies of guilt, and pay the old girl off accordingly?'

'Not the ones I'm aware of. But you might be lucky, of course.'

'Maybe if I start by talking about Sam – sort of neutral territory – it'll go better.'

'Maybe it will.'

Laura fiddled with an earring as she tried to imagine speaking to Nick. It wasn't something she looked forward to. 'You know, I think I'd rather live in somebody's disused pigsty than plead with him. I come over all peculiar, just thinking about it.'

'I think disused pigsties are a bit hard to come by, actually. No, no, it won't come to that. In fact,' Rosemary leaned forward earnestly, 'if I were you, I'd go back to the house and stake your claim to it. He might not even know you've left. It's only been three days, after all.'

Laura shook her head 'No, I don't want to do that. Maybe I'd better see if Matthew has any ideas.'

'Matthew? Oh, right – your son.'

'The one who's more likely to be on my side. Not that Nick didn't try to nobble him. It might have worked with Helena, but not with my boy.' She lifted her chin proudly.

'Nick discussed it with them, did he?'

'Can you believe it? He told them before he told me!'

'They say the wife's always the last to know.'

'They say right,' snarled Laura.

'Like me with my redundancy,' Rosemary commiserated.

Laura gave herself a little shake. 'Look, this won't do. You need to be working on those trees, so you can get out of here and sort things out, not gossiping with me.'

'I like gossiping.'

'So do I. Even so...'

'I'm going to have to look further afield for the answer. Daniel said something about a Malaysian owning Winterbourne before he bought it. I happen to know a lovely man in the Department of Forestry at Kuala Lumpar University. If I can get hold of him, he might have some ideas.'

'Kuala Lumpar?'

'I know. What time is it there, do you think?'

'Something like seven am, I should think. Have you got his number?'

'No such luck. I *did* have it, once. We met at a conference, some years back, and exchanged details. I suppose Billie might be able to find it for me.' She sighed. 'I'm too tired for any of that now. And if Daniel dies, the trees aren't going to matter, are they?'

Laura gave her a stern look. 'I don't believe I heard you say that. What about the trees themselves? Don't you want to save them, for their own sake? Such magnificent things deserve to be helped, don't they?'

Rosemary chuckled. 'Ooh, I do love a good talking to. You sound exactly like my mother. Of course, you're right. I'll be back on track in the morning, but to be honest, I think I've had enough for one day.'

Laura grinned. 'So have I,' she said.

When she woke at seven next morning, Laura remembered a dream where the word *Withersedge* had been shouted at her by a thin young woman, and Vickie Trent, wearing a shapeless floppy hat, threw flowers onto a big red coffin in a shallow grave. Things did not seem a lot clearer once she was awake.

'Are you in a rush to be somewhere?' she asked Rosemary, over breakfast.

'Not at all. Why?'

'Can we look up "Withersedge" on your computer, do you think? It's niggling at me.'

'We can try, but I bet we'll get some awfully weird results.'

Back in Rosemary's room, they booted up the laptop, and Rosemary ran a search on Google for the word. 'Thousands of sites,' she sighed. 'Although most of them don't seem…' She peered at the screen. 'Look – The Royal Borough of Withersedge! It's a place. Shall I open it?'

'I don't know.' Laura looked over her shoulder. 'What's that one? "They Got Away With It". Sounds interesting.'

Rosemary clicked, and waited for the website to appear. 'It's unsolved murders. Jack the Ripper, Adelaide Bartlett, Madeleine Smith…dozens of them. What's it got to do with Withersedge, I wonder?' She scrolled down slowly. 'Ah! There it is. "The Wicked Witch of Withersedge". How funny.'

'I remember! Delia Kettle. I was a young probationer. They made me sit through the entire trial, and then she got off. The jury liked her, I think. Her hus-

band was a butcher, a rather unpleasant man, by all
accounts. He died very suddenly, and Delia claimed on
his life insurance. The insurers thought it was suspicious and wouldn't pay out, so she took them to court.
The police suddenly developed an interest, and she
ended up being charged with murder. First degree. But
there never was much evidence, and the jury didn't
like insurance companies, so she was acquitted. Young
wife and mother, wanting her just desserts. I must say,
I was pretty much on her side myself.'

'There's a picture of her. See?'

'It is Mrs Potts, isn't it. Nearly thirty years
younger, but still her.'

'Definitely. She's even wearing an early version of
the hat.'

'So she is. And now she's at Winterbourne.'

'I like her sense of humour,' Rosemary chuckled.

'Oh?'

'Mrs Kettle and Mrs Potts. It's wonderful.'

'Oh, yes.'

'But she couldn't have pushed Daniel out of the
window, even if she did poison the butcher all those
years ago. I saw her only about half a minute before he
fell.'

'She might have doctored Sam's pills, though.'

'Why? Why would she do that? And how? Even if
Sam did die of heart failure in the car, it's almost certainly down to natural causes.'

Laura narrowed her eyes. 'I remember liking Delia
Kettle, for her courage, and defiant manner, but I
wouldn't have trusted her an inch. She was clever, too.
Maybe this dottiness is all just an act. She's really a
cunning killer, taking advantage of poor Daniel and
Alicia.'

'Rubbish. People don't do that sort of thing in real
life. Even if she killed the butcher for the insurance
money – did she *get* the insurance money, by the way?'

'She did, yes. Set free without a stain on her character. Obviously they had to pay out.'

'Well, then. She had a good reason for it. What in the world could she have to gain by bumping off Sam Trent?'

'I don't know – but I'm going to try to find out.' Laura picked up the phone beside Rosemary's bed and listened.

'It's dead,' she said. 'The phone's out of order.'

Rosemary stared at it helplessly for a few seconds, and then giggled. 'It's not plugged in – the computer's in the socket, look.'

Laura watched as Rosemary swapped the leads, wishing she understood more about electronics.

'That's better,' she said, listening to the phone again. She dialled a number. 'Yes – can I speak to Sergeant Thyme, please?'

Rosemary's eyes widened. 'Your husband?' she whispered.

'My son,' said Laura.

Police Sergeant Matthew Thorne had to be called to the phone from the canteen, where he had just settled down to a large strong coffee. He picked it up at his desk, across the room from Constable Beth Graham, a woman he was perpetually trying to impress.

Nobody had told him who was calling, but he assumed it would be a member of the public with some helpful information concerning the robbery case he was working on. When he heard his mother's voice, his heart sank.

'Mum!' he gasped. 'Is something the matter? I heard about poor old Sam. What a terrible thing to happen.'

'Yes, I know. I saw him, you know, only a few minutes before the crash.'

'You said you were going to him and Vickie, so I did wonder if you were involved. I didn't know how to get hold of you. You must be in quite a state.'

'I'm all right. I've made a new friend —' She smiled across the room at Rosemary, '— she's being a great help. Actually, Matt, we seem to have blundered into something that might be linked to Sam's death.'

'Oh?' His tone was cautious. 'What do you mean?'

'I probably shouldn't say too much for now. But you can do a bit of research for me.'

'Oh yes?'

'Have you got a pen?'

'Yes, Mum.' A glance towards Constable Graham revealed her studiously attending to a file on her desk.

'Well, I want you to have a quick look at a case that happened back in the seventies, a woman called Delia Kettle. I want you to…'

'You know I can't do that,' he interrupted.

'Yes, you can. Now write it down. Delia Kettle. 1972. A place called Withersedge. She poisoned her husband and got away with it. All I want you to do is find out what happened to her.'

'No, Mum. I really can't.'

'Yes, Matthew, you really can. Just for me. There's a good boy.'

'I… Oh, well, all right. I'll have a try.'

'You promise?'

'All right. Yes I will.'

'You're a good lad.'

'Okay. I've got to go now, Mum. Are you sure you're all right?'

'I'm quite sure. Now keep in touch, won't you?'

'Okay. Bye, Mum.'

Constable Graham was clamping her lips tightly together in an effort not to smile. A tiny snort escaped her. Matthew glowered at her. 'Haven't *you* got a mother?' he asked.

Rosemary eyed Laura with undisguised admiration. 'That poor boy,' she said.

Laura preened herself. 'You have to pull rank sometimes,' she grinned.

'Well, let's keep up the good work. Time to try for a result from Professor Hashim. What d'you reckon? Must be early evening where he is.'

Laura nodded. 'Seven or eight pm, I'd guess. Maybe a bit later.'

'Right. I got his number from Billie while you were still at breakfast. Let's see how the miracle of modern technology matches up, shall we?'

A miraculous seven minutes later, Rosemary was terminating her very fruitful conversation with the Professor.

'That's very helpful indeed,' she said. 'Thank you very much. Bye now, and give my regards to…um…Madam Hashim.' She put the phone down and looked at Laura. 'Well, what *do* you call the wife of a Malaysian Professor?'

Laura spread her hands to show her ignorance. 'What did he say, then?' she asked.

Rosemary handed her the large jotter pad, its top page almost covered in notes.

'Gosh!' said Laura. 'Look at all this! Heart rot fungus. *Inonotus hispidus*. Acacia mangium tree. Indian paintbrush fungus. *Igniarius*. Armillaria root disease. *Phytophthora cinnamomi*. Oh, I like that one.' She said the name again, rolling it round in her mouth. '*Phytophthora cinnamomi*. It's like poetry, some of this.'

'Most of those are very unpleasant little parasites, I might tell you,' said Rosemary. 'And none of them completely fits the symptoms in Daniel's trees. The trouble is, the organism responsible has probably been forced to adapt to our conditions. These are all from the rainforest, which isn't at all the same sort of environment as they have in Winterbourne.'

'No,' Laura agreed, with mock seriousness. 'I can certainly understand that part of the problem. It's just the long words that I find bothersome.'

'Oh, shut up,' chuckled Rosemary. 'You're taking

the mickey.'

'Not at all. I'm extremely impressed. So what happens now?'

'It'll be down to the lab work, in the end. I'll have to go and take more samples from the trees themselves, and have a thorough look at the way the problem seems to be spreading. You can help with that – we need to do more digging at root level, in case it's travelling underground.'

'Is that likely?'

'Not very, but the Professor seems to think it should be checked. *Phytophthora* is a root rot that can cause something like the symptoms we're got here. And there are a few others.'

'Well, let's get to it, then,' said Laura, standing up.

Rosemary followed more slowly. 'Hold on,' she pleaded. 'I've got to have a bit more of a think first. It won't help to just go rushing in without a proper plan.'

'You can think as we drive,' said Laura. 'I don't know about you, but I really do need to be *doing* something.'

'All right,' Rosemary said. 'I'll see you downstairs in ten minutes.'

In the Land Rover, they talked first about the trees, before moving on to the subject of Daniel. 'I'd love to go and visit him in hospital,' said Rosemary. 'Do you think we could?'

'Anybody can visit anybody in hospital, I suppose,' said Laura. 'But it's best not to upset the close family, in my experience.'

As soon as they arrived at Winterbourne, they both noticed a different car on the gravel sweep. 'My God! I know that car,' said Rosemary. It was a two-door sporty job, expensive and inconvenient for ordinary purposes. 'Just let me get my hands on him!'

'Who? What?' spluttered Laura, suddenly left several paces in the rear, as Rosemary marched briskly up to the front door of the house and rang the bell.

Laura caught up, as Mrs Potts opened the door. 'All right, all right,' they heard her muttering, before looking hard at Rosemary.

'I want to see Professor Marchant,' Rosemary said loudly.

'I dare say you do,' grinned the old woman, blocking the doorway.

'Oh, get out of the way,' growled Rosemary, and pushed past her. Laura, after a brief skirmish, managed to follow her.

In the elegant drawing room, voices could be heard. Without hesitation, Rosemary swept across the hall and into the room. 'Julian!' she cried, breaking into the conversation he was having with Alicia.

'Rosemary!' he responded, turning pale.

'How dare you!'

'I heard there'd been an accident. Poor Daniel —' She gave him no chance to finish his sentence.

'You loathsome toad. You double-dealing slimy verminous —'

'You got my letter,' he summarised, taking a step away from her.

She pursued him, still firing enraged epithets at him. 'You cheap, grisly, dismal little —' When he reached the sofa, she caught up with him, and punched him full in the face with all her strength. He toppled backwards onto the cushions, blood already appearing between the fingers he clasped across his nose.

Alicia had been sitting in an armchair throughout, and made no movement or sound now. Laura, in the doorway, stood aside as Rosemary made a fast but dignified exit, and then followed her back to the garden.

'That was magnificent!' Laura panted. 'What weight do you normally fight at?'

'I've never hit anybody before.'

'Well, you have a natural talent for it.'

Rosemary doubled over in sudden hysterics. 'Thank you very much,' she gasped. 'I feel wonderful.'

'So I can see.'

'I just don't understand how I could ever have fancied him,' Rosemary went on. 'He's nothing but a self-serving toerag.'

'You and he have a history, then?'

'Didn't I tell you? Yes, to my eternal shame. We had eight months together. *Eight months*! I must have been mad. Mind you, I never thought he was right for the job. The four of us who've got the sack were on the brink of writing to the Board of Governors listing all Julian's defects as Principal. I might not feel so outraged if I'd actually posted it behind his back.'

'I'm not sure I followed that,' said Laura.

'Never mind. Just take my word for it, he deserved that smack in the mouth for about fifty very good reasons.'

'Is it allowed, though?'

'Is what allowed? Punching one's ex-boss? Very possibly not.'

'No, no, I didn't mean that. I was talking about your – fling – with him. Members of staff consorting. I thought it wasn't allowed.'

'Julian's the Principal. There's nobody above him. He can do what he likes, as long as the Governors don't find out.'

'He's not married then?'

'He was. She saw the light and left him four or five years ago. Nice woman, actually.'

'I get the picture,' said Laura.

For a moment they waited beside the Land Rover, wondering whether to continue with the garden work or beat a rapid retreat. When nobody came out of the house, no sirens disturbed the rural peace, they concluded there would be no reason to leave. Laura went on a brief bindweed-zapping spree while Rosemary studied the sick trees yet again. After a few minutes, the peace of the garden was broken by the sound of a small plane flying low overhead.

'Hey!' called Rosemary. 'What does he think he's doing?'

'There was some writing on the side,' said Laura. 'I just caught a glimpse. It looked like Cavendish Pictures.'

'You think it's a film company, taking some footage for a movie? We might be in it, if so. Wouldn't that be exciting!'

'More likely to be one of those aerial photographers,' Laura guessed. 'Or maybe it was just someone showing off to his girlfriend. Plenty of people around here probably count flying as one of their hobbies.'

Rosemary gazed after the plane as it headed into the distance. 'Must be rather nice,' she said wistfully. 'To have your own plane, I mean.'

'Wonderful,' Laura agreed. 'Apart from all the faffing about, and the cost and the frustrations with the weather.'

'Cynic,' Rosemary scoffed. She paused for a moment, obviously deep in thought. 'Actually,' she said, 'I think I might have had an idea. What if there's a photo of this place, showing these trees? You can tell a lot from the way they look from above. And it would be useful to see how they've changed in the past year or two. We could look up Cavendish Pictures and see if they're local.'

'We could, if you think it would help.'

They found a pub the other side of Devenish, and Laura bought Rosemary a whisky. 'You need cheering up,' she said.

'I need calming down, not cheering up. And how'm I going to drive after this?'

'I'll drive. I've always wanted to have a go at a Land Rover.'

'Really?'

'No, not really. It scares the daylights out of me. I've never been much of a driver. But today will be different. Drink up. To hell with men!'

Rosemary drank thoughtfully. 'Have you ever met a good one?'

'Can't think of any. If they're not all over you, they're all over somebody else.'

'Some of them are lovely.' Rosemary sighed reminiscently.

'Gosh, that worked fast,' Laura observed. 'Don't get silly on me, will you.'

'Why don't you have a drink as well?'

'Driving, remember,' Laura smiled. 'I'm saving myself for this evening.'

'Where are we going this afternoon?'

'To the hospital. I think it's called St Mark's. I passed it yesterday, on my bus.'

Rosemary was intrigued by Laura's knowledge of hospital procedure. 'I am a bit rusty,' she admitted. 'But I used to have a lot of hospital visiting when I was a WPC. Spent half my time in Casualty in the first year or so. Catching up with drunk drivers and wife-batterers. Taught me a lot, I suppose.'

'I'm not sure I ought to ask for details, in spite of being very tempted.'

'Another time,' Laura nodded. 'Now let's get our story straight.'

They were in the car park of St Mark's General Hospital, at three-thirty in the afternoon. Each was relying on the other for courage, trying to persuade themselves that their motives were based on concern for Daniel and not merely old-fashioned curiosity. Rosemary squared her shoulders. 'The fact is, I'm a genuine friend of Daniel's. I have every right to visit him. It's just that…Alicia thinks of me as nothing more than a sort of glorified gardener. She won't understand what I want.'

'She'll wonder why you couldn't just ask her how he is,' Laura supplied.

'Precisely. And after I punched Julian, she might think I'm…well…'

'Insane? Drunk?'

'Unreliable.'

They sat for a few more minutes, until Rosemary spoke again. 'Maybe you could do the talking. That's if Alicia sees us. She's very likely here, after all – though I can't see her car.'

'There must be two hundred cars here,' Laura pointed out. 'Not to mention another hundred or more in the surrounding streets.'

'Right. Okay. So – you could say you'd heard about the accident…'

Laura shook her head. 'I have no imaginable reason to be concerned about Daniel Kellaway,' she said flatly. 'Face it.'

'So, you're just here to keep me company, then. No problem.'

They approached the main entrance, trying to appear purposeful, reading the various signboards aloud to each other. 'Accident and Emergency, Maternity, Radiography…' recited Laura. 'None of those seem to fit the bill.'

'If he's still in a coma, he'll be in the one of those special places – what do they call it?'

'ICU,' Laura said. 'Intensive Care.'

'That's it. We'll find that, then.'

'They won't allow visitors into IC, unless they're close family.'

'Nonsense,' Rosemary snapped. 'I don't believe you.'

They proceeded down a wide corridor, peering curiously through small windows in wide double doors leading to mysterious wards and treatment rooms. 'I always forget how much I hate hospitals,' Laura said.

'Can't do without 'em,' Rosemary breezed. 'I had a great-aunt who was a hospital Matron. Terrifying woman.'

'We really shouldn't be here. It's crazy.'

'Oops!' said Rosemary suddenly, and gripping Laura by the sleeve, yanked her through the next door on their right.

Laura shook her off, trying to get her balance and her bearings. 'What's going on?' she demanded.

'Didn't you see? Alicia and the doctor were coming towards us.'

'Oh. Er…' Laura had just realised where they were, assisted by a man standing in an unmistakable stance, his back to them. The jerky splash of urination completed the picture. As she spoke, he turned round to stare at the two women over his shoulder. 'No cause for concern, sir,' Laura added briskly, staring hard at a pipe running from ceiling to floor. 'Just a routine inspection.'

Rosemary began tapping the pipe pointlessly, eyes wide with hilarity.

'Well, that seems to be in order,' Laura continued. 'So sorry to disturb you.' And she opened the door back into the corridor. Peering around both Laura and the door, Rosemary caught sight of the retreating figures of Alicia and Dr Whittaker. 'That was close,' she said, as Laura tiptoed out of the gents to join her. 'They've just disappeared round that corner.'

'Who?'

'Mrs Kellaway and her ever-faithful doctor friend. Who do you think?'

'They were together?'

'Yes!' said Rosemary emphatically. 'As usual. Honestly, I really think there must be something going on.'

'It does look bad,' Laura agreed. 'On the other hand – why *wouldn't* they be talking about Daniel? It's not exactly surprising, when you think about it.'

'You didn't see them,' said Rosemary darkly. 'Now – I vote we go that way.' She pointed in the direction from which the pair had come.

Shakily Laura agreed. 'I am not enjoying this at all,' she said. 'I just wanted you to know that.'

'I loved your "routine inspection, sir" routine. Sheer genius.'

'Well, I had to say something. That poor man!'

'He'll probably think it was all a hallucination. Now, shoulders back. Let's see if we can look like bona fide visitors.'

They explored miles of corridor on two floors before finally locating Daniel's ward. Laura repeatedly pleaded with Rosemary to abandon the project, in vain. 'We're here now,' Rosemary said. 'And we're sure to find him eventually.'

The ward was encouragingly labelled 'Recovery Room,' and was supervised by a nurse at a station a few feet from the door, which also had a card with 'Mr Kellaway' written on it in felt tip pen. When the nurse disappeared to answer a flashing red light over another door, Rosemary and Laura pushed their way into Daniel's room.

The patient was lying motionless on a high white bed, attached to a drip, and flanked by several machines. His eyes were closed, and one leg was plastered from knee to toe and suspended from a pulley system in the ceiling.

'He isn't going to tell us much,' Laura observed. 'Can we go now?'

'Well, at least he's still alive,' Rosemary argued. 'Poor man. Look at his skin.'

Laura was already doing precisely that. Her first sight of Daniel Kellaway was proving to be rather a shock.

'Revolting!' she shuddered. 'How can he *bear* it? All that tissue destroyed. It's ghastly.' She leaned over Daniel's bare arm, lying on top of the bedsheet. 'I've never seen anything so awful.'

'Actually, it's not as bad as when I last saw him. The blisters have subsided.'

Laura groaned. 'They must have been at a loss to know where to begin. That Doctor Whittaker must be completely useless, letting it get so bad. At least there might be a silver lining to his fall from the window. Maybe they've got better medication in here.'

'He's in a bad way, though. Broken leg, too, look.'

'Yes, I noticed that.'

'Maybe we ought to go now.'

'Definitely. Please.' Laura went ahead, glancing quickly to right and left, and stepping briskly into the corridor. Rosemary had to trot to keep up with her.

'Hey, slow down,' she panted. 'Your legs are longer than mine.'

Laura fractionally modified her pace. 'I suppose we're safe now,' she acknowledged. 'But I never want to do anything like that again. I felt like a criminal.'

'Chicken. We didn't do anything wrong. Poor Daniel, lying there all by himself. It was *nice* of us to go and see him.'

'A totally pointless exercise, as it turned out,' Laura reminded her.

'Oh, pooh,' said Rosemary rudely.

It was with a shock that Laura realised, later that day, that it was still considerably less than a week since Nick had dropped his bombshell. Rosemary's investigations into the diseased trees had taken her up to her room, with laptop and textbooks, and Laura found herself sitting moodily in the hotel lounge, waiting for the bar to open. There seemed to be far too many unhappy thoughts swirling around her head, and little prospect of much good cheer in the near future. When Robin came to tell her there was a phone-call for her, it seemed like a providential rescue from imminent depression.

'Mum?' came Matthew's voice. 'How are you doing?'

'All the better for talking to you again. I mean, you have to feel sorry for any girl who'd get mixed up with a man like your father.'

'Ha ha. Look, I'm phoning about Sam. Dad just called me. Apparently the funeral's on Monday. We thought we'd all go.'

'All of you? All three?'

'Right. Helly's very upset about it, with him being her godfather and everything. He's always been very good to her.'

'Yes he has. He sent her a card to our house, actually. I hope your father gave it to her.'

'I don't know.' Matthew sounded impatient. 'The point is, I thought I should warn you. Assuming you're going to be there as well, I didn't want you and Dad...well, you know. Forewarned, sort of thing.'

'That's thoughtful of you,' Laura said, struggling with the sudden sense of panic that was engulfing her. Seeing Nick again so soon was not going to be easy. In fact, it was going to be utterly dreadful. All the clichés from films and novels swirled around her head, from polite distance to screaming abuse, and back again. 'I expect I'll cope,' she added. And then, 'Oh, Matt – did you look up Delia Kettle for me?'

'Give me a break, Mum,' he pleaded. 'It was only this morning you called me. I've got work to do, you know. There's this big robbery case —'

'All right,' she interrupted. 'I know you're busy. Just don't forget, that's all.'

'I'll do what I can. And I'll see you on Monday. Take care, Mum, won't you.'

'Don't worry about me,' she said. 'Thanks for phoning. That was very nice of you.'

'Bye, then.'

'Bye, love.'

Normally the idea of a family gathering would have

delighted her. Now it merely seemed fraught with bottled-up emotions and things a person couldn't possibly come out with at a funeral.

The distractions provided by events at Winterbourne Manor had faded, at least for the time being. The discovery that Mrs Potts was none other than Delia Kettle had been exciting at the time, but seemed to have little real importance. Laura had no wish to confront the woman, or make unfounded accusations. If Alicia Kellaway was having a fling with the doctor, then so what? People had flings all the time, and no good was ever done by drawing attention to it. And although that might conceivably give the man a motive for disposing of Daniel, the fact was that Daniel was lying safely in hospital, showing some signs of recovering from his ghastly skin condition as well as, presumably, regaining consciousness eventually.

But, as always, these thoughts led straight to ever-deepening suspicions. However firmly she tried to persuade herself that there was nothing dubious going on, the facts came along and smacked her in the face. These facts involved means, motive and opportunity galore for the disposal of both Sam and Daniel. Like scattered pieces of jigsaw, they must surely fit together, if only she could get hold of the key to it all. The big picture had to be staring her in the face, if she just had the sense to see it.

But, as yet, she could find no reason for Mrs Potts to arrange for Daniel to fall out of a window, or for the doctor to issue lethal medication to Sam. She remembered Vickie, walking down the street hand in hand with a strange man. She relived the glorious moment when Rosemary had punched Julian Marchant in the face, and asked herself whether *he* might have been instrumental in Sam's death and Daniel's fall. And then she swept an imaginary hand across the stubborn puzzle, impatient with the whole business.

At least it had filled the waiting time. Rosemary's

tread was heard on the stair, and the tell-tale tinkle of glasses as Robin got the bar ready for first orders. Laura got up, to meet her friend. 'Drinks on me this evening,' she said. 'I still haven't toasted that left hook you threw this morning.'

Rosemary pulled a face. 'Thanks. I could do with it. I'm still completely at sea over this tree problem. At this rate I'll be able to claim a whole new malady – The Boxer Virus. Trouble is, I still won't be any closer to knowing how to cure it.'

'Just cut the whole lot down and burn them,' Laura suggested.

'It might even come to that,' Rosemary said miserably.

Chapter Eight

'Do you know – when I first saw you, I thought you'd come here for a funeral,' Rosemary confided, next morning. 'I thought that was why you were crying, and had those two great big suitcases with you.'

'Well, now I really am,' Laura said. 'You must have had a premonition.'

'So, it's Monday, then? Quite quick, under the circumstances.'

'Burial at the church in Devenish, eleven o'clock.'

'At least you don't have far to go.'

Laura tried to laugh. 'The irony is – in spite of filling two large cases, I didn't bring anything remotely suitable for such an occasion. I'll have to go back to the house to find a dark suit.'

'How will you get there?'

'Train and taxi, I suppose, same as I got here.'

'You can borrow the Land Rover if you like.'

Laura raised her eyebrows. 'Really?'

'You made a fair job of it yesterday, didn't you?'

'Well, I wasn't bad, but I can't say I enjoyed it much. That second gear trick is murder on the wrist.'

'You'll get the hang of it in no time. Just remember – if she won't start, you tap the starter motor with the spanner I keep under the driving seat. It works every time. Anyway, I think it's sorted itself out now. It's been fine for the past three or four days.'

'You don't fancy coming with me, I suppose?'

Rosemary gave her a sympathetic look. 'I don't think so,' she said gently. 'I get the feeling this is something you need to do on your own.'

Laura sighed loudly. 'I'm sure you're right. It's just…'

'I know. Poor old you.' Rosemary patted her hand. 'But if you make sure you turn everything off, and do all the boring stuff like that, you won't have to go again for ages. Maybe not ever.'

Laura frowned. 'I'm not sure whether I like that idea or not. My lovely garden! Oh, dear – I do miss my garden.'

'Well, tomorrow you can help me with some serious digging at Winterbourne. That'll keep you occupied.'

'Thanks very much.'

The Land Rover played all kinds of games with her during the journey home. The gearbox had a mind of its own: one minute it would slide from first to second to third like the smoothest synchromeshed system ever made; at others it screeched and stuck and almost broke her fingers. The steering took some concentration, too, veering wide on some bends, if the speed was a fraction too high. But on the whole, she remained on friendly terms with the thing, and arrived outside her former home feeling she'd achieved something.

The broken window was the first thing she noticed. Obviously Nick hadn't been back, and none of the neighbours had seen the damage – but to Laura it stood out like a shameful beacon. How could she have done that? Amongst all the other jobs, she would have to tape some card over it, from the inside.

She had a key to the front door in her bag, and she let herself in, glancing around in the hope that none of the neighbours were watching. The last thing she wanted was to be questioned by Maggie Frost or Jennifer Williams. While pretending concern, they would be far more interested in hearing the gory tale of betrayal and abandonment. And above all, they would want to know what was in store for the house. Property prices had become an obsession in the street, and anybody risking a change for the worse would have the residents' committee to reckon with.

The house smelt of dust and something pungent in the direction of the kitchen. Already it had a neglected feel, as if all the years of happy family experience had wilted and turned to ash. This was nothing like that sense of being welcomed back after a holiday, where you explored your own territory with an odd sense of curiosity, seeing it with new travel-broadened eyes. This was a moment full of darkness and fear, and a certainty of something finished. No longer could she settle back here, pulling it around her like a comforting old coat. It was tainted, corrupted by Nick's disloyalty.

Laura tried to tell herself that this was a kind of progress. To have realised that the house no longer qualified as a home made her future decisions much easier. She now had to work through a preordained set of actions, designed to set herself free of the place, and turn to a whole new phase in her life.

And this she proceeded to do. Kicking aside the scattering of mail on the doormat, she marched across the hall to the cupboard under the stairs. There, she threw the master switch in the fusebox, cutting off the electric power. She closed the stopcock under the kitchen sink, and made a laborious call to British Telecom telling them she wanted the line discontinued. She then gathered up the letters and magazines lying on the hall mat, and rapidly flicked through them, sorting junk from bills and other items of interest.

One letter jumped out at her, making her heart lurch. It was addressed to Nick, in a familiar handwriting. The date on the postmark was the day she had left the house. Because the writing was unmistakably that of Sam Trent, she opened it.

Dear Nick

How's things? I hope Helena got the card I sent. I never did get a notification of her last address, so I'm relying on you and Laura to forward it.

Anyway, I'm writing in response to yours of a couple of weeks ago. I'm flattered that you'd like me to act as

Executor of your will, and of course I'll do it, if you're sure you want me. I must admit I've had rather a lot of this sort of stuff just lately, with my business partner insisting on sorting out his affairs. He's ill, and prone to dark thoughts of mortality. All very wearing, to be honest.

If I'd thought of it sooner, I could have returned the compliment and asked you to do the same service for me. I made my will last year, at Daniel's insistence. Vickie isn't too thrilled about it, but it seems only sensible for Daniel and me to leave our share in Kellaways to each other. Vickie won't go short, if the unthinkable were to happen.

Anyway, we'll have to meet up one day soon, and you can run the basics past me, and I'll sign on whatever dotted line you need me to. It would be good to see you, in any case. It's been much too long – again. Where does the time go?

Better get on. Lots of love to Laura.

All best

Sam.

Laura wiped away a tear as she read the letter twice through. How ironic that Sam should write about his will and 'the unthinkable' only a day before his own death. She hadn't known that Nick was making his will – and a sudden realisation showed her why. He'd been planning to include the Tart! Had he said anything of this to Sam? Had he asked his friend to say nothing to her, in the unlikely event they were to run into each other?

No. She shook herself crossly. Sam had been completely convincing when he'd told her he'd heard nothing at all about Nick's affair. Paranoia was not part of her repertoire, and it was no time to start now. Much more likely was that Nick would explain the situation when he and Sam met, and that it hadn't occurred to Sam to refer to the business when Laura showed up on his doorstep. Wills were touchy subjects at the best of times, and she could well understand why he might choose to duck the subject, at least on that first evening.

The part about Daniel Kellaway meant little to her at first. There didn't seem to be much mystery about it. Daniel was now the sole proprietor of the garden centre business, and good luck to him. Both wives were apparently aware of the situation, with little cause for resentment.

Except that Vickie Trent had been agitated about something to do with money. She had been annoyed and distracted. Had something happened in that last day or two, after Sam wrote the letter to Nick?

Putting the letter back in its envelope and slipping it into her bag, she went upstairs. The memory of the exchange with Nick, only a week earlier, was vivid. Standing in the bedroom, she repeated every word of it to herself, feeling the same surges of fear, rage and contempt as before. And then she said aloud, 'That's it. Not finished, I know, but accepted.' She savoured the thought behind the words. Mandy the solicitor had been right – people did adapt quickly. She no longer thought of herself as a wife and certainly not as a *housewife*. It might be far from clear what happened next, but one thing was sure: she was never coming back to live in this house.

A careless glance out of the window as she moved towards the wardrobe in search of funeral clothes made her pause in sudden pain. The garden! In the week she'd been away a lot had changed. Buds had burst into flower, flowers had drooped into that shapeless stage before they turned into seedheads. Buttercups and dandelions had magically appeared between the rose bushes, the moment her back was turned.

Never mind, she told herself fiercely. You can always make a new garden – or work in other people's. Plants were plants, wherever you went. A simple walk in the countryside could take you to a paradise of wild blooms and stately trees. Meanwhile, there were still several days' work at Winterbourne Manor, unless Rosemary made a miraculous breakthrough in her researches.

Thank goodness for Rosemary, she thought then. Without her new friend, what would this week in the White Hart have been like? Grieving for Sam as well as her collapsed marriage, she'd have sunk into self-pity and despair. Probably she'd have turned to eating and drinking too much, and phoning poor Matthew in the middle of the night.

Which in turn reminded her that Matthew was supposed to be digging up the old police records on Delia Kettle alias Mrs Potts, and passing on any forgotten details of the case. He hadn't been very co-operative when she'd asked him the favour, admittedly, but she knew her boy. Matthew Thyme could never refuse his Mum anything.

The suit looked reasonably clean and tidy, and she carefully inserted it into a carrierbag she found in the wardrobe. There wasn't anything else she wanted to take with her. The few pairs of shoes in the rack were all either uncomfortable or worn out. A drawer full of scarves and gloves and petticoats could easily be abandoned. It was almost a relief to walk away from them.

Downstairs again, she went into the kitchen. The unsavoury smell was traced to the swing bin, which she dealt with as quickly as she could. When she found the mouldering casserole, sitting forgotten in the fridge, she had to hold back a sudden threatened storm of tears. How long ago it seemed now, that she had cheerily prepared it for herself and Nick. That and all the other contents of the fridge joined the bin liner in the wheelie bin outside, along with all the junk mail.

She did another tour of the house, closing doors, making sure all the windows were securely fastened. The broken window was fixed with a double sheet of cardboard taken from a Cornflakes packet. She collected together a few ornaments and pictures, and stowed them under the bed in the main bedroom, thinking in a vague way that if anybody did break in, they wouldn't find the things that mattered. Not that any would-be burglar was likely to get past Maggie Frost or Jennifer Williams. Their antennae for anything of that nature were more acutely tuned than anything a state-of-the-art surveillance system might achieve. The real truth was, she acknowledged, that these were things she didn't want Nick to have. And it was more than likely that Nick would come back to the house one of these days.

The Land Rover did its not-starting trick when she tried to drive away. She turned the key again and again, with no result. Closing her eyes for a moment, she faced the inevitable. By now, Maggie and Jennifer, and probably Susie and Fran from further down, would all have noted the vehicle outside the Thyme house. They'd be watching from behind their curtains to see what it signified. When Laura herself climbed in, sat there a few minutes, climbed out again armed with a spanner, opened the bonnet and banged the engine beneath it, they would not believe their eyes. Hoping desperately that she had hit the starter motor, and not the carburettor or windscreen washer by mistake, she tried again. Like magic, it fired. Trying to keep her head low, she sped to the end of the street, without a backward glance. Only later did she appreciate what the motor had done for her, in distracting her from thoughts of finality and failure. 'Thanks, old girl,' she murmured, patting the steering wheel.

Rosemary had her own morning of nostalgia, contrary to expectations. Billie phoned the White Hart, asking to speak to her. She almost refused to take the call, until sense prevailed. What more could they do to her, anyway?

'Rosemary? How's it going?'

'Slowly.'

'Oh. Well, I thought you should know that Fergus and Deirdre have decided to challenge the redundancy decision. They want you and Tom, of course, to join with them. I said I'd sound you out about it.'

Rosemary didn't hesitate. 'Sorry. They'll be fighting a losing battle, and life's too short for all that sort of stuff. Can you tell them I wish them luck and everything, but to count me out. I'll see them again sometime – but not just yet. I've got a lot of thinking to do, but it's all *forward* thinking. Do you understand? I'm hoping to forget all about Malmesbury for the time being.'

But when she put the phone down, she found herself wallowing in reminiscences of her time at the college. Eighteen years was a long stint in the same place, despite all the changes she'd seen it go through. She'd been good at the job, probably the best lecturer they'd had, in the way she could hold the students' attention and make them think for themselves. She'd dodged a lot of the administrative flak, sticking to her own certainties about what was important. But it had got her in the end. Nobody was ever going to flout the system successfully, in the long run. And if you rocked the boat, they fired you. Simple as that.

She remembered sweet moments when a struggling student passed with far better marks than predicted, or a long field trip ended with a companionable singsong in the minibus. Oh well, she sighed, all good things come to an end, and there's life in this old cat yet.

But her next thoughts drifted to a subject less easy to confront. Her mother was not going to take the news of her abruptly ended career very lightly. She would carp and criticise and accuse Rosemary of being feckless. She would ask tedious questions about pension rights and security. Which would be a bit rich, considering what a rebel Mrs Boxer had been all her life. But at least she would like Laura; that could be assumed with perfect confidence. The two had quite a bit in common, come to think of it: independent, plain-speaking, undaunted women, both of them. Laura had been a real find. Without her, there would have been long bitter evenings in the hotel, musing over life's injustices and wondering where the next laugh was coming from.

The apparent mysteries at Winterbourne Manor were a bonus, on top of the trouble with the trees. If it hadn't been for Laura's questioning habits, Rosemary probably wouldn't have thought twice about Sam's death or Daniel's fall from the window. She'd have taken it all at face value and got on with the job. As it was, she found herself deeply into wild imaginings about Doctor Whittaker and Vickie Trent, or was it old Mrs Potts and Julian Marchant? Mentally, she juggled the names, bringing in Alicia Kellaway for good measure, although unable to see how she could be implicated in Sam's death. Presumably she had no idea that her housekeeper had once been charged with murder, either. The suspicions that Rosemary harboured concerning an affair between Alicia and the doctor reflected much worse on the man than the woman. After all, Alicia already had everything a woman could wish for, in that wonderful house and garden. The doctor might well want a piece of that, and Alicia might want a piece of the doctor, but as far as Rosemary could see, she had that anyway. It was probably just a flirtation, in any case. There didn't seem to be any question about Alicia's devotion to her husband.

But none of this concerned Rosemary personally. Only if she could somehow demonstrate that the loathsome Julian Marchant was in reality a criminal mastermind would she find personal gratification in the eventual outcome. Poor Daniel aroused her pity, but he was getting good care at the hospital, and whatever happened next was completely out of Rosemary's hands.

It did, however, remind her of the idea about aerial photographs. With nothing better to do, she went downstairs and asked Robin for a local phone book. Businesses were listed in the first section, and Cavendish Pictures leapt out at her, at the top of a page. The address was in Fairchester, where Laura had gone to find a solicitor. Without hesitating, Rosemary called the number.

A man answered, his voice deep and rather elderly-sounding.

'Oh, hello,' Rosemary said. 'Am I right in thinking you take aerial photographs?'

'Indeed you are. Can I be of service?'

'Well, I was wondering whether you keep copies of pictures you've taken, going back a few years.'

'We keep some,' he said, sounding wary. 'And since we've gone over to digital, we store them all on disk.'

'When was that? The changeover, I mean?'

'Nearly three years ago. I'm not at all sure it was a change for the better, to be honest.' She heard a heartfelt sigh and imagined him as a lifelong user of long lenses and manual focus.

'Could I come and see you, do you think? It's all rather difficult to explain over the phone.'

'Of course you can, my dear. I'm always pleased to have a young lady come to see me.'

Rosemary gave a girlish giggle and took down the directions. 'I'll try and make it this afternoon,' she said.

Laura was back just in time for lunch, which they had at the White Hart. Rosemary was surprised at the flood of relief that washed through her, at the unique sound of the Land Rover drawing up outside. Smiling to herself, she wondered whether it was her motor or her friend she was most pleased to see.

'How was she?' she asked Laura, the moment she stepped into the hotel foyer.

'Who?' Laura frowned and blinked.

'The Land Rover, of course.'

'Oh! She's a beauty. We're the best of friends.'

'She started then?'

'Well, no, actually. But it turned out she did me a bit of a favour by being so baulky. And the trick with the spanner worked a treat.'

'Come and have a drink, then, and tell me all about it.'

They lingered over lunch, despite Rosemary's appointment in Fairchester.

'You can come with me if you like,' she said, having told Laura about it.

'Just try to stop me,' Laura said. 'It sounds really interesting.'

'We can probably be there and back by around four.'

'Are we in a hurry?'

Rosemary shook her head irritably. 'Not really, I suppose. It's just that if we do find something out about the trees, I'll be keen to go and see how it affects what I've been doing.'

'You can go tomorrow. I don't suppose Alicia cares whether or not it's a weekend.'

They were still slowly finishing up their coffee when they heard a voice in the hotel foyer. 'Is Mrs Thyme here?' it demanded.

'Who's that?' Laura wondered. 'I know the voice.'

She got up and went to have a look. 'Vickie!' she exclaimed. 'What are you doing here?'

'Oh, Laura, thank goodness I've found you. I can't think who else I can talk to.'

Laura did her best to suppress the quick memory of how Vickie had received her only a few days earlier, when she'd thrown herself on her friend's charity. After all, the poor woman had just been widowed.

'Come through to the lounge, and tell me what's the matter,' she invited. 'Shall I order you some tea or coffee?'

Vickie nodded vaguely, and Laura turned to Robin, who was hovering at the reception desk. 'Tea?' she mouthed at him, and he nodded obligingly. *I'm going to miss Robin*, Laura thought.

Rosemary appeared in the doorway of the dining room. 'Anything I can do?' she asked.

'Oh, yes. You should hear all this as well – I suppose.' Vickie frowned at her. 'You knew Sam, didn't you?'

'Well…not really. But I'm an old friend of Daniel's. I can make myself scarce if you'd rather talk to Laura on her own.'

'No, it's okay. I'm sorry to interrupt you.' Vickie shook her head as if dazed. 'I don't know what to do, you see. I don't know what it all means.'

Laura remembered her glimpse of Vickie hand in hand with a strange man, and her consequent suspicions. This didn't seem like a woman with a guilty secret – much more like a bewildered soul, in receipt of information that had thrown her right off balance.

'I've had the police round this morning, you see,' she went on, as Laura led her to a cosy corner of the hotel lounge. 'They're talking about foul play. Pursuing investigations, they said, because they're not satisfied with the findings of the post-mortem. I told you, didn't I, that they were talking about anomalies, on Tuesday.'

Laura nodded. 'So they're still not satisfied?' she said. 'Does that mean the funeral's been postponed?'

Vickie shook her head. 'No, no. They've done all they need to with the…with Sam's body. They think he'd been taking too much Digoxin. It strained his heart until it couldn't cope any more. They asked me so many questions, Laura. On and on, for ages. They searched the house for medication. Now they've gone to his office to see if he kept pills there. It's *horrible*. They seem to think *I* did something to hurt Sam.'

Laura took Vickie's trembling hand in hers, with a swift glance at Rosemary. Robin arrived with a pot of tea and three cups, which Rosemary arranged on the low table in front of them. Nobody spoke for a few minutes.

'Are you saying they've started a murder investigation?' Laura asked eventually.

'Well, they didn't say that word – but I suppose that must be what they meant.'

'It doesn't sound like much evidence. Maybe Sam was just careless,' Rosemary contributed. 'After all, he really did have a weak heart, didn't he? And he was working so hard, with Daniel out of action.'

Vickie nodded. 'That's what I told them. He was over at Winterbourne every other day, taking orders from Daniel, then back to the office, then visiting all the garden centres, checking up on things. He never stopped. But they insisted they'd found high levels of Digoxin and its derivatives in his system, much more than might be expected from the prescribed dose.'

'So are they interviewing the doctor?' Laura asked. 'Isn't he the best person to settle all this?'

Rosemary made an inarticulate sound, which seemed to arise from a state of some excitement, when Laura turned to look at her. Laura could almost read her thoughts – centred on a suspicion she'd had of Bob Whittaker more or less from the start. Plus, it appeared, a new idea, that Rosemary was anxious to voice, but not in Vickie's hearing.

Vickie heaved a quivering sigh. 'That wouldn't make sense. Why would Doctor Whittaker want to harm Sam? He was really upset when he heard the news.'

'It could have been carelessness,' Laura suggested.

'Mmm.' Vickie took a long swig of the tea. 'It's a terrible feeling, you know, wondering whether somebody deliberately killed your husband. You feel so dreadfully *helpless*. And confused.'

Laura sat up straighter, and looked Vickie full in the face. 'Can I just ask you something?' she said.

Vickie blinked and nodded. 'Of course.'

'I saw you in Fairchester, a couple of days ago. You were with a man...'

'Oh, yes. Wednesday. That was Tony.'

'Tony?'

'My brother. Didn't you ever meet him? He was helping me with the funeral arrangements. He's been very kind, but he has to go off to Rome tomorrow morning, and he won't be back until late on Sunday, for the funeral.'

'Rome?' echoed Rosemary, irrelevantly.

'Yes. Actually, he works for the Vatican, as an administrator. He's based there. He's a very good man.'

Laura reran her image of Vickie holding hands with this Tony, trying to reinterpret what she'd seen. Perhaps it did make sense that a brother with Italian habits would hold his sister's hand, especially at a time of distress. It did, of course.

'Oh,' she said. 'No, I never met him.' Neither could she remember ever hearing his name mentioned. All she could recall was that Vickie had two older sisters.

'Why? Did you think I had a lover?'

Vickie's accuracy flummoxed Laura. 'Well...' she mumbled. 'No, not really.'

'You did! Do you also think I poisoned my darling husband?'

'No, no, Vickie, of course not. Come on, love, calm down and finish your tea. Everything's going to work out right, you'll see.'

Vickie gave her a hard stare, ignoring the tea. 'It won't, though, will it? How can it come right when Sam is never going to come back? I'm never going to see him again. He was fifty-four, Laura. That's much too young to die.'

She got up from the low settee. 'Well, thanks for listening, but I think I'd better go. I'm sure you mean well, but quite honestly, you haven't made me feel the least bit better.'

Laura wrung her hands. 'I'm so sorry. Please don't be angry. Tell me what I can do to help on Monday. Nick's going to be there, you know. And Matthew and Helena as well. We were all very fond of Sam, you know that.'

Vickie put a hand to her throat. 'I don't know anything, do I? I don't know what people are thinking, who's plotting behind our backs, what Sam thought he was doing taking all those pills. I don't know *anything*.' Her voice rose, and Laura made a movement towards her. But Vickie put out a hand to ward her off. 'No, leave me alone. I'm going home now. I suppose I'll see you next week.'

For a moment, Laura had feared that Vickie would order her to stay away from the funeral. Her relief made her weak. 'Thanks, Vick,' she said. 'I'm terribly sorry to have upset you. I didn't mean it. It was really crass of me.'

'Never mind,' sniffed Vickie. 'Pretty well everything upsets me at the moment.'

When she was gone, Rosemary let out a groan. 'That didn't go very well, did it?'

'You can kick me if you like,' said Laura.

Laura and Rosemary were relieved to climb into the Land Rover and head for Fairchester, after the difficult encounter. Laura kept making small moans, every time she thought of how she'd virtually accused Vickie of having an affair. Rosemary finally lost patience.

'Come on, old girl. It's not the end of the world that you upset Vickie. From what you said, she's never been much of a friend to you, anyway.'

'That's true. It's just bad timing, I suppose. After this morning, taking my leave of the house, it feels as if I'm free floating – hardly anybody knows or cares where I am, I have no idea what's going to happen next. It's unsettling.'

'Look at it this way – most women would give ten years of their lives for this sort of freedom. You're not answerable to anybody, you can go anywhere you like. Things'll turn up, you see. And don't forget – you've got me.'

Laura reached across and patted Rosemary's shoulder. 'Yes,' she laughed. 'I have got you, haven't I.'

'And I've got you. I was only thinking this morning – how grim all this would be if I was on my own.'

'So was I! Just the same thought.'

'And that means we should make the most of our freedom. Time enough for funerals and sick trees and crazy housekeepers in the morning. For now we're going to meet a randy old photographer.'

'If you put it like that, what can I say?' Laura grinned.

Chapter Nine

Cavendish Pictures was based in a very small building, not far from Laura's friendly solicitor. Apparently overlooked when any reconstruction work had been underway, the photographic shop looked and felt like a remnant of a former age. On two floors, with a low-slung gable over the single upstairs window, it was coyly identified by a modest sign above the door.

'It's like something out of Dickens,' said Laura. 'How sweet!'

'I wonder where they keep the aeroplane,' Rosemary said.

'Perhaps it's much bigger when you get inside – like the Tardis,' Laura joked.

'We'll soon find out.' Rosemary pushed open the door, and they stepped inside.

A small man, who looked to be well over seventy, was sitting at a black teak desk, surrounding by filing cabinets. On the desk in front of him was a computer, and on two of the walls there were rows of aerial shots of houses, mostly large with generous gardens. Rosemary immediately began to scan them for Winterbourne Manor.

'Good afternoon,' said the man, in a gentle voice. 'Can I be of service?'

'Oh, I'm sorry. I'm Rosemary Boxer. I phoned you this morning, about your archives.'

'I remember,' he nodded. 'You didn't tell me very much. I'm eager to know just what it is you're looking for.'

'Well…' she began.

'Sit down, ladies, before you start. It's cramped, I know, but I'm sure we can accommodate you.'

Laura's comparison with a scene out of Dickens seemed to be increasingly accurate. Two chairs stood the other side of the desk, and she and Rosemary settled into them. They half expected to be offered tea, or

Madeira wine.

'Now,' the man invited. 'We should start at the beginning. My name is Nicholas Grindley. I began this little enterprise close to fifty years ago, and my son and grandson both now work with me. It's a modest living, but we survive.'

'You must be looking forward to your half-century,' said Laura admiringly. 'I love these small family businesses.'

'We aim for good service,' he said unassumingly. 'Now, please. I interrupted you.' He turned to Rosemary, eyebrows raised.

'We're interested in Winterbourne Manor,' she said, readily. 'In particular, the trees in the avenue. It's all a bit technical, but I was hoping to learn something about their recent condition, if I could examine a picture of them taken from overhead.'

'Winterbourne Manor, eh,' he said dreamily. 'Lovely place. I suppose it's owned by some faceless bureaucrat these days.'

'Actually, I think you might have taken a picture of it yesterday. And no, the owner isn't really like that at all. He's a nice man. And his wife seems quite sweet, too.'

'I haven't had yesterday's work through yet. Ronnie brings it all in, twice a week. But I gather it isn't the recent picture you're looking for?'

'No,' Rosemary said patiently. 'As I said —'

'I remember Winterbourne fifty or sixty years ago. Joe Whittaker and I were good friends in those days. We used to climb some of those trees together.'

'Joe Whittaker?' Laura leaned forward.

'That's right. The Manor belonged to the Whittakers for a century or more. Very pleasant people. Middle class merchants, I suppose you might say. Joe's grandfather made a fortune manufacturing harness and such for hansom cabs. Of course, the market dwindled dramatically once the motor car took over.

They finally sold up, regrettably. Nobody expected them to hang on as long as they did, even though they made enormous efforts to keep up with the times. Nothing else they turned to ever seemed to succeed.'

'Whittaker, as in Doctor *Bob* Whittaker,' Laura pressed.

'Bob must be Joe's grandson. His father, Eric, married very young, the same as Joe did. The boy went into medicine.'

Rosemary was still trying to stick to her main point. 'Do you have any pictures?' she urged.

He frowned slightly, and stared at her for a few moments. 'No, I wouldn't think so. Now, how should I phrase this, in these delicate times? The Whittakers were not the type of people to find a use for our sort of product. They were much more concerned with what they could see for themselves than what might be observed from above. And after them, some foreign johnny bought the place. To be perfectly honest with you, I don't think I had the heart to photograph it. I always had a soft spot for Winterbourne. And you say the trees are sick? That's a shame, it really is.' He shook his head slowly, and sighed. 'Nothing lasts, you see.'

'I'm doing everything I can to save them,' Rosemary tried to reassure him. Although they wouldn't be the ones you climbed, anyway.'

'Well, I'm sorry if I wasn't of very much help. I do wish you both well, ladies.'

He stood up, giving a clear signal that the encounter was at an end. Rosemary held out her hand for the expected shake. But Mr Grindley did not respond. Something had evidently saddened him to the point where he wanted them to leave immediately. Laura was the first to reach the door, urging Rosemary to follow with small sideways twitches of her head.

'Well, thank you very much for your time,' Rosemary said. 'It's been really nice to meet you.'

'Goodbye,' said the old man, watching them go with moist eyes.

'Well, what did we make of that?' Laura demanded, almost before the door had closed behind them. 'Poor old chap seems to be losing his grip.'

'We stirred up a few ghosts for him, I think,' said Rosemary thoughtfully. 'How very surprising, don't you think, that Doctor Whittaker should be so closely linked to Winterbourne?'

'I wonder if the Kellaways know about it.'

'Good question. If they're relatively new to the area, they might easily have no idea. Although you'd think somebody would have mentioned it.'

Laura fiddled with an earring, which generally seemed to assist the thinking processes. 'It might explain why he spends so much time there. Did you get the impression he played there as a child, and might be resenting it going out of the family?'

Rosemary tapped her front teeth reflectively. 'He might remember happy times there, as a small boy, before it was sold. That's why he grabs any chance to visit now. Maybe he wasn't even trying very hard to make Daniel better, just to give himself an excuse for nostalgic calls at the old place.'

'But would he be actively trying to get it back? And how?'

'Good question.'

Laura's eyes narrowed. 'Hang on. I think I can see how it could work. Did I tell you about the letter from Sam I found at the house?'

'I don't think you did, no.'

'It was a bit near the bone, actually. All about making wills. Nick had asked Sam to be his executor, and Sam wrote back saying he'd had a basinful of wills lately, with Daniel insisting he was dying, and wanting to get his affairs sorted.'

'How does this connect with Doctor Whittaker?'

'It's only a theory. But Sam and Daniel jointly own

Winterbourne Manor as well as the business. The letter said they'd left their halves to each other. Something to do with the business and tax. So, if Daniel had died instead of Sam – and let's face it, that looked to be the likely outcome, this time last week – then Sam would have owned the house and the garden centres outright.'

'You're saying the doc murdered Sam, so that wouldn't happen?'

'Right. Because as it is, Daniel is now the sole owner of the whole shooting match. And his heir can only be Alicia. So if anything happened to him — '

'Which it jolly nearly did.'

'Indeed. Then Alicia and her boyfriend would be in clover.'

'But Daniel's still alive, so the whole plan's failed,' Rosemary pointed out.

'For the time being,' Laura agreed, with a dark look.

'Sounds pretty complicated,' sighed Rosemary.

'I know. And it's only a theory. It's probably all wrong. After all, the doctor seems quite a nice chap, and Alicia's a devoted wife.'

'And what about Vickie?'

'She's got the house she lives in. She seems to be reasonably well catered for. Sam said something about that in the letter. He hadn't forgotten to ensure that she didn't go short.'

'So if Daniel had died when he fell out of the window, the two wives would be running the business, Alicia and Doctor Whittaker would be living in the Manor and everybody would be happy? Is that what you're saying?'

'Something like that.'

'And what about your Delia Kettle?'

'Ah!' Laura raised an approving finger. 'That's the best question of them all.'

Despite the failure to glean anything about the

trees, they felt their trip to Fairchester had been well worth the trouble. With a sense that it had been a very long week, they agreed that the coming weekend would be devoted to idle enjoyment.

'So what exactly are we going to do?' Laura asked. 'I'm not sure I can just switch off altogether.'

Rosemary frowned. 'I know what you mean,' she agreed. 'Well, for one thing, I'll probably give Professor Hashim another call.'

'That won't take long.'

'No. Hey – tell you what! Why don't we give the Kellaway Garden Centre the once-over? We could go on Sunday.'

Laura's face brightened. 'I love garden centres,' she said. 'We might even have lunch there, if it's got a cafeteria.'

'Bound to have. They all do these days.'

Having something to look forward to made all the difference. They drove back to the White Hart feeling decidedly pleased with themselves.

But by late on Saturday morning, they were both feeling restless. Rosemary had tried phoning the Professor, only to be told that he had gone on a business trip for a few days, and was impossible to reach. Their suppositions about Doctor Whittaker's designs on Winterbourne Manor caused them a lot of concern.

'What if he tries to bump Daniel off while he's in hospital?' worried Rosemary. 'It must be awfully easy to do.'

'It isn't easy at all,' Laura insisted. 'All the drugs have to be signed out, and he'd be terrified of being caught. The real worry will be when Daniel gets home again. I wonder how much Alicia knows? That's the big hole in the picture.'

'I can't believe she's working in cahoots with the doctor. She's so devoted to Daniel, nursing him the way she does. Let's hope his skin trouble doesn't recur. The chances are, he'll be back to normal once he gets out of hospital and his leg mends.'

'I hope you're right. Maybe all this has scared Whittaker off, and the whole thing's over and done with.'

'You know, there are ways of driving a person to suicide,' Rosemary went off at a tangent. 'The doc could have been subtly undermining Daniel, week after week, until he lost all his will to go on. Otherwise, I don't really see why he'd have got so desperate.'

Laura raised her eyebrows. 'Gosh, I do. That gruesome skin disease, getting steadily worse, must be unbearable.'

'Right,' Rosemary nodded. 'So that's our conclusion, is it? The doctor did it, in both cases.'

'It's our firm hypothesis,' corrected Laura. 'I'm not sure we're quite ready for a conclusion just yet.'

They kept to their idea of visiting the garden centre, having asked Robin for precise directions. 'It was Daniel's first one,' Rosemary explained. 'He opened it six years ago, and now he's got a dozen of them. He hasn't wasted any time, I must say.'

'Did he live near here then? When he first got started, I mean?'

'Oh yes, I think so. I remember him talking about the area when he was at college. He probably had his eye on Winterbourne for years, as well. He'd have known about it all his life, and must have been thrilled when it came on the market just as he and Sam were in a position to buy it.'

'Wow!' Laura was more than impressed by her first glimpse of the place. 'It's enormous!'

'It's his showpiece,' Rosemary said. 'None of the others are quite up to this one. But I must admit I didn't think it would be quite as grand as this.'

They spent well over an hour drifting from one section to another, indoors and out. Water features, fencing, terracotta pots, paving stones, statues...

'When are we going to get to any actual *plants*?' joked Laura. 'So far, it's been everything but.'

'Over there, I think,' said Rosemary, waving to an extensive area with countless rows of trees, shrubs, perennials and late bedding plants. 'I suggest we have lunch first and then give that bit the once-over.'

'Agreed,' said Laura. 'This is such fun – I could stay all day.'

The cafeteria was filling up fast, and they quickly bagged a table near a large window. Next to them another two women were just getting started on large salads.

'Daniel must be so pleased with himself,' Rosemary said. 'It's a real empire, isn't it.'

'Must be raking in a hefty profit, too,' said Laura.

'More than they know what to do with, apparently. Hence the endowment to Malmesbury.' She scowled. 'I still wish I'd managed to sabotage that little transaction. Julian Marchant will take every ounce of credit for it, and carry on making his usual mess of the place.'

'Not your problem any longer.'

'True. But I can't help feeling sorry for the students. They deserve better. You know, he's going to establish a Chair in Plant Genetics, and you know what that means, don't you?'

'Tell me.'

'GM.' Rosemary rolled the two syllables in her mouth, making them sound sonorous and sinister. 'He's mad keen to get into all that stuff. Thinks it's the future, whatever the consumers might say.'

'He's probably heading for a fall, then. I can't see people ever going for it.'

'I hope you're right.'

At the next table, the two women were talking intently, heads close together. As Laura and Rosemary fell silent, odd words caught their attention.

'Alicia…Room upstairs…the *poor* man…suicide…'

The woman speaking was vibrant with excitement, her voice beginning to rise.

'And I said to her – how will he possibly cope without Sam Trent? We were standing right outside Daniel's window, where he must have heard everything. I never realised until I heard he'd jumped only a little while afterwards. I mean – I felt *awful*. What if I'd said something to send him over the edge?'

'Oh, Cynthia, don't! Didn't she try to move you away?'

'No, that was the funny thing. She came trotting out of the house and more or less *forced* me to stand there. I kept expecting her to ask me in for coffee or something, but she just kept me talking, right there. Where he could hear it all.'

'She can't have done it deliberately.'

'No, I don't suppose she did. But it was all very unfortunate, I must say.'

Laura and Rosemary exchanged a long meaningful glance, before settling down to their lasagne and cottage pie respectively. They chatted idly about gardens and gadgets until the other women got up to leave. Then they almost exploded with pent-up excitement.

'Who was she, I wonder?' Laura said.

'Some neighbour, I assume. Poor Daniel! I wonder how much she said that he could hear. Why didn't she realise at the time?'

'You don't, do you. I mean, look how she was just now, shooting her mouth off right next to us. She's just a compulsive talker, regardless of who can hear her.'

'She seems to know Alicia quite well.'

'The Kellaways must be pretty high profile around here, with that house and this place. Probably nearly everybody knows them, one way or another.'

Laura shrugged, and finished her ice cream. 'Nice,' she said, with satisfaction. 'Now let's go and look at the shrubs. I saw a fabulous ceanothus out there.'

Although they knew there was no sense in buying any plants, they felt embarrassed to go away empty-handed, so Rosemary selected a pair of secateurs and Laura, belatedly remembering Helena's recent birthday, splashed out on a wall clock from the gift section. 'This place really has got everything,' she remarked. 'You could do all your Christmas shopping in here.'

'How will you get it to her?' Rosemary asked.

'She'll be at the funeral tomorrow. I can give it to her then.'

This reminder cast a shadow over Laura's mood, and she stood in the check-out queue feeling that the best of the day was already behind her.

As they waited, a familiar voice came from just over their shoulders. 'And another thing. They must be ever so worried here, with Sam gone and Daniel in hospital. What if he never comes out of the coma? What happens then?'

Laura could not restrain herself. She turned round, to confront the woman from the cafeteria. 'Aren't you being ever so slightly insensitive?' she demanded, in a low voice.

The woman's eyes bulged, and she gave a kind of squawk. 'And who might you be?' she gasped.

'A very close friend of Sam's, as it happens. And who are *you*?'

'Cynthia Battson, if it's anything to you. I live just down the road from Alicia and Daniel. I was at Winterbourne the day of Daniel's...accident.'

'Then you should know better than to spread gossip,' Rosemary put in tartly, at Laura's elbow. 'It never does any good, you know.'

'Gossip? I have no idea what you mean. I'm just speaking the plain truth.'

'Oh leave it,' said Laura, feeling suddenly tired. 'I should have kept my mouth shut.'

'No, you can't leave it there,' persisted the neighbour. 'I want to get to the bottom of this. My son-in-law is the assistant manager here, which means I'm directly involved. He's worried sick that his job's going to disappear. They all are. And nobody's said a word to them.'

'Hang on,' Rosemary said. 'Let's get outside and talk about it in a civilised manner. We're holding up the queue, look.'

Once all the purchases were paid for, the four women gathered in the car park, the atmosphere between them very much calmer. Laura apologised for her aggression, claiming to be upset about Sam. Cynthia Battson accepted with good grace. 'Perhaps, if you have any influence with Alicia, or Mrs Trent, you could get them to explain just where everybody stands,' she said. 'It isn't fair to leave them in limbo like this. Obviously Neville is hoping there'll be an option for some sort of buy-out, or whatever they call it. He's very ambitious, with all *sorts* of ideas —'

'Cynthia!' warned the friend, who had not been introduced.

Laura's hackles rose again. 'Daniel isn't dead, you know,' she said sharply. 'There's no reason to suppose anything will change here. If I were you, I'd tell your Neville to settle down and wait for promotion in the normal way.'

Cynthia Battson flushed pinkly, but said nothing.

'The fact is, we don't have any influence,' said Rosemary, feeling slightly sorry for her. 'And I'm sure you'll hear something as soon as Daniel recovers consciousness. Until then, there can't be anything definite to say, can there?'

Ignoring Laura, Cynthia addressed herself to Rosemary, sensing a less critical approach. 'Possibly not,' she conceded. 'But just let me tell you this – there are a great many stories going around, and the longer people are kept in the dark, the more they're going to start inventing things. And who's to say they're not right, anyway?'

'Stories?' echoed Rosemary. 'What sort of stories?'

'Like somebody's behind all this,' Cynthia said darkly. 'That Sam and Daniel are both victims of some sort of takeover plot. After all, the Kellaway garden centres must be worth a fortune. And you can't deny it all looks very fishy.'

Rosemary and Laura took a moment to digest that. Then Rosemary took out the Land Rover keys. 'Well, time we were off,' she said. 'We'll give Alicia your message, if we see her.'

'Well, just be sure that you do,' came the parting shot.

They didn't say very much in the Land Rover, each busy with her own thoughts. Finally, Laura tried to sum up the day. 'We hadn't thought of that, had we,' she said.

'What?'

'The garden centres, and the effect of everything that's happened. It's all going to change for them now, isn't it? New managers, jobs being rejigged to compensate for Sam not being there. There must be a lot of strong feeling going on.'

'But you don't think somebody *arranged* it, do you? Some ambitious little jobsworth wanting to get a few rungs higher up the ladder? Prime suspect being the ambitious Neville.'

'I really don't know what to think,' said Laura.

Chapter Ten

The church at Devenish was typical of any of a thousand English village churches. A squat tower and a large undulating graveyard presented a timeless image that was curiously reassuring. People stood in small groups in the road outside, and along the path to the church door, when Laura arrived ten minutes before the appointed time. Evidently the hearse had not yet appeared, but thinking it couldn't be much longer, she decided to go into the church and take her place near the back. There was no sign of Vickie – presumably she would be coming in a limousine following behind the hearse.

Much more immediately worrying than the prospect of encountering Vickie was the knowledge that Nick and the children would almost certainly be here, in a group that excluded her. Already Laura felt the loneliness of estrangement; not just from Nick, but from Helena and even Matthew as well. A degree of awkwardness was unavoidable, with the new alignments in the family, and the sudden blank where the future had once been.

Following a middle-aged couple she didn't know, Laura entered the church. The familiar musty smell hit her, along with the rows of pews and softly-playing organ. Never a regular churchgoer, there was, all the same, a sense of comfortable welcome in the place. Another dull day meant that the light coming through the stained glass was muted, but the church was certainly not dark. Laura saw her husband – ex-husband – instantly. He was four or five rows from the back, flanked by his son and daughter, head bent in apparent serious thought, if not actual prayer.

Laura's first reaction was a deepening sense of isolation and betrayal. How dare Matthew sit there like that? How dare they gang up, behaving as if it didn't matter whether she was there or not? Admittedly there was plenty of space next to Matthew for her to slide into. And it was probably no coincidence that it was Matthew, rather than Helena or Nick, who was nearest the aisle. With painfully thumping heart, Laura went to take her place.

Matthew turned quickly towards her, leaning sideways for an awkward hug. 'Hiya!' he said. 'You okay?'

Laura nodded dumbly, wondering how on earth she was going to get through the next hour or two. The presence of Nick, in full uniform, just beyond their son, was like a crouching tiger waiting to maul her. And Helena, invisible at the end of the pew, was almost as worrying. Why didn't she lean forward and send her mother a welcoming smile? 'What's the matter with Helena?' Laura asked Matthew, not quite whispering, but in a low voice.

He shrugged. 'We'll sort all that out later. Let's just think about Sam for now.'

'You're not in uniform,' she noted.

'Day off.'

'Ah.' She was glad, on the whole. People would have stared uncomfortably hard at the sight of two obvious policemen.

The church was filling rapidly, and a sense of anticipation began to grow. Alicia Kellaway arrived hurriedly, and took a place on the end of a pew several rows further forward than Laura's. She appeared not to know the people she'd joined, merely nodding at them in a rather formal fashion. As Laura watched her, more for distraction than from any real interest, she suddenly realised that the man in the next pew forward was Doctor Whittaker. Alicia put a hand gently on his shoulder, causing him to turn round and smile.

Then the organ changed key and volume, and everybody stood up, as if pulled by invisible strings. Laura felt herself bursting with a host of strong emotions, among them the memories of three other funerals she had attended with her husband. Both her parents and Nick's father had died over the past ten years: expected deaths which had been sad but not devastating. Nick and she had been kind to each other, listening to the reminiscences and helping with the practical stuff. They had sat shoulder to shoulder in church and crematorium, shoring each other up.

Now he would barely glance at her, and had somehow succeeded in turning her daughter against her as well. Combined with the shock and simmering sense of guilt over the untimely death of Sam Trent, it all proved too much. As quietly as she could, Laura sobbed into a very inadequate handkerchief.

The funeral service passed in a haze of eulogies and hymns until the final procession down the aisle as the coffin was carried to the grave. Vickie, following the pallbearers, paused at the pew containing the Thyme family, and met Laura's eye. A wealth of emotion passed between the two of them, woman to woman, suffering all the untidy nameless feelings that women always seemed to get landed with. Laura managed a tiny smile and Vickie moved on.

Throughout the service, she had kept herself from turning to look at Matthew or Nick or Helena. But now, waiting to leave the church, she could no longer avoid them. Dread seized her afresh, at the prospect of having to talk to Nick and her daughter. Matthew she could cope with. In fact, in a rush of very uncharacteristic weakness, she grabbed his arm and held onto it tightly.

Squaring his shoulders, Matthew responded, placing a comforting hand over his mother's, and nudging her out of the pew. Behind them, Laura could hear Nick give one of his loud sighs. The familiarity of it pierced her like a bayonet.

Outside, people once again stood about in small groups. Vickie and a man Laura recognised as the hand-holder from the previous week, along with a trio of youngsters who might have been nephews and nieces, circled the grave as the coffin was lowered. The other mourners hung back, ranged roughly according to a hierarchy of connectedness to the dead man. The churchyard was almost full, and Sam's grave was situated in an obscure corner, approached by a narrow path between large old headstones. Alicia Kellaway stood alone, looking around with an air of an animal at bay, despite the elegant clothes and perfectly groomed hair – or so it seemed to Laura. Presumably she was hoping to speak to Vickie, like everybody else, but was reluctant to push forward. There was no sign of Doctor Whittaker. Probably had appointments waiting, Laura concluded.

'Are you going to the lunch?' Matthew asked Laura.

'Oh, God! No, I don't think so. Are you?'

He shook his head.

'Nick?' It was the first time she had addressed him, and it felt as if she'd scaled a very high wall to do it.

'No, no,' he said.

'Poor Sam,' she went on. 'I was the last person to see him alive, you know.'

'Yes, I heard.'

She gave him a more direct look. 'Are you here personally or officially?'

'Both.'

Finally she turned to face her daughter. 'Helena? It feels like ages since I saw you. How are you, darling?'

The girl shifted her weight from one foot to the other, and avoided Laura's eye. 'Okay,' she muttered.

None of this was new. Many a time Laura had demanded of the world in general, 'When is this girl going to stop behaving like a teenager?' Helena was now twenty-two – surely old enough to dispense with moods and mysterious resentments.

'It was very nice of you to come.' Then she remembered – Sam had been Helena's godfather. As a little girl, she'd been very much attached to him, treating him like an uncle. Her loss was just as great as Nick's or Laura's.

'I loved him,' Helena said, simply. 'He was always wonderful to me.'

'When did you last see him?'

'About a month ago. He took me out to lunch. We had a good chat.' Tears filled the girl's eyes. 'It's terrible to think I'll never see him again.'

Laura was deeply touched, more tears starting up in her own eyes, in sympathy. Before she could reach out and give her daughter a hug, Nick was there, a fatherly arm thrown around Helena's shoulders. Laura retreated a step. Inevitable comparisons filled her mind – Nick and his new sexy Emily, much the same age as his own daughter, contrasted with the innocent attachment between the childless Sam and Helena. If Nick had wanted to act as mentor to his colleague's daughter, why couldn't he have followed Sam's example? Laura wouldn't have objected to that at all. Instead, he'd crossed the boundary between adult friendship towards a younger woman, and lustful involvement with her. It might be a common event, even understandable in a purely biological context, but Laura could not help being consumed with contempt for the man she had always regarded as her equal, her partner, the father of her children.

All of which reminded her of what she carried in her handbag. She extracted Sam's letter and approached Nick with it, like a messenger waving news from the battle front. 'This was at the house,' she said.

He took it, fingering the torn upper edge. 'You opened it?'

'Of course I did. It was obviously from Sam. In the circumstances...'

'Yes, yes.' He pulled the letter from its envelope and quickly read it. Laura noticed a flush creep up his cheeks.

'You were going to change your will, without telling me.' She stated it as a fact, pointless to deny.

He waved a hand at her, his gaze still on the letter. Finally he looked up. 'Sam left everything to Kellaway, then. I was wondering about that.'

Laura almost stamped her foot. 'Never mind Sam, what about *us*?' she snapped.

Nick threw Matthew a look: a man-to-man appeal for help in calming an embarrassingly emotional woman. 'Not here, Mum,' Matthew said quietly.

She clamped her lips together, frustrated, but aware that they were right. 'All right,' she muttered. 'So what if Sam did leave it all to Daniel? Isn't that perfectly normal for business partners?'

'Probably.' Nick was clearly deep in thought. 'But it isn't what he told me he was going to do.'

'When?'

'Must be a year or so ago now. Vickie was showing an interest in becoming a third partner in the garden centres, and they were discussing how it might be worked out.'

'And they mentioned wills?'

'No, not directly. I suppose I just assumed that if anything happened to Sam, she would step into his shoes. I wonder what happened to change all that?'

'You know about Daniel's illness, I suppose? I think that started about a year ago. Maybe that changed Sam's mind. Maybe he thought that if Daniel wasn't going to be up to the job, it wouldn't be fair to land Vickie with everything. Or maybe she backed out when it all looked like heavy going.'

'Illness? I knew he'd fallen out of a window – but I hadn't heard he was ill before that.'

Suddenly Laura just wanted to sit down some- where and forget all about the Kellaways and their complicated lives. She wanted to turn the clock back to a month ago when life had been predictable. She wanted Nick to transform himself back to the man she had loved and trusted.

'Sorry,' she gasped. 'I can't do any more of this.' And she turned away, staring blindly down the churchyard path to the road beyond. As she started to move towards the lychgate, she became aware of Vickie, walking slowly back towards them, the burial accomplished. There were people alongside her, the most prominent of them the affectionate brother, fresh from Rome, and once again holding her hand. Laura thought he looked rather oily, like a stereotypical undertaker rather than one of the mourners.

From behind her, a woman hurried past, walking on the grass to overtake. 'Vickie!' she called.

'Oh, Alicia,' said the widow, tonelessly. 'Thank you for coming.'

'Of course I came. But I've got to rush now. Daniel, you see…well, I do have rather a lot to do.'

'Oh, yes. Well…thanks.' Vickie had clearly had enough of condolences and explanations and demands. Alicia trotted briskly away towards the long line of cars parked opposite the church.

Vickie's eyes met Laura's then, but with no flicker of friendly recognition. Laura tried to smile, to rekindle the long relationship that lay between them, to share at least a little in Vickie's grief. But it didn't work. The returning smile was no more than a brief kink of the mouth, the eyes cold and dull.

It was all too much, and Laura dropped her gaze, unsure of what she should do next.

'Mum.' Matthew put a hand on her upper arm. 'We can go now. It's all done.'

It had all passed so quickly, seen as if through a blizzard. Surely that couldn't be the end of it? She shook her head. 'No, I have to speak to Vickie,' she said.

This was not easy. A large number of mourners had now surrounded the widow, trying to speak to her before taking their leave. Laura waited patiently, hardly caring whether her family stayed or went. At last she was again face to face with her friend. 'Vick,' she said, 'please keep in touch. I feel terrible about Sam. I know I'll see you at the inquest, but before that, it would be good to have a chat. I'll try to come and see you later in the week.'

Vickie raised a weary eyebrow. 'Yes,' she said vaguely. Then, 'Helena came, I see. And Nick. Do they want to talk to me?'

'I'm sure they do. It's just – there are so many people.'

'A good turnout,' murmured Vickie. 'A lot of them are from the business, of course.' Then she seemed to remember something. 'Sam left some money for Helena. Since we haven't any children, you see…' she tailed off. 'Just a bit. All the business property goes to Daniel, and I get the house. But he always loved your girl. He was jealous of you for having a daughter, when he and I…'

Laura reproached herself again for her nasty suspicions. Vickie had every right to be jealous of her and Nick for having their two healthy children, when she herself had been childless. It was a good and happy thing that Sam had 'borrowed' Helena from time to time. But it had never occurred to her that he would leave her money.

'That's terribly generous of him,' she said.

'Sam was generous.' Vickie's eyes widened. 'He didn't deserve to die like this, Laura. Not so young. Somebody has to be responsible for it.' She turned to look at Nick, who had moved to the lychgate. 'I want to speak to Nick. To tell him they have to find whoever did this to me.'

As if aware of her need, the policeman came back, against the flow of mourners leaving the churchyard. 'Vickie,' he said, holding out both hands to her. 'I am so very sorry. Sam was a good kind man.'

'Yes he was.' Laura heard many other remarks

beneath those three words. *And I never told him so. And see where it got him.* And finally *Not like you, you bastard.* This last, Laura acknowledged, was all her own and very unlikely to be part of Vickie's subtext at all.

'You can have confidence that there'll be a full investigation, you know. I'm sure you're being kept properly updated.'

'Oh yes. But it won't bring him back, will it?'

Nick had no reply to that, and Laura watched him walk jerkily towards his car, his shoulders stiff with the awkwardness of the situation. Ordinarily she would have felt sorry for him – he had lost a friend, after all. As it was, she could only wish he would go and leave her in peace.

Matthew had missed most of the exchange. 'What was all that about?' he asked.

'Vickie isn't co-operating very well with your father's efforts to console her. You can't blame her, poor thing. She still doesn't know exactly how and why Sam died. It must be awful for her.'

Matthew scratched his head. 'Doesn't sound like much of a case, from what I hear.'

Laura gave him a searching look. 'I think there are very good grounds for a full investigation, actually.' A sudden thought struck her. 'Gosh – I forgot Helly's present. Don't go away – I've left it in the church porch. I'll have to go and fetch it before she disappears.'

She trotted back up the church path, and retrieved the parcel in its blue plastic carrierbag. Seeing that Nick and Helena were getting into his car, she kept up the fast trot to catch them.

'Steady on, Ma!' Helena cautioned, seeing her mother's pink face. 'Don't overdo it.'

'This is for your birthday,' Laura puffed, thrusting the bag at her. 'I hope you like it.'

'Oh – thanks.' Helena seemed very ill at ease. 'I

thought you'd forget, with everything that's been going on.'

'As if I would.' Laura leaned towards her daughter, and aimed a kiss at her cheek. Helena accepted it stiffly, and smiled. 'We've got to be off now,' she said. 'Dad's due back at work soon.'

'It was good of you to come,' Laura said. 'I'm sure Vickie appreciated it.'

Helena gave another brief smile. 'I was very fond of Sam,' she said.

Laura watched as Nick started the car, without a word to her. With a sense of unreality, she realised how distant he had become, in a single week. And yet everything about him was still acutely familiar. It made her insides churn, trying to understand it all.

'So, what now?' Matthew asked, when his father and sister had driven away.

'Oh...I...' Laura realised she hadn't given any thought to how she'd get back to the White Hart. At worst, she'd have to walk the two miles between the villages.

'Why don't we go and have a bit of lunch?'

'Where? I don't want to intrude on the funeral – they've taken over the Saracen's Head, and there's nowhere else in Devenish.'

'I know a good place, three or four miles away. Come on.'

There was nobody else she would rather be with, just at that moment and she gratefully took him up on the suggestion.

Matthew took her into a small pub garden and bought her a large white wine. She hardly noticed when he put it down in front of her. At every turn there seemed to be worry and sadness, fear and panic. Helena's manner had hurt far more than might have been expected. What had Nick said to her? It all felt terribly unfair.

But Sam Trent had just been buried, and that was

where her thoughts ought to be directed.

'You don't mind that Sam always favoured Helly, do you?' she asked Matthew, with a mother's anxiety for equality between her children.

Matthew laughed. 'I minded for about half an hour when I was eleven, but since then I've just accepted it as a given. To be honest, I thought she could do with all the favour she could get.'

Laura's heart lurched. Was this turning into one of those sessions where your adult offspring treated you to a summary of all your defects as a parent? Up to now, she had been mercifully spared any such analysis. 'What do you mean?' she choked.

'Oh, sorry! It wasn't meant to sound like that. Just that she always seemed to put herself down, to make everything hard for herself. Some people are just born like that.'

'Are they?'

'Don't you think so?'

'I think it's more likely that they go through a stage of non-cooperation or whatever you like to call it, when they're very small, and sometimes the mother over-reacts, and after that it's very difficult to rebuild the easy trusting relationship. Believe me, Matt, I've given this a lot of thought. Helly was a terrible baby, by any standards. I can't pretend that I enjoyed her very much in those early months.'

'Whereas *I* was perfect.'

'You were. For a first one, you were miraculous.'

'It's all a mystery to me. But I do remember Helena being a right little beast most of the time.'

'Your father handled her far better than I did. He was unwavering in his adoration of her. Which is why I don't actually understand where Sam came in.'

'Whatever the explanation, she surely doesn't have anything to complain about.'

'*Does* she complain?'

'You know she does.'

The conversation turned to other matters as they waited for their ploughman's. 'You haven't had time to check up on Delia Kettle for me, I suppose?' This felt to Laura like safer territory than old family difficulties. 'It's not really important, anyway. Just idle curiosity.' She told him a bit more about how she had recognised Mrs Potts, and how the word *Withersedge* had stuck in her mind.

'I'm really not supposed to do that sort of thing. It's privileged information, Mum.'

'I'm sure that's not true. If I had a car or a computer and enough energy I could look it all up in a newspaper library, or on the internet. After all, that's where I found her originally.'

'I doubt if the details of the trial would be on the net. It's all rather a long time ago, and it doesn't sound as if it made much impact even at the time.'

'Well, just give it ten minutes, to humour me, okay? There's a good boy.'

Matthew winced. 'Don't call me that.'

'Sorry. Actually, it's not so much the trial – I remember most of that for myself. It's what happened to her afterwards. Where did she go? What did she do with the insurance money?'

Matthew sighed. 'Now, honestly, Ma, that really *is* privileged information.'

'But you'll do it anyway, won't you. Just for me? Besides, I always quite liked Delia. It's a shame she's deteriorated into the daft old thing she is now. Working for some *nouveau riche* couple in a house that's much too good for them can't be a lot of fun.'

Matthew was keen to divert her. 'You don't like the Kellaways?'

'I still haven't properly met him, but she's all right in a synthetic sort of way. Every hair in place, a lounge that hardly seems real, and a garden to die for.'

'And this woman, Rosemary. Tell me more about her.'

Which did the trick very nicely. Laura smiled for the first time all day, and launched into a paean of praise for her new friend.

Meanwhile Rosemary herself had been diverted by a phone message from Alicia Kellaway. After dropping Laura at the funeral, she had gone back to the White Hart for her equipment, meaning to spend the morning at Winterbourne.

Robin met her at the front door, having heard the Land Rover approaching along the village street. He held out a sheet of paper towards her. 'Message for you,' he said.

Rosemary's first inevitable thought, with funerals the theme of the morning, was that something had happened to her mother. She grabbed the paper and scanned it anxiously.

Alicia Kellaway. 10.35am. Please phone. 01664 765333 after 12.30.

Rosemary looked again at the time. The call must have come just as she and Laura were leaving for the church. If Alicia had gone to the funeral, she must have phoned moments before setting out – and be intending to go straight home again afterwards. 'Is that all?' She looked at Robin 'Didn't she say anything else?'

He shook his head.

'So why all the drama?'

He frowned. 'What drama? I just happened to be in the foyer when I heard you, so popped out to meet you.'

'Oh, okay. It doesn't sound very urgent, but I'll do as she asks.'

Promptly at twelve-thirty, she made the call. Alicia answered quickly, sounding somewhat ruffled. 'Oh, Miss Boxer, thank you for phoning back. It's Daniel, he'd like to see you.'

'He's recovered consciousness then?'

A slight pause before she answered, 'Well, obvious-ly. He's actually feeling a lot better, but they want to keep him in hospital for a while longer. I've moved him to a private room, and he's very comfortable. The thing is, he says he'd like to speak to you. With Sam's death, the situation has changed regarding the busi-ness, and he has something important to tell you.'

'You're sure he wants me, and not Professor Marchant?' Rosemary tasted bile as she uttered the name of her betrayer.

'Quite sure. I told him, you see, about the – um – disagreement between you and your superior, and he found it rather amusing.'

'Well, I'm happy to have entertained him. When should I visit him, do you think?'

'I think perhaps not until tomorrow afternoon. He's having tests on his leg in the morning, and a few other procedures. Don't forget he was seriously ill before the accident.' For the first time, Rosemary clearly heard anxiety in Alicia's voice. Not surprising, she thought. Things must feel very uncertain for the poor woman.

'It must all be a great worry for you,' she said sym-pathetically.

'Thank you,' Alicia responded coolly. 'So, I would suggest perhaps late tomorrow afternoon for your visit. Of course, being a private room, there are no restrictions.'

That's right, thought Rosemary, *make sure I've got the message that you can afford to go private, why don't you?*

'All righty,' she chirruped. 'I'll be there, if you tell me the name of the ward.' She paused, trying to think through what happened next. 'Do you mind if I come over to the garden again this afternoon, for some more work?'

'If you must,' Alicia sighed. 'I have to say, it does seem to be taking you an awfully long time.'

'I know. I'm quite embarrassed about it, to be honest. But I think I'm getting very close. I've narrowed down the general area of concern, and have a laboratory working on samples, plus a renowned expert helping me. It won't be long now, I promise.'

'Whatever,' said Alicia, sounding much less like the grand lady of Winterbourne Manor, and much more like a disaffected teenager.

'Bye, then,' said Rosemary.

She asked Robin if she could have coffee in the lounge, and sat for ten minutes wondering why she felt so agitated. Alicia Kellaway had no reason to be especially friendly towards her; the poor woman had more than enough to cope with, without having to worry about some obscure difficulty in the garden. Even so, there had been some sort of conflict in her tone, as she passed on the message from Daniel. Was it perhaps that she suspected Rosemary of being her husband's former lover? However irrational it might be, women seldom took kindly to meeting predecessors, and a certain frostiness was quite understandable, if that was indeed the explanation. In which case, Daniel was culpable for not reassuring his wife that he and Rosemary had never been more than good friends.

The day stretched ahead, with Laura's return unpredictable and Winterbourne Manor somehow uninviting. The truth was, she had very little work still to do in the garden itself. Unless Alicia hired her to generally tidy the place up and check for the condition of other vulnerable plants, she could only continue to grub around the affected trees and take even more samples. Although a dedicated professional would be justified in going to such lengths, Rosemary was dubious as to the benefit. The more she thought about it, the more she wanted to speak to Daniel. He could authorise a more general inspection, and even some hands-on garden maintenance. Whatever he wanted to tell her about the endowment and such matters was secondary in her mind to the puzzle of the poorly trees.

She had not arranged to collect Laura from the funeral, since there was no way of knowing when she would wish to leave. 'There's sure to be somebody to give me a lift,' she had said. 'Probably Matthew can drop me back here.'

Suddenly decisive, she stood up and brushed biscuit crumbs off her jeans. What difference could it make if she visited Daniel today, rather than tomorrow? Alicia had given no real reason for postponement, and if Daniel lapsed back into unconsciousness before she could obey his summons, Rosemary would feel frustrated and guilty. The only explanation she could think of for delay was to give him time to gain strength, and perhaps Alicia had been assuming she wouldn't like such short notice. Surely it would be a kindness to respond quickly.

The Land Rover started easily, and she was soon on the road to St Mark's, remembering with amusement her previous visit with Laura, and how they'd surprised the poor old man in the gents. He must have thought he'd imagined the whole thing, afterwards.

Armed with the name of Daniel's ward, there was none of the frantic rushing up and down corridors there'd been the last time. Even though it was on a different floor, approached by a different staircase, she quickly located it. This time she breezed up to the nurse at the central work station, and asked for Mr Kellaway, who was in a private room.

The room, when she was shown into it, was not very different from the previous one, Rosemary noted with interest. A television was attached to the wall facing the bed, the window was shielded by high-tech blinds, and there was carpet on the floor. But a hospital bed was a hospital bed, and Daniel lay there as before, with his plastered leg propped up at an awkward-looking angle.

But this time, he was wide awake.

'Rosemary!' he cried, breaking into a broad smile. 'I thought you were coming tomorrow.'

'Well, you know me. Always impatient to get a move on. It's not a nuisance for you, is it?'

'Not a bit. It's perfect. You can even have some lunch with me, if you like. One of the perks of going private.'

'Well, that sounds too good to refuse. Thanks very much.'

She sat in the comfortable chair provided, and listened to Daniel ordering a second lunch. His skin was remarkably improved from the last time she had seen him. Despite purple scarring still blotching his cheeks, there was none of the blistered inflammation of a few days earlier. It was the first thing she commented on when he turned to her with another smile.

'I know,' he said. 'It's miraculous. Between you and me, I wonder just what that muck was that Bob Whittaker insisted we use. Mind you, it could just as easily be due to all the drugs they've pumped into me here. They tell me I was in a bad way when I came in. My whole system was getting infected, and they weren't sure how the leg would mend, the state I was in.'

'You look like a new man.'

His expression changed to one of embarrassment. 'I was right at the end of my rope, this time last week,' he admitted. 'I couldn't see any hope at all, whichever way I looked.'

'Poor old you,' she sympathised. 'It must be have been gruesome for you.'

'You know what the final straw was?'

She shook her head.

'A neighbour called in, and started talking to Alicia, right under my window. I heard every word. A woman called Cynthia, who loves the sound of her own voice. She was so patronising and horrible, it was as if they were discussing a dying dog. That's how I heard it, anyway. And I couldn't justify putting poor Alicia through any more of it. She was being so brave and sweet, holding everything together – far more than any man had a right to expect.'

Rosemary nodded. 'I bumped into that neighbour at your garden centre, yesterday,' she said. 'She sounds a real blabbermouth.'

'I think she's perfectly well-intentioned – but don't you find that sympathy is often the last thing you want?'

'Absolutely,' Rosemary said, trying to sound brisk and unsentimental.

'And all on top of Sam dying. I simply couldn't take it in, at first. I've only just begun to think through the implications.'

'Daniel, you've been unconscious for days. How could you think *anything* through?'

'Well, yes. But before that. All I could see was my own useless misery. Sam had been losing patience with me for a while, and who could blame him? But he was my friend. We go back a long way. It just felt like a cruel loss.'

'Of course it did. Obviously.'

'And now everything's different regarding Kellaway Garden Centres. Do you see?'

'Not entirely,' said Rosemary carefully.

'Well, I've got some stark decisions ahead of me now. Either I have to find another partner, or —'

He was interrupted by the arrival of lunch, which was very different from what Rosemary had expected. It was hot, tasty and decidedly nourishing, and she took hers to a table by the window, to be out of the way as Daniel's was laid out on a tray in front of him. She had plenty of time to wonder what he had been about to say, and how it might affect Malmesbury University and the abhorrent Julian.

Politely, she waited for the nurse to leave, and for

Daniel to remember where they'd got to. A certain awkwardness about her own situation prevented her from prompting him, even when they were alone again. A few minutes later, she was to sorely regret her good manners. Before Daniel spoke again, another visitor arrived and the chance was lost.

'Oh!' Alicia yelped, at the sight of Rosemary. 'I thought we said tomorrow.'

'Yes, yes, we did,' Rosemary assured her. 'But you made it sound quite urgent, and I thought it would be all right if I came today instead.'

Daniel spoke with his mouth full: 'I'm glad you did. They're doing some unpleasant tests on me tomorrow. Needles and so forth. I'm glad to have my mind taken off all that.'

Alicia remained just inside the door, her gaze flicking from Daniel to Rosemary and back. 'Have you been here long?'

Rosemary shrugged, and looked at Daniel. 'Twenty minutes or so, I suppose.' He nodded his agreement.

Alicia seemed very thrown by Rosemary's presence. She had a large leather bag in one hand, and wore a smart jacket and skirt. 'Are those my clean pyjamas?' Daniel asked her, pointing to the bag.

'Oh! Yes. And some of Mrs Potts's carrotcake. She's missing you terribly. Hardly knows what to do with herself.'

'How touching,' he mumbled, with ill-concealed sarcasm. 'I can't pretend the feeling's mutual.'

'Daniel! Don't be nasty. The poor old thing doesn't know where to put herself, with all this disruption. She's dusted and vacuumed the entire house about five times in the past two days.'

Rosemary began to feel she might be surplus to requirements. She bolted the remains of her lunch. 'Well, maybe I should be going,' she said, rather hoping Daniel would stop her. 'Thanks for the lunch. Should I pay for it?'

The couple both looked at her. 'Don't be silly,' said Daniel.

Alicia's face softened. 'It was good of you to come,' she said. 'I can see Daniel's enjoyed talking to you.'

'Yes, but – ' said Daniel. 'I was going to – ' He stopped himself, with a glance at his wife. 'But it wouldn't really interest you, my love. How long can you stay?'

'As long as you like,' she smiled at him. 'I'm entirely at your disposal.'

At last Alicia moved to the bedside, and leaned over him for a kiss on the mouth. Remembering how unpleasant his skin had been previously, Rosemary wondered how long it had been since they'd had any significant skin-to-skin contact. With a rush of fond feeling, she gathered up her shoulderbag and prepared to leave. 'It's wonderful to see you looking so much better,' she said. 'I'm sure the leg will heal up in no time, and then you'll be as good as new. You probably did yourself a favour, falling out of that window.'

Instantly she knew she'd blundered. Two wooden faces confronted her, saying nothing.

'Sorry,' Rosemary said. 'Tactless thing to say. Take no notice. I'm forever putting my foot in it. But let's face it —'

Alicia cut her off. 'Daniel still isn't out of the woods,' she said. 'There's concern for his lungs, and of course he was unconscious for several days. There could be permanent damage arising from that.'

'Brain damage, do you mean?' Rosemary looked at Daniel. 'I don't think so. Look at him! He's a new man!'

'You don't know anything at all about it,' Alicia argued, with unmistakable irritation.

'Now, now,' Daniel soothed. 'Don't start fighting over me.' He gave a silly laugh that did nothing to relieve the tension. 'Thanks for coming, Rosemary. It was good of you to go to the trouble. I'll see you again soon, I'm sure. You can tell me all about the trees then.'

'The trees?'

He raised his eyebrows at her. 'Of course the trees. That's why I asked you to come. I've been really worried about my lovely trees.'

Matthew dropped Laura back at the White Hart at three that afternoon, just before Rosemary got back from the hospital. They met in the foyer, as Laura was rather aimlessly drifting out for a stroll, having changed out of her dark suit. They both started speaking at once.

'How did it go?' said Rosemary.

'Why aren't you at Winterbourne?' asked Laura.

By mutual agreement, they headed for their riverside walk on the outskirts of the village, intent on catching up with the events of each other's day.

Laura talked mainly about Vickie Trent, to begin with, resisting Rosemary's efforts to get her onto the more interesting topic of Nick, and how it had felt to see him again. She then skipped deftly on to Matthew and how sweet he had been to her.

'Did you ask him any more about the Witch of Withersedge?' Rosemary interrupted.

'Yes, but he hadn't got round to looking it up. He says he'll do it in the next day or two. He isn't too happy about it, though. Says it's classified information or something.'

'Pooh!' scoffed Rosemary. 'I bet he's tickled pink to be asked. Shows you respect his status. Men love that. He'll be back on the phone before you know it.'

'Maybe,' Laura said dubiously.

'Anyway, stop dodging the really important stuff, and tell me what it was like being with Nick? Did you sit next to him?'

'No, Matthew was between us. And Helena on the far end. She was very tight-lipped with me. Worse than Nick, if anything.'

'Taking her Daddy's side. Treacherous little beast.'

Laura gave a rueful laugh. 'I must admit, those were more or less my thoughts. She can be a very unsatisfactory daughter.'

'Sounds a bit like me and my Mum. There's always some niggle between us.'

'Well, in this case, I blame Nick. He's said something to turn her against me, I know he has. It'll all come out eventually. Things always do.'

'When everybody's dead,' said Rosemary crossly. 'You can't rely on that. Phone her, or write or something. Get to the bottom of it. Life's too short to let things work themselves out. You have to give them a push.'

Laura laughed again. 'You're so proactive, aren't you.'

'Impatient. Reckless. Foolhardy – that's what you mean, isn't it.'

'I wasn't criticising.'

'Well, it's true. Guess where I went at lunchtime.'

'Tell me.'

'To St Mark's, to visit Daniel.'

Laura stared at her. 'You didn't! How is he? Has he woken up from the coma? Did Alicia know you'd gone?'

Rosemary made a *slow down* motion with both hands. One by one she answered the questions, describing the visit in as much detail as she could recall.

Laura listened with rapt attention, relieved to have changed the subject so successfully. 'So – do you think he really wanted to talk about something else, but not with Alicia listening?'

'I'm not sure. After all, she herself said something about the endowment and things being different since Sam died. So it can't have been that. When I mentioned his fall, they both froze. It was a bit tactless, I suppose.'

'Just a bit, yes. It really isn't done to start talking about people's suicide bids. Especially as it sounds as if you were implying it was rather a good thing.'

Rosemary put a hand over her mouth, appalled at

the implications. 'Gosh, yes! It must have sounded awful. But honestly, I was right, in a way. He does look infinitely better than he did a week ago. He admitted that himself.'

'Of course, people do sometimes want to talk about that sort of thing. If Alicia hadn't been there, he might have been happier to describe his feelings, how depressed he'd been and all that.'

'He did, though. Early on, before Alicia arrived. She was surprised to see me – and a bit miffed, from the look she gave me.'

'Wanted him to herself, I suppose. She was at the funeral, you know – and rushed off mumbling something about Daniel.'

'She does seem to be very devoted.'

'Despite your suspicions about her and Doctor Whittaker.'

'Mmm. Was *he* at the funeral?'

'Oh, yes. Alicia sat behind him, and put a hand on his shoulder. Then he must have made a quick getaway, because I didn't see him outside the church at all.'

'There you are, then. There *is* something between them, even though she truly loves Daniel as well. Women can be very complicated, you know. I remember once – ' and she went on to recount a slightly shameful story from her youth when she had kept two men dangling, sure she was equally in love with them both.

'I think I'm beginning to grasp how you are with men,' said Laura, with a hint of admiration. 'I can't say it's like that with me. I really don't think I'll mind if I never get involved with another one.'

Rosemary shivered in horror. 'What a thing to say!' she protested.

The afternoon turned chilly, with a thick layer of grey cloud blotting out the sun, and the two slowly returned to the White Hart, tired from the events of the day. After supper, they revived and on a sudden whim, took themselves out to a film at the cinema in Fairchester.

They stopped at a small pub on the way back to Downminster, spending an hour over their drinks, not talking very much. Rosemary had to take it slowly, thanks to the Land Rover's poor headlights. 'I'm sure you should get better bulbs or something,' Laura said.

'I probably should, but I don't often use her at night. To be honest, I generally have an escort to drive me after dark.'

Laura snorted. 'And now you've got to make do with me. Sorry about that.'

'Don't be silly. You know I've had a great time. Hello! What's this?'

For a moment, Laura thought it was déjà vu – a rerun of the morning they'd found Sam's car upside down in a ditch. Then she recovered herself. This was simply two cars drawn up, one behind the other, leaving just enough space for passing vehicles to get by. Two people were standing behind the nearer car. Rosemary and Laura both leaned forward for a better view.

'That looks like Alicia,' said Laura. 'Don't you think?'

'And the other's a chap. Hang on – I think it's Doctor Whittaker. Well, well – caught in the act.'

'I don't think so,' Laura disagreed. 'Look!'

As they slowly drove past, they both clearly witnessed Alicia push the doctor away with both hands on his chest, making him stumble backwards. Without pausing to see the consequences, she turned away from him, waiting for the Land Rover to get clear.

'Should I stop?' Rosemary wondered.

'What for? It's embarrassing enough as it is. She's sure to realise it's us.'

'What if she's knocked him into a gatepost or something? He might need help.'

'He'll be fine. He didn't even fall over. Drive on,

woman. It's got nothing to do with us.'

'Poor man, though,' Rosemary worried. 'Do you think he was making unwelcome advances?'

'Whatever I think would be pure guesswork.'

'But their cars are both here – that means they didn't go out together. Possibly just a chance meeting. Even so, I *knew* there was something going on. I've seen them together twice before now and both times the vibes were unmistakable. I think we're on the right lines about him wanting to get Winterbourne Manor back. He's been making advances, and she's had enough.'

'Well, we'll probably never know the whole story, so you'd better try to forget all about it,' Laura advised. 'I'm doing my best not to think about the Kellaways or the Trents or anything to do with Winterbourne Manor.'

'Easier said than done,' Rosemary said. 'Specially for me. I still have to cure those wretched trees.'

When they got back to the White Hart, Robin had gone off duty for the night, but there was a note attached to Rosemary's key, with a rubber band. 'They should get pigeonholes, like a proper hotel,' said Laura.

'Oh, no. This is far more characterful. Now, I wonder what this is all about? Taking messages for me must be keeping Robin busy today.' She unwrapped the sheet of paper, and quickly scanned it. 'Oh, this sounds promising!' she exclaimed.

'What?'

'Professor Hashim phoned. Says he has a new lead, and could I call him back.' She looked at her watch. 'Best leave it till tomorrow now. He is a kind man.'

'Have you told me everything about your – well – *relationship* with him?'

Rosemary dimpled girlishly. 'Not quite. We – er – had a bit of a fling, actually. At that conference I told you about. These things happen at conferences.'

'Wasn't he married?'

'He said not. I believed him. I gather the current wife is quite a recent acquisition.'

'It doesn't sound as if you're sure.'

'You needn't take that tone. I'm always absolutely firm about married men. Won't touch them with a bargepole. Nor with anything else, either, come to that.'

'I'm relieved to hear it.'

'Anyway, he's still got a soft spot for me. I've consulted him three or four times over the years. He really is a top expert these days, you know. He gets paid by governments to analyse the effects of pollution on plants.'

'You don't think Winterbourne's problem is to do with pollution, do you?'

Rosemary grinned. 'Well, the thought did occur to me that Mrs Potts might be poisoning them with some horrible concoction. But I couldn't think of any reason why she might do that.'

'Except to upset Daniel.'

'Oh, no, she *loves* Daniel. Alicia was saying this afternoon, in the hospital, how the poor old thing is pining for him. It sounded quite pathetic, in a way.'

'We're doing it again,' Laura sighed.

'What?'

'Obsessing about the Kellaways. Well, that's it for one day. I'm off to bed.'

'Nighty night, then.'

'Night night.'

Laura dreamed that night of her daughter Helena, dressed in a short black leather skirt and daubing paint onto Rosemary's Land Rover. When Laura tried to stop her, she turned a savage face on her mother, and told her she hated her because she never cut bread properly. Then they were in a large garden and Helena was tearing up several small trees with her bare hands, throwing them over a nearby hedge.

She woke up breathing heavily with distress. As soon as she got a chance, she'd phone her daughter, and try to find out the reasons for the rift between them. Things really couldn't go on as they were.

Rosemary was loading something into the back of the Land Rover when Laura went in search of her after breakfast. 'Still at it?' Laura said. 'You must have made an early start.'

'I thought it would make sense to have as much information as possible before I phone Hashim. First I'm going over to the lab to see if they've found anything. They've had time for at least some preliminary ideas.' Rosemary spoke breathlessly, and Laura looked into the vehicle to see what had made her puff so much.

'What's all that?' she asked, pointing to a large cardboard box.

'It's the book Billie brought me, plus my laptop and all the notes I've been making. Oh, yes, and a bagful of soil from around the roots of the trees. Actually, I think I might need some more, before we're done.'

'What for?'

'If I'm to do the job properly, I ought to establish how far this infection, or fungus or virus or whatever it is, has spread. I'm taking what I've collected so far to the lab, but I've a nasty feeling there'll be much more to do yet. I'll probably have to take samples of soil at twelve-inch intervals in all directions for – say – twenty feet.'

'You're joking! That'll take ages.'

'Not really – especially if you help me. Besides, what else is there to do?'

As if in answer to the question, a familiar red car drew up beside them, and Doctor Whittaker's head appeared through the driver's window.

'Morning,' he said. 'Another nice day.'

Rosemary darted a quick glance at Laura, her

expression clearly saying *Well, well, well.* 'Hiya!' she chirped at the doctor.

'Have you got a minute?' he asked, getting out of the car.

'All the time in the world,' said Laura.

'The thing is – last night. That was you, wasn't it?' He examined the Land Rover. 'I don't think there are many of these old girls still around.'

'More than you might think,' said Rosemary. 'But yes – that was us. And it's really none of our business.'

'It must have looked very strange to anybody passing just at that moment. The thing is, Alicia's been under an awful strain. Daniel's illness, and now his accident. Well, I'm sure you can understand —' He looked from one to the other, with an appealing gaze.

'Well —' Rosemary began.

'She did seem very angry with you,' Laura said mildly.

'That's just it.' The doctor rubbed a distracted hand over his hair. 'She wasn't. Not really.'

'Look, this has absolutely nothing to do with us,' Laura insisted. 'You don't owe us any sort of explanation. It was just bad luck that we happened to drive past when we did.'

Whittaker laughed bitterly. 'It felt as if the whole world was driving past us during those ten minutes. Vickie Trent came by a minute or two after you.'

'Oh?' Rosemary's eyebrows went up. 'Did she stop?'

He shook his head. 'I don't think she saw us, actually. We were both back in our cars by then. But she might have recognised the vehicles.'

'Another time, you might want to conduct your – um, discussions – somewhere a bit more private,' Rosemary suggested.

'There won't be another time,' he said firmly. 'That's what I wanted to tell you. Whatever impression you might have gained – and I'm not just talking about last night – it's a false one. Daniel Kellaway is no longer my patient. I won't ever be visiting Winterbourne Manor again, or having anything to do with that family.'

'Right,' said Laura with a brisk nod. 'Message received and understood.'

'What d'you think happened?' Laura asked Rosemary, when Doctor Whittaker had driven away.

'I think Daniel's been causing rather a stir. Not only might he have picked up the vibes between his wife and the doc, but his skin condition clearing up the way it has must have made people wonder about the treatment he'd been having. Double embarrassment for the poor old GP. It strikes me, they've given him the push – literally, if last night's any indication.' She exploded into a hearty laugh. 'That was good, wasn't it. Gettit? Given him the push!'

'Yes, I get it,' Laura smiled absently. 'I wonder where that leaves our guesses about the doc wanting to get his hands on Winterbourne again? Maybe they've just decided to lie low for a bit until the excitement's died down.'

'Then what?'

'I have no idea.'

Rosemary tutted impatiently. 'Well I think we've got it wrong. Alicia might have been flirting with the chap, but I'm sure she's basically a devoted wife. She must have seen the error of her ways, after almost losing Daniel. It's shaken her up, and last night she was making sure the doctor was under no misapprehensions as to where he stands.'

'Maybe so. That still leaves him under suspicion for what happened to Sam.'

'Well, he's not going to get what he wants now, is he? Daniel's getting better, and Alicia's gone right off him. You could almost feel sorry for him.'

'Almost,' said Laura with a dash of scepticism.

Rosemary squared her shoulders. 'Now, that's

enough of that. Are you coming to the lab with me?'

'Might as well. Ten pee says she won't start.'

'You're on.'

Rosemary won the bet, and they were quickly on the open road to Bitterton.

The talk returned to the topic of mothers and daughters, Laura still worrying about Helena, and Rosemary beginning to feel she should be keeping her mum better informed.

'Tell me a bit more about her,' Laura invited.

Rosemary was more than happy to oblige, with a wry chuckle. 'She's eighty years old, and could probably beat me in a hundred-yard dash. She has opinions about absolutely everything, and the greenest fingers in the world. Anything grows for her. She's also a nifty car mechanic. This thing was hers originally, you know.' She patted the steering wheel. 'She still doesn't trust me to look after it properly.'

'Sounds daunting.'

'Too right.'

'Difficult to live up to.'

'Exactly.'

'But I can't see that it's like that with me and Helena. I'm just a boring housewife in her eyes, with stick-in-the-mud attitudes and a hopelessly out of date taste in music. She overtook me when she was about twelve, in any kind of mother-daughter contest.'

'But you were contented with yourself, weren't you? You felt you were in the right place, doing what you wanted to do?'

'More or less. Why would that upset her?'

Rosemary shrugged. 'I don't know, but I'd guess it made her feel she had to find something similar for herself. Some comfy niche, or vocation or – I don't know. Your example suggested to her that there was a slot for everybody, if only they could find it. Am I making any sense?'

Laura considered. 'Not entirely,' she admitted. 'But you're probably on the right lines. Except that now I've been turned out of my comfortable little world, you'd think she'd be – well, at least *interested*. She doesn't seem to want to know me at all.'

'Because the boat's been rocked – or capsized completely. She's probably scared. She doesn't know where she is with you any more.'

'She's always disapproved of me. Criticised my lack of ambition. Told me I was getting old before my time. It often felt as if she was the mother and I was the daughter.'

'Not like me, then. I've never been allowed to grow up. Whatever adult thing I try to do, my mum acts as if it's just a bit of frothy nonsense. She's going to have a ball when she hears the latest.'

'You haven't told her?'

Rosemary shook her head. 'That's the next thing on the agenda, I s'pose. And I'm not looking forward to it one bit.'

It was half past three when they returned to Winterbourne Manor, wearing suitable clothes for digging, since Rosemary had been advised by the lab that she would indeed need to take more soil samples. The sky was clear, but despite that, a brisk east wind made it feel more like March than May. 'Better keep moving,' Laura said. 'Find me something energetic to do.'

'We're both doing roots. You take that tree over there, and I'll do this one. As far as I can tell, yours is unaffected, so we need to be careful about cross contamination. You need a clean trowel.' They looked blankly at each other. 'And I only brought one with me.'

'Oh dear.'

'Tell you what. Those outbuildings behind the house. There's sure to be a tool store of some kind. They won't mind us borrowing a trowel – after all, we're doing their work. Come on.'

A path led around the house, on the opposite side from the balcony where Daniel's sickroom was. A good-sized brick barn stood across a yard from the back of the house. 'This is lovely, isn't it,' sighed Laura.

'Gorgeous. Look at that ampelopsis.' She nodded at a vigorous Virginia creeper covering much of the barn. 'Must have been there for decades, to have got to such a size.'

'Lucky Alicia. She must love living here.'

'She does if she's got any sense,' Rosemary agreed. 'And think how galling it must be for Doctor Whittaker, seeing his wonderful ancestral home belonging to somebody else.'

'Sickening,' Laura agreed.

They pushed open the barn door, and stood for a moment adjusting to the gloom inside. There were strong smells of herbs and other plants, which they quickly traced to bunches of dried leaves and stalks tied to beams overhead. 'Enough to run a market stall,' Rosemary observed. 'Look at them all!'

Laura stared upwards, trying to name the various plants. 'There's plenty of rosemary and thyme here, for a start,' she laughed. 'Mrs Potts must be a splendid cook, if she uses all these in her sauces.'

'It's like a little factory. Look at this workbench. Pestle and mortar, chopping board, grinder, storage jars. She must keep terribly busy.'

'What's this?' Laura had found two large jars of ointment. 'Look, this is the same as that tub we saw Mrs Potts carrying out of the chemist, last week. Hydrocortisone cream. We were right – it must be what they put on Daniel's skin. Poor chap, spending his whole life slathered in this muck.' Idly she took a dab of the cream and rubbed it on the back of her hand. 'Well, maybe it isn't too bad.'

'Dried foxgloves, plus hyssop, dill, oregano...' Rosemary was still identifying the bunches hanging from the beam. 'Well, well. This is amazing.'

'But no sign of a trowel,' Laura reminded her.

A shadow blocked the light from the open door. The silhouette was alarming at first sight, with an overlarge head, and one hand thrust forward in a threatening manner. Rosemary squeaked.

'Oh, I got you now,' said the figure, which had stepped forward and turned out to be Mrs Potts clutching a wicked-looking kitchen knife.

'We're looking for —' Laura began to explain.

'What do you think you're doing in here?' the woman demanded.

'I'm trying to tell you,' Laura said.

'You'm poking about, that's what.'

'We wanted a trowel, that's all.' Laura's voice was completely calm. Rosemary moved carefully so that Laura was between her and the knife. After all, she reasoned, her friend had experience of this sort of thing. The best thing Rosemary could do was to stay out of the way.

'Poking about ain't allowed. This is private property, this is.'

'Yes, of course it is. That's quite understood. We're terribly sorry. We'll be going now, then.'

'Clear off, both of you.' Mrs Potts waved the knife at them. 'And don't come back!'

With very little dignity, the two made their escape, Rosemary already close to collapse from a sudden acute need to giggle hysterically. Once in the avenue again, she let rip.

'That woman is a real case,' said Laura, also laughing. 'I'm not sure she's safe to be let loose. Private property, indeed! And that knife!'

'I almost fainted when I saw it. I've never had such a fright in my life.'

'She seems to carry a knife about as a matter of course. Didn't you say she had one that day you saw her in the shrubbery?'

'Right. She did. I assumed it was for cutting plants. It probably was. Once I calmed down, I didn't get the feeling she intended to use it on us.'

'No. Actually, I feel a bit sorry for her, even now. Poor old thing. She must have had a hard life.' Laura looked back at the barn, consideringly. They walked more decorously into the full sunlight of the parterre.

'Not if she got the insurance money from her butcher husband. And look at her now, living in this wonderful place, with nothing to do but mix herbal concoctions. Makes herbal tea, too, I expect. She gave Sam something bland when the rest of us had normal tea. The first day I came here, that was. Seems ages ago now.'

'Ooh!' Laura suddenly started rubbing the back of her hand. 'My hand stings.'

'Let's see. Gosh, it's covered in blisters. What've you done?'

'It's where I put that cream on. It seemed fine at first. I'd forgotten about it.'

Rosemary looked up at the sky, where the sun was sinking slowly and vividly.

'Phytophototoxic,' she muttered. 'Reacting to sunlight.'

'My God!' Laura stared at Rosemary, open-mouthed, as she realised the truth. 'She's been doctoring Daniel's cream! What a cruel thing to do. Imagine feeling like this all the time. It's criminal!'

'And there's you feeling sorry for her,' Rosemary teased.

'Not any more. I'll have to try and wash this off. It's burning.'

'I think you'll need the doctor. Washing won't get rid of it now.'

Laura took out a big white hanky from her jacket pocket, and wrapped it round her hand. 'That's a bit better. Keeps the sun off it, at least. But – listen, this doesn't make sense. Daniel was kept in that room all the time, with a window under the eaves. There can't have been much sunlight in there. None at all, most of the day.'

'That's quite right.' Rosemary tapped her front teeth with a fingernail. 'There must be an answer, but I can't find it for the moment. Anyway, let's worry about you, for now. Can you drive, do you think?'

'Why? Aren't you coming with me?'

'I want to check something out here.'

'Well, my hand can wait. I want to stay with you. You're up to something.'

'Come on, then.'

Rosemary led the way through the shrubbery, and down the narrow path they'd explored before. 'Yes!' crowed Rosemary. 'Just as I thought!'

She pointed at the patch of giant hogweed they'd discussed a few days earlier. 'Those stems were cut down deliberately, by Mrs Potts. She extracts the sap in that workshop of hers and mixes it into those big tubs of cream. I would think a single stalk would last weeks and weeks, if she's careful.'

'But *why*? What's the point of it? It's not going to kill him, is it?'

'It might,' Rosemary said. 'If the tissue damage was severe enough to cause septicaemia. Or maybe the intention all along was to drive the poor chap to suicide. Send him bonkers with the pain and misery of it all.'

'Yes,' said Laura patiently. 'But *why*?'

Rosemary met her eye, frowning slightly. 'Good question,' she said.

Chapter Twelve

'I think I will have to go and find a doctor,' Laura decided, as the burning in her hand refused to abate. 'Are you still determined to stay here?'

Rosemary thought about it. 'You know what,' she said, 'I think we've been under-estimating Mrs Potts. We know, after all, that she's almost certainly killed once in her life. We've got evidence that she's been torturing poor Daniel. I don't feel at all happy just leaving it as it is. She might take it into her head to attack Alicia, now there's just the two of them in the house. If she's got some idea of getting hold of their money, then it would make sense to bump the wife off as well.'

Laura tried to think this through. 'But Daniel's still alive,' she said. 'Won't she just give up now?'

'If she thinks nobody's onto her, she'll have plenty of opportunity to have another go at him, when he comes home. I know it sounds a bit over the top, but I'd feel terrible if something happened to Alicia. I'm going to go in there and warn her. She must be at home – her car's here.'

'But —' Laura hardly knew where to start. The pain in her hand was distracting her from lucid thought.

'Look. Go to Doctor Whittaker. Tell him about the cream, and show him your hand. After all, it lets him off the hook, doesn't it? It's all down to Mrs Potts, adulterating the perfectly innocent ointment. If you tell him the whole story, he's sure to take notice, and want to help us sort it all out. See if he'll come back here with you, so we can show him what's in that barn. With him on our side, we'll be in a much better position to go to the police, and save the Kellaways.'

'How am I going to get there? Aren't you going to take me?'

Rosemary produced a set of keys. 'I told you – take

the wagon. I really do think I'd better stay here. The old witch might get away, if I don't do something.'

Again Laura cradled her hand. 'All right, then. I'll give it a go. Now, you be careful. I think it's rather rash of you, I must say.'

'Oh, I'll be okay. Mrs P. won't hurt me if Alicia's there, now will she?'

'Good luck, then,' Laura said, to Rosemary's retreating back.

Driving the Land Rover with a swollen left hand was not easy. Changing gear became a nightmare, and Laura did her best to stay in third all the way to town. She tried not to think of all the junctions and round-abouts and unforeseen obstacles that would force her to move down to a lower gear. After only a mile, she came to the conclusion that she couldn't do it.

Instead, she headed for Dowminster and the White Hart. She'd have to get Robin to call the doctor from there, and wait for him to fit her in amongst his other obligations. After the encounter with him that morn-ing, she thought it would be relatively easy to per-suade him to come.

Robin was very solicitous, settling her into the lounge and bringing her a very early pre-dinner sherry, once he'd phoned Whittaker. 'On the house,' he said. 'I'm really enjoying having you and Miss Boxer here.'

'Are you?' Laura laughed. 'You're barmy. We must be real nuisances.'

'Not a bit,' he said. 'You're absolute treasures.'

'That's ever so sweet of you,' she sighed. 'People like you are a beacon in a dark world. Do you know that?'

'Steady on!' he pleaded. 'Now where's that doctor? He said he'd only be ten minutes.'

'I'll be all right,' she insisted. 'You just get on with whatever you were doing.' Reluctantly, he did as she advised.

Left on her own, Laura tried not to worry about

Rosemary. She imagined the scene, where her friend would quickly locate Alicia and calmly recount the events of the morning. Probably the result would be a phone-call to the hospital, where the truth about Daniel's skin disorder would be relayed, hastening his recovery, perhaps. Then Mrs Potts would be summoned, and told that her behaviour made it necessary for her to instantly quit her position at Winterbourne.

That was where Laura began to worry. Would Rosemary and Alicia be strong enough to enforce the departure of the wicked old woman? Would they have the good sense to phone the police before tackling her? Her mood changed as she thought this one through. *Was* it good sense, after all? It seemed a shame to put the old girl through another trial, however much she might deserve it. If she could just be sent packing, with dire warnings as to her fate if she ever did anything to harm another person again, that might be a more humane course of action.

She looked at her watch. Twenty minutes since Robin phoned the doctor. Where *was* the wretched man? Her hand felt better, and she peeled back the hanky to see how it was doing. It was inflamed, but there were only a few small blisters. Presumably the toxin was much diluted in the hydrocortisone cream, and she had only been exposed to sunlight for a minute or two. If Whittaker didn't arrive in the next few minutes, she was inclined to give up on him, and go back to Winterbourne. It felt self-indulgent and unnecessary to be sitting there doing nothing while Rosemary might be embroiled in all kinds of difficulty.

At Winterbourne, Rosemary was working slowly through the house, afraid to call out in case Mrs Potts leapt out at her, but intent on finding Alicia and warning her of the danger she was in. She had it all quite clear in her mind – what she would say, and how the two of them would confront the old woman. Except the memory of the scene in the barn kept recurring uncomfortably. There had been two of them then, both frightened into paralysis by the long knife in Mrs Potts's hand.

It would be different this time, she assured herself. She was prepared, for a start. And it would surely be easy to persuade Alicia to summon the housekeeper to an interview in the lounge or dining room, where she would obviously not bring the knife with her. Everything would be kept calm and clear, with firm statements of the evidence showing her ill-treatment of Daniel and the unavoidable conclusion that she must be dismissed.

She explored the ground floor first. At each door, she stood listening before gently opening it and going in. The lounge was deserted, and Rosemary took a moment to admire properly the lavish furnishings. A lot of money had obviously been spent in this room, but the overall impression was cold and uninviting. The last time she'd been in there was when she'd punched Julian, she remembered, with a self-satisfied smile. She even thought she could see a small brown spot on the Chinese carpet that could have come from Julian's bleeding nose. It was a very pleasing thought.

Back into the hall, and across to the dining room, which she had not seen before. A shining antique table was surrounded by six dining chairs, each upholstered with a rich brocade. Like the lounge, it seemed to be based on ideas borrowed from glossy magazines, with no sign of any mundane human use. Nothing to indicate than anybody ever ate in here at all, and certainly never held stimulating dinner parties for friends and neighbours.

Finally, she ventured upstairs, glancing behind her every few steps, to ensure she wasn't being observed. At the top of the wide staircase there was the landing she remembered, and a second flight leading to the room that had been Daniel's sickroom. It was more obvious up here that the house had been extended more than once, with odd angles and different levels revealing the points where the additions had been made.

And because this floor contained the more intimate bedrooms and bathrooms, where a stranger could have no possible excuse for intruding, Rosemary's heart began to beat very much faster. She rehearsed again the speech she wanted to make to Alicia. She could explain herself perfectly well, after all. She was on a mission of mercy, saving Daniel's unsuspecting wife from who knew what danger. She had to be surreptitious, for fear of meeting Mrs Potts and arousing her murderous rage. But somehow, however many times she repeated all this to herself, she still felt like a burglar.

Pausing to listen, she could not avoid the conclusion that the house was empty. Nobody upstairs or downstairs. Alicia must be outside, or in one of the other buildings ranged around the house. There was little point in investigating further, she decided. If Alicia was on the second floor, in Daniel's sickroom, her footsteps would be audible. It seemed very unlikely that she would simply be sitting quietly in a room that must hold many painful associations. And yet, maybe she was doing exactly that. Rosemary remembered the anxious solicitude that the woman had shown towards Daniel in the hospital. She might have gone up there for a spell of melancholy reflection at how dreadful the past year had been for them both, with Daniel's skin so awful, and the doctor so unsuccessful in curing it.

But if that was the case, then Rosemary really ought not to intrude. She would feel awkward and embarrassed. Perhaps, after all, she ought to wait for Laura to come back, and talk the whole thing through with her one more time.

As she hovered indecisively, she heard a tread on the stair. Alarmed, she shrank back into a shadowy corner, peering around a large oak chest to see who might be approaching.

With great relief, she caught sight of Alicia Kellaway's head and shoulders, as she mounted the stairs. Eagerly, she stepped out of her hiding place. 'Oh, good, it's you,' she said. 'I've got something I really must tell you.'

Impatiently, Laura went to the front door of the White Hart to scan the street for any sign of the doctor, being careful to keep her hand well wrapped against the sunlight. She looked first to her left, in the direction she assumed Doctor Whittaker would come from, and then, for good measure, to the right, and was surprised to see, only two strides away, Vickie Trent approaching.

'I wondered whether I might see you here,' Vickie said calmly, as Laura did a double take. 'I'd like a few words, if you've got time.'

'Well...' Laura hesitated. 'I'm waiting for someone, as it happens, but there's no sign of him at the moment.'

'It won't take long. I just needed to talk to you about Sam. I've had another call from the police, you see.'

'Come into the lounge,' Laura urged her. 'I'm sorry, but I probably only have a few minutes to spare.'

Briskly she led Vickie to a pair of armchairs near the door, where she could hear if Doctor Whittaker arrived. 'Have they told you anything new?' she asked.

'Not new, exactly, but confirming their earlier findings. Sam definitely had an overdose of Digoxin in his system, and there seems to be little doubt that it put a fatal strain on his heart. The thing is, there's no evidence at all that he was prescribed too high a dosage by Doctor Whittaker. And some of what they found was in a different format – not pure chemical Digoxin. They think it must have come from a foodstuff or something. They made me go through everything he'd ever eaten in the last week of his life. I mean – as if I *could*! He was at the garden centre practically the whole time. They've got that cafeteria, and the shop sells all kinds of things. I told them they'd have to go and look for themselves.'

Laura remembered Cynthia Battson and her ambitious son-in-law, Neville, and began to wonder whether the police might finally be onto something.

'I'm sure they'll find the answer eventually,' she said.

'You *would* say that,' Vickie accused. 'You always do stick up for the police.'

'I suppose I do,' said Laura mildly.

Vickie's thin face twisted with a surge of emotion. 'I'm sorry,' she moaned. 'But it's driving me mad trying to think it all through. Sam knew how strong the medication was. I'm sure he wouldn't have taken any extra Digoxin deliberately – which means it was either accidental, or somebody was giving it to him disguised as something else.'

'Oh, goodness,' Laura said helplessly. Her hand was stinging again, distracting her attention.

'I won't rest until I know,' Vickie insisted, suddenly intense. 'If somebody gave it to him on purpose, then I'm going to make very sure they pay the penalty for it.'

'Quite right,' mumbled Laura, hearing the slam of the front door as she spoke. 'Oh, I think that might be the person I'm waiting for.'

It struck her then that it might seem odd to Vickie that Laura was meeting the doctor here at her hotel. If possible, she would very much prefer not to have to explain the events of the morning, until everything had become clearer in her own mind.

'Look – you stay here for a bit,' she ordered. 'You look whacked, and I'm sure you'd like a coffee. I'll go and ask Robin to bring you one. It's on me, of course. I'm just sorry I have to rush off like this. I'll speak to you soon.' And she was out of the room before Vickie could reply.

Doctor Whittaker was all apology and concern.

'Perhaps we ought to go up to your room,' he said, as Laura stood before him, blocking the way into the lounge. 'I don't expect Robin wants to turn his lounge into a surgery.'

'Fine by me,' said Laura, leading the way towards the stairs, and silently thanking her luck. 'Oh – hang on for two seconds, would you?'

She ducked back towards the dining room, where she could hear some clattering. Finding Robin putting new menus into plastic sleeves, while Caz the waitress laid tables, she quickly asked for a coffee to be taken to Vickie. Then she went ahead of the doctor to her bedroom.

'What happened?' he asked, as she revealed her stricken hand.

'I think it's called phytophototoxicity,' she said. 'I was in contact with the juice of the giant hogweed. Or so it would seem.'

'Ah!' he nodded. 'Psoralens.'

'Pardon?'

He smirked at her. 'That's the substance in the sap that causes the trouble. It reacts to ultraviolet light, and destroys cells. Luckily, I think you've escaped any permanent scarring.'

'Unlike poor Daniel Kellaway.'

'What?' He jerked upright, dropping her hand.

'After what we saw this morning, Rosemary and I are convinced that sap from giant hogweed plants has been mixed into the cream you prescribed for Daniel, and that's what gave him that terrible skin condition.'

'Impossible,' he said. 'You're raving.'

'You won't say that when I tell you the whole story,' she assured him, and proceeded to do just that, before he attended to her hand.

But the doctor was a lot harder to convince than Laura had hoped. 'It doesn't make any sense,' he insisted. 'Mrs Potts is certainly eccentric, but nothing more than that. She's not certifiably insane. She functions within her own limitations. Have you seen the way she keeps that house spotless? And she cooks magnificently. More than that, I'd say she was genuinely fond of both Daniel and Sam Trent. Remember, I have seen quite a lot of her over the past months.'

'I hadn't forgotten,' said Laura, giving him a knowing look. 'But I rather thought you were more interested in the lady of the house than the general factotum. And perhaps more in the house itself than Mrs Kellaway.'

'I'm afraid I don't know what you mean,' he said stiffly.

'Well never mind that for now. The main thing is - you have to believe me about Mrs P. Her real name is Delia Kettle, and she was charged with poisoning her husband, in 1972.'

'But not convicted?'

'That's right. The thing with poisoning, you see, is that it's very easy to cover your tracks. You can leave something for the victim to eat or drink, in a week's time, and be off across the world with a cast iron alibi. And in her case, she probably knows just what's likely to go undetected, and what tastes tolerable.'

'Most poisons taste revolting.'

Laura gave an impatient *tut*. 'That's not the point. Rosemary and I have uncovered incontrovertible proof that Daniel's ointment was contaminated. At the very least, you ought to come back with me and remove it from the house. It's dangerous.' She waved her hand at him. 'I'm living evidence of that, if nothing else.'

Which reminded them both of why they were together in Laura's hotel room. 'Let me bandage that for you,' he said. 'It needs to be kept out of the light. I can remove most of the harmful agent, but best be on the safe side.'

He opened his bag and took out a bandage and a small plastic bottle. Leading her to the washbasin in one corner of the room, he thoroughly cleaned the whole hand before applying the bandage. Laura waited quietly, doing her best to be patient.

When he was finished, Doctor Whittaker sighed, and Laura gave him another searching look. The man did look very drained, with dark shadows under his eyes and a droop to his shoulders. She was just about to make some encouraging and sympathetic comment, when the phone on the bedside table rang.

She picked it up with an apologetic little shrug. 'Hello?'

'Mum? It's me, Matthew.'

'Hello, love. What can I do for you?'

'Nothing. I'm doing something for you. You asked me, remember.'

'Ermm,' she mumbled, trying to unscramble her thoughts. 'Yes.'

'For heaven's sake! Here's me, breaking all sorts of rules, to do as you ask, and you can't even remember what I'm talking about.'

'Oh! Yes, of course. Delia Kettle. Sorry, love – I was just talking about her, too. What a silly old fool I am.'

'Well, listen. There isn't much, but you might as well have the whole thing now I've ferreted it out for you.'

'I'm listening.'

'The police in Norfolk were quite convinced she was guilty of poisoning her husband, despite the jury letting her off, so they kept an eye on her for a while. She never gave them any trouble, although her young daughter turned out to be rather a handful. She went for a couple of her teachers, apparently. Quite a little savage, she sounds. Anyway, after a few years, they moved away from Withersedge and nothing's been heard of either of them since.'

'Oh, well. I suppose that's that, then. Ancient history.'

'Actually, not quite. Alicia skipped probation when they moved, and officially she's still wanted, even though it's more than twenty years ago. So, if you're likely to come across mother or daughter, you might bear that in mind.'

'Yeah – I'll turn her in. Wait a minute. What name did you say?'

'Alicia. Alicia Kettle. She'd be in her late thirties now, I suppose.'

Cutting him off without any farewells, Laura stared blindly at the doctor, her mind in turmoil.

'Did you know?' she asked him.

'What? Did I know what?'

'That Alicia is Mrs Potts's daughter.'

He laughed, a single high donkey-like bray. 'No, of course not. Of course she isn't. What a crazy idea.'

'Think about it,' she urged him. 'Just for a minute. It explains all sorts of things. Firstly, why she would tolerate such an unstable person in her house. Secondly, how did the old bat get away with doctoring the cream… Oh, God!' She put her hand to her mouth in horror as a whole new batch of implications hit her. 'Come on!' she cried. 'We've got to get to Winterbourne as quick as we can!'

The doctor didn't move. He was staring at a corner of the room, eyes fixed, as his brain tried to absorb a hundred astonishing thoughts all at once.

'Well, if you won't come, I'll go by myself,' Laura said impatiently.

'Alicia…' he mumbled. 'She was always so *sweet*.'

'Never mind that now. I'm worried about

Rosemary.' Her voice was already indistinct as she rushed down the stairs.

'All right. Wait for me.' Belatedly he hurried after her, and threw himself into the Land Rover beside her, as the engine roared into life.

Despite her hurry, Laura had taken a few seconds to peer into the lounge as she passed. There was no sign of Vickie Trent.

In his comfortable private room at St Mark's, Daniel Kellaway took a phone-call that left him feeling deeply disturbed.

'Daniel? It's Vickie. How are you now?'

'I'm improving by the minute,' he told her cheerily. 'They're talking about letting me go home in a day or two.'

'That's good. Look, I've just come from Dowminster. I've been talking to Laura Thyme. You know she and her husband have been friends of ours for years, don't you?'

'Um…I'm not sure. Is she the woman who's helping Rosemary with my trees?'

'Yes, yes,' snapped Vickie, the strain and impatience clear in her voice. 'She came here when her husband left her, last week. She and Rosemary met at the hotel and seemed to hit it off. She was the last person to see Sam alive.' Her voice cracked, and she had to take a few seconds to steady herself.

Daniel made soothing noises, wondering what she wanted from him. He didn't think she had just phoned to ask after his health.

'Daniel, can I ask you something? It might sound strange, but I can't think who else to turn to.'

'Fire away,' he invited.

'Well, you might not know that the police are very suspicious about the quantity of Digoxin that Sam had in his system when he died. It seems it's highly toxic if you take too much of it.'

'Like most plant poisons,' Daniel agreed, thinking of the lectures he'd sat through on the subject. 'So?'

'So the question is, where did the additional dosage come from? We've been through his prescriptions, and I've accounted for all his tablets. My first reaction was to blame Doctor Whittaker for over-prescribing —'

'And quite right too,' Daniel went off at a tangent. 'You know, it looks very much as if the cream he was giving me for my skin was actually *exacerbating* the problem. The man's a liability. He should be struck off. I don't mind telling you, Alicia's had some strong words with him, and we're not on his list any more. So if he's been just as careless with Sam, I won't be a bit surprised.'

'No, Daniel, listen. The doctor's in the clear. In fact, I think he's been very conscientious. It strikes me that Sam must have been getting Digoxin in some form from some other source. That's what I'm asking you. Can you think of any way he might have been taking it at the garden centre? Do you think they serve something in the cafeteria that contains it?'

'Good God, I wouldn't think so. Mind you, there's a lot of weird and wonderful stuff in the shop. We franchise out to all kinds of New Agey outfits. One of them sells herbal potions of various sorts. I can't say I ever took very much notice of the contents.'

'Oh, well – it was just a try. I'm sorry to bother you. I'm all over the place today, trying to find out what must have happened.'

'I know,' Daniel said gently. 'I feel it, too. Sam was my best friend, as well as my partner. He's left a great gap in our lives.'

'Thank you,' Vickie sniffed. 'I really am pleased that you're getting better. Will you be going home soon?'

'Don't ask me. I've been having a whole lot more tests today, and with any luck they'll tell me what's what. I must say, I can't wait to make my escape. And

it's such a strain on poor Alicia. She doesn't deserve all
this bother. I can tell you one thing – when I'm back
on my feet, I'm really going to make it up to her.'

Too late, he realised this was rather a tactless thing
to say. On the other end of the phone, Vickie made a
choked sound, suggesting a tearful attempt to say
goodbye.

'I'll see you soon,' he told her. 'Better go now.' And
he replaced the receiver with a sigh.

* * *

It took Laura five minutes to convince Doctor
Whittaker that he should call the police. 'But surely —
' he blustered. 'I mean, you don't really think —'

'I think Rosemary is going to need back up. I think
it might already be too late. For heaven's sake, man,
just press nine three times. How difficult can that be?'

'Slow down, will you,' he pleaded. 'You'll have us in
a ditch at this rate, and the 999'll be for us, not your
friend.'

'Listen. If Mrs Potts has been poisoning people,
and Alicia Kellaway is her daughter, then they're sure
to be in it together, aren't they? So when Rosemary
tries to warn Alicia about the old woman… well, who
knows what might happen?'

He shook his head. 'I can't believe *anything* would
happen. Even if you're right, all they'll do is present a
united front, and tell her she's got it all wrong. Come
on,' he urged her. 'This is a civilised country. What are
they going to do?'

She flashed him a scornful glance. 'Get real,' she
said, witheringly. It was something Helena had said to
her a million times. It sounded rather satisfying on her
own lips.

'Anyway, I *know* Alicia.' Even he heard the false-
ness in this statement. 'Or I thought I did,' he muttered.

Laura's brain was working feverishly. There were a

number of assumptions that she and Rosemary had made over the past few days which now needed urgent reassessment.

'Everybody thought they knew her, and everybody got it wrong,' she said. 'The sweet devoted young wife, turning to the dedicated doctor for solace in her time of trouble. But in fact, she's been using you, don't you see? Flirting with you, and spinning you along, just to make sure you didn't get suspicious about what was really happening. And it worked brilliantly, didn't it. There was even a time when everybody thought *you* were to blame for Sam's death, and even Daniel's fall. You, Doctor Whittaker, have been the prime suspect for quite a few days now.'

'Good Lord. I had no idea.'

'It was obvious you fancied Alicia, for a start. Rosemary spotted that after about three minutes of seeing you together.'

'She threw herself at me,' he insisted. 'Just as you say – I thought she needed a shoulder to lean on, with Daniel being so ill. But – well, it did get a bit further than that.'

'I bet it did.'

'She was very nice to me,' he went on sadly. 'I suppose I have been rather a fool over her.'

'That's enough. Please, *please*, make that call. Otherwise, I'll have to stop and do it myself.'

Finally, with a shaking thumb, he did as she instructed. 'Hello? Police, please...Yes, this is Doctor Whittaker from Dowminster. Listen – I have very good reason to think there's some serious trouble going on at Winterbourne Manor, in Devenish. There's a woman's life in danger. I think you should get over there straight away. No, I'm sorry, I don't have any more details, but I really am worried. Yes, that's right... Thank you.'

He looked at Laura, still fully focused on covering the miles to Winterbourne at maximum speed. 'I think that should get them moving,' he said with some satisfaction.

'You did a splendid job,' she assured him. 'Well done. Oh, God, now what?'

A tractor was chugging contentedly along the lane in front of them, leaving no room at all to pass. Laura hooted vigorously, only causing the driver to turn round and wave at her, a friendly grin on his face.

'He thinks you're another farmer, in this thing,' noted the doctor. 'He thinks you'll be happy to crawl along behind him. He'll be glad of the company.'

'Then he's got another think coming,' she growled, wrenching the steering wheel abruptly to the left. Tilting alarmingly, the Land Rover overtook the tractor on the inside, where a field gateway provided a brief widening of the lane. They missed the front wheel of the farm vehicle by millimetres as they pulled very bumpily back onto the tarmac. The doctor gave a terrified squawk.

'Not far to go now,' she puffed.

'There's something wrong,' the doctor said. 'We're listing.'

'I do not believe it,' shouted Laura. 'It's a flat tyre.'

'Must have been that stone you hit in the gateway. Probably buckled the rim.'

'Well, I'm just going to keep driving on it,' she announced. 'It's not far.'

'Give me strength,' prayed Doctor Whittaker.

'Something to tell me?' echoed Alicia. 'And what might that be, that's so urgent you have to come snooping around my house?'

The frosty tone wasn't surprising, Rosemary reminded herself. 'I'm so sorry,' she said. 'I know it must look strange. But Laura and I have just had a very peculiar encounter with your housekeeper, in the barn outside. She actually threatened us with a knife. And in the circumstances, we felt it was our duty to reveal to you what we know about her. To be honest, Mrs Kellaway, we think you're in considerable danger, here alone with her as you are.'

Alicia's expression contained interest, certainly, but also something rather more like malice. Rosemary tried to believe that it was all directed at Mrs Potts. 'Go on,' Alicia invited. 'Please do explain yourself.'

'Well, you obviously had no idea of this, but your Mrs Potts is in fact a woman named Delia Kettle. She was charged with the murder of her husband, in the 1970s, and although she was acquitted, there is still a lot of suspicion hanging over her. The thing is, you see – it was *poison*.' She uttered the last word in a low voice, hissing it as if it clinched her argument beyond any doubt.

'Poison?' echoed Alicia, in a high light tone, almost singing it.

'Shh. She'll hear you,' Rosemary said, glancing down the stairs in alarm.

'I'm afraid I still don't fully understand what you're suggesting. You think my housekeeper is planning to poison me?'

'No, no. At least…possibly. But that *knife*. She definitely seemed capable of using it.'

This time Alicia really did laugh. 'I don't think so,' she trilled. 'But perhaps we ought to confront her with your suspicions. See what she has to say for herself.'

'Oh, no! I mean – are you sure?'

'Of course. It's by far the best thing to get it all out into the open. After all, she might have a perfectly reasonable explanation. The thing is, you see, *we* live here, and you don't. You're an interloper in our house, sneaking about watching us, and inventing all sorts of wild stories about us.'

Rosemary was slow to notice the sudden change of tone. When she did, she felt bewildered, but not particularly worried. She had already persuaded herself that the woman was justified in resenting her intrusion. And she didn't think she'd done a very good job of explaining herself, now she thought over what she had just said.

'I'm sorry,' she said again. 'I don't think you've fully understood what I've been trying to —'

Alicia ignored her, and went to a bell push at the end of the corridor. 'We had this installed, you see, when Daniel was still in the master bedroom. So he could summon myself or Mrs Potts if he felt poorly. I'm not sure he ever actually used it, but I expect it works well enough.' Her voice had a dreamy distracted edge to it, as if she was really thinking about something else entirely. 'It rings in the kitchen, and in the barn outside.'

'So – what are you going to say to her?'

'I'll probably let you do the talking. I'm still having a bit of trouble believing your story, you see. It's all rather incredible, don't you think?'

'It's certainly very strange. But you must believe me, I wouldn't have troubled you with it if I didn't think you were in genuine danger. I'm very concerned for your safety, do you see?'

'That's very noble of you. Ah – here she is.'

Rosemary watched as the knitted hat appeared around the twist of the staircase, followed by the head and then entire person of Mrs Potts. In her hand, she clasped the same wicked knife as before. This, Rosemary felt, was really very worrying.

'What do you want me for?' The old woman looked at Alicia enquiringly.

'This lady —' she waved a hand towards Rosemary, who had taken several steps backwards in the last few seconds, 'she's been making all sorts of accusations. I think we're going to have to deal with her, Mummy.'

'Mummy?' Rosemary whispered the word, looking from one face to the other and back again. 'Mummy! Oh, my God!'

Daniel tried three times to telephone Alicia from his hospital room, when she failed to appear for her promised visit, and each time he got no reply. He imagined the phone ringing in the empty house, and wondered where on earth she and Mrs Potts might be. The old housekeeper hardly ever went out anywhere, and she could usually be relied upon to answer the phone, even if she was sometimes rude to the caller. With mounting frustration and anxiety, he racked his brains as to the reason for her silence. Some sixth sense told him that there was something going on, something wrong at Winterbourne Manor. The conversation with Vickie had started him thinking about Sam, and the garden centres and the future, and it all made him feel lonely and abandoned. Sam had always been there for him, ready to listen and bounce ideas around with. And when Sam wasn't available, Alicia had always been an excellent confidante. Now he wanted to talk things over and nobody was there for him.

Finally, he called the White Hart, where he knew Rosemary Boxer was staying. With luck he would catch her, and ask her if she'd noticed anything strange going on at the Manor. She might even agree to drive over and check that everything was all right with Alicia.

But Robin told him that Rosemary had been out all afternoon, and that Laura had hurt her hand. She, however, had made a very sudden exit, accompanied by Doctor Whittaker. Daniel almost howled with frustration, desperate to know what everybody was doing, what was happening to his wife and his house and his garden centre. Something was going on and all he could do was lie in this stupid hospital and fret about it.

And then, everything changed to a different tempo. A small army of medical personnel descended on his room and announced that it was time for yet more tests. He would have to go to X-ray, and then to an examination room. It would take about an hour, they thought, and no, there was no chance of postponing it while he made one more phone-call.

In any case, he realised, there was nobody else he could reasonably call. Whatever might be going on, would have to happen without him.

Rosemary was ashamed of herself for screaming. It didn't help one bit, and made her attackers all the more confident of victory. All the thrillers she'd ever watched seemed to come to mind, simultaneously. Usually, the cornered victim managed, by lightning calculations along with sheer energy and determination, to dodge the aggressors and escape undamaged. She didn't think this was going to happen in her case.

Mrs Potts was still standing at the top of the stairs. Alicia was between them, slightly to the left, where she had gone to press the bell push. To the right was the second staircase leading to the upper floor. Behind her were three doors leading into bedrooms or bathrooms. The sensible thing would be to retreat to one of these rooms, barricade the door, and climb out of a window, which was only one floor up, and very probably furnished with a creeper or drainpipe to assist descent.

Rosemary did not do the sensible thing. Instead, she rushed for the second staircase. Halfway up it, she found herself thinking that instinct was a very unreliable thing and she had probably taken the worst possible line of action. She could have pushed Mrs Potts backwards downstairs and escaped past her. Or rugby tackled Alicia, so she fell on top of the old woman and sent both of them tumbling down the stairs.

But it was too late for all that. Both her attackers were right behind her, and she was going to have to trust to her defective instincts a while longer. There were only two doors on this landing, and one of them was open. She dashed through it, and slammed it forcefully behind her.

It was Daniel's sickroom, she realised immediately. It had several items of moveable furniture, two of which she hurriedly dragged across the door. The table on which the medications had stood, along with a large vase of flowers, was disappointingly flimsy, but it was the perfect height for fitting under the door handle. Again, she recalled a dozen adventure stories where items were effectively wedged in this way. It even seemed likely to work – at least for a few seconds. But much stouter reinforcement was needed. She grabbed a sturdy chair, and shoved it up against the table. Then she leaned her own weight on the chair. It was not an ideal strategy, she concluded, as she desperately inspected the remaining contents of the room.

Everything was very neat and tidy. No flowers or medicaments remained. The bed was stripped, and the curtains thrown open. A strange-looking gadget stood beside the bed, which Rosemary briefly considered as an additional piece of her barricade. Then she found herself wondering what it might be, noting that it had a power lead, and odd vertical panels.

The truth hit her suddenly. A sun lamp! The source of the ultra violet light that activated the hogweed toxins on Daniel's skin. This substantial new piece of the puzzle only served to increase her rage against Alicia for her treachery. On the other side of the door, there was a persistent thumping, as the two women strove to break into the room.

'Leave me alone!' she shouted. 'You won't get away with this. You're both murderers.'

Muffled exchanges could be heard, but on the whole the two aggressors were unnervingly quiet. They had stopped trying to manipulate the door handle, and thundering at the door. Thankfully, Rosemary observed how well-made the thing was, from good solid oak that would withstand any amount of battering. If only there'd been a lock and key, she'd have been safe for a fortnight.

There was, though, considerable cause for anxiety. If they'd shouted at her, Rosemary would at least have felt she knew where she was. The sinister hush made her wonder if they were planning some new way of getting at her. Were they going to unscrew the door hinges, for example?

Doggedly, Rosemary refined her barrier, wedging the chair under the table, and hauling the bed itself across the room to prevent the chair from moving. It wasn't very good. If she'd had the chance, she'd have started all over again with a totally different configuration. As it was, she didn't dare release the door handle, even for a second.

Panting heavily from her exertions, she moved towards the window. This was where Daniel had fallen; a fact that strongly deterred her from trying to jump off the balcony. But it was worth investigating, in case there might be a ledge or handy tree branch that might enable her to get away from the sickroom.

There was nothing, and when she looked back into the room, she saw that the table had somehow been jiggled away from the door handle, and the bed, chair and table were all inching inexorably across the floor as great force was applied to the door from outside. Alicia and her mother were simply pushing, showing astonishing strength, and liable to achieve their purpose quite soon.

All Rosemary could do was scream. She stood on the balcony, and inflated her lungs. '*HELP!!!*' she bawled. And again, 'Somebody *help*.'

Time seemed to stand still then. Sounds of grunting exertion came from the room, birds sang in the trees outside, and an aeroplane passed overhead. Rosemary found herself wondering whether in the end she would be more afraid of the knife and Mrs Potts or the drop to the ground below. Of course, there was no guarantee that she wouldn't end up experiencing both.

Cursing the habits of rich people, whereby they chose to live out of earshot of each other, she screamed again.

'That won't help you,' panted a voice from the doorway. Mrs Potts was half into the room, her shoulder to the door, the hand with the knife waving threateningly.

'Push harder, Mummy!' Alicia was apparently putting her own weight behind the task, to judge from her voice. Rosemary wondered whether it was completely insane of her to hope they both had heart attacks from the effort.

And when the answer to this came back as affirmative, she tried for a more rational approach.

'What do you think you're going to do to me?' she demanded. 'You're already in trouble, but nothing like as much as if you attack me with that knife. How would you argue your way out of that? Eh?' Her shaky voice undermined her message, she feared, but it all sounded quite convincing in her own ears.

'We'll be long gone before anybody finds you,' puffed Alicia. 'We've done it before and we can do it again.'

Unhappily, Rosemary accepted that this sounded perfectly feasible. It might be another hour or more before Laura returned in the Land Rover. Meanwhile, Rosemary's stiffening body would lie undiscovered under the balcony, or on Daniel's bed, and her killers would be off and away to some remote hiding place.

Again she cried for help, her screams soaring across the lovely gardens, to fall on the ears of small animals, and even perhaps a dog or two, but no human rescue was at hand.

Or so it seemed. Suddenly, as the furniture in the room slid another six inches under the onslaught of her attackers, and Mrs Potts finally stood there brandishing the knife, a siren was to be heard.

Idiotically, Rosemary remembered the sirenless ambulance that had come for Daniel. Why had they turned it on this time? Was it really a police car – or might it be a fire engine? And were they really coming for her? Or would they charge straight past, intent on a chimney fire or overturned tractor somewhere further down the road?

Shaking herself, she turned to Mrs Potts, who was involved in an undignified scramble over the table, chair and bed, followed closely by her daughter. 'You're too late!' she cried. 'The police are here. Can't you hear their siren?'

'Never mind that,' snapped Mrs Potts, extracting her own leg from those of the chair which had fallen sideways.

'Ah…Mummy,' said Alicia, throwing her head up to listen. 'Wait a minute.'

In reply the older woman merely snarled, and made a strong forward movement. She was crawling across the bed now, with only a few feet between her and her target.

Rosemary pushed the casement windows closed, to create one final barrier, and leaned against them. Below her, the siren had grown very much louder.

After her phone-call to Daniel, Vickie sat motionless in her living room for several minutes. The truth now seemed clearer to her. The manager of the garden centre, Neville Grant, must have been scheming to get his hands on the place. Familiar as she was with the finances of the place, and the personalities who worked there, it seemed all too obvious that Neville had been finding a way of giving Sam some herbal concoction containing Digoxin.

But there were many unanswered questions, and nagging doubts still to be overcome. Where did Daniel's illness fit into the picture? Neville never went to Winterbourne, and couldn't possibly arrange for him to be damaged.

Unless... into Vickie's mind floated the image of the crazed housekeeper with her ludicrous hat. Was it possible that she'd been contacted by Neville and persuaded to somehow ensure that Daniel didn't recover?

Crossly, she shook her head, muttering aloud, 'This is all madness. What's the matter with me?' She paced the room, trying to think it all through yet again. But Vickie was no detective. Her talents lay with business matters and persuasion. She had kept Sam up to the mark, never letting him lose sight of his own interests. When Daniel had decided to endow that stupid University Chair, Vickie had been furious. Despite Sam's insistence that there was nothing anybody could do to change Daniel's mind, she had persisted to the end in trying to prevent it. Now, she wondered what would happen. The endowment had never needed Sam's direct co-operation, so his death would not make any material difference.

And yet, somehow Vickie suspected it would not now happen. By a piece of female irrationality, her thoughts returned to Neville Grant.

'Mummy!' Alicia's voice contained urgency and clear authority. Mrs Potts paused in her battering at the balcony window.

'What?' she snapped over her shoulder. 'What do you want?'

'We'll be trapped if we stay here. We'll have to run.'

Rosemary heard the words indistinctly as she pressed herself against the wall of the house in one corner of the balcony, waiting desperately for the police to work out what was going on. She was hoarse with shouting, but they still hadn't located her, despite some purposeful gravel-crunching sounds coming from the front of the house. When she realised that Alicia was calling a halt, she could hardly breathe for the suspense, unable to believe that Mrs Potts was stoppable.

But it seemed she was. Peeping into the room, she saw the younger woman drag her mother back across the jumble of furniture and out of the door. It seemed too much to hope for, and Rosemary waited a moment to be sure she could credit the evidence of her own eyes.

Then a wave of rage washed through her at the thought of what had almost happened. She had to make sure the women didn't escape. If the police were still milling about in the front, wondering what to do, and discussing procedure and codes of practice and risk levels and back-up, there would be nothing to stop Alicia and Mrs Potts making a dash for it from the back. Behind the house were fields and patches of woodland, with a maze of small winding lanes and old footpaths. Anybody familiar with the terrain could probably make an escape as effectively as any fox going to earth. For all Rosemary knew, there was a quad bike in one of the sheds, which would certainly give them a nice head start.

Furiously, she wrenched open the window and climbed back into the room. Throwing aside the chair and small table, she followed the two women out onto the landing and down the stairs. 'Hey!' she yelled. 'Help!' Was the front door locked? If not, surely the police would come into the house when they heard her?

On the ground floor, in the large hallway, there was no sign of movement. Still in a state of rage, Rosemary ran to the front door and pulled it open. Two uniformed policemen stood there, looking startled at her appearance, but businesslike.

'Quick!' she gasped. 'They'll get away if you don't act fast. Round the back! They'll be round the back and away over the fields.'

It was understandable, of course, that they would

want additional information, but she was impressed at the briskness with which they obtained it.

'Who are we looking for, madam?' asked one.

'Two women,' Rosemary panted, already leading them round the side of the house. 'Mother and daughter.'

'Are they armed?'

'The older one has a knife. I wouldn't think there's anything else.'

They were already behind the house. 'What kind of knife?' asked the policeman.

'A wicked long kitchen knife. But I think they'll be gone by now.' Despair was flooding over her at their failure to act quickly. Calming down slightly, she tried to think rationally. 'We *must* catch them,' she urged. 'They'll know how to escape without being seen. There must be ditches and paths they can use.'

The policeman who hadn't yet said anything shook his head reassuringly. 'As it happens, I know this area very well myself. If they run off that way, all that'll come to is a dirty great dual carriageway, and by my reckoning, it's just on rush hour by now. They'll never get across it alive.'

Rosemary paused, before pointing down the avenue of sick trees. 'What if they go that way?'

The officer considered this briefly and then cocked his head at Rosemary. 'Have you ever tried running over a field of young maize?' he asked. She shook her head. 'It's not easy,' he told her. 'Not easy at all. Very tiring for anybody, and two ladies might find it quite a business.'

'So where *are* they?' Rosemary wailed.

'We'll have to find that out, won't we?' he said. 'I wouldn't think they'd gone very far. Please try to relax, madam. Everything's under control.'

But his manner belied his words. Speaking tersely into the radio phone attached to his uniform, he seemed to be requesting reinforcements. In her bewil-

dered state, Rosemary found herself admiring the effi-
ciency. They might, after all, have spent long minutes
trying to discover the details of the case. Only then
did she wonder who had alerted them in the first place.

'Go and sit in the car,' she was ordered. 'You'll be
safe there. Until we apprehend these people, we can't
be sure just what might happen. Do you understand?'

Rosemary nodded, glad to be told what to do. She
retraced her steps around the side of the house, glancing nervously towards the barn where Mrs Potts had
accosted her and Laura. It felt like days ago.

'This is impossible,' the doctor repeated, as the
Land Rover flapped along, on the naked wheel rim.
The tyre had disintegrated over the first mile, leaving
chunks of itself behind them.

'Nearly there now!' insisted Laura. 'There's been
no sign of the police, so it's all down to us to make
sure Rosemary's all right.'

'Yes, yes.' In spite of himself, his anxiety levels had
risen dramatically in the past few minutes.

At last they were there. Laura slewed the vehicle to
a halt on the gravel drive. Miraculously, the police had
already arrived. She stared at their car in disbelief and
thankfulness. But where was Rosemary? And Alicia?
Everything was silent and still.

Behind them, another police car drew up.

'What's going on?' shouted a tall young officer.

'I'm not sure,' Laura replied. 'But I can tell you
that the woman who lives here, Mrs Kellaway, has
been carrying on a major deception. Her mother is
pretending to be her housekeeper, and she is in fact a
dangerous criminal. My friend doesn't know, you see.
About Alicia being her daughter. She was going to
warn Alicia, but now – well, I have no idea.' She gazed
around her helplessly. The policeman eyed her doubt-
fully, struggling to make any sense at all of what she
had just said.

Rosemary reached the front of the house just after Laura arrived in the limping Land Rover. Before she could react, one of the first two policeman appeared at a trot, shouting to nobody in particular, 'The back door to the house is locked. Nobody can have come out that way.'

The conclusion hit them all simultaneously. 'Then they're still in the house,' said Rosemary 'There isn't any other way out – you'd have seen them if they came through the front.'

Then she turned her attention to Laura and Doctor Whittaker, standing confusedly on the gravel beside the Land Rover, with its pronounced list to one side, and the shredded tyre. 'What the *hell* have you done to her?' she squealed.

'Never mind that now,' Laura snapped. 'What's going on here?'

'Alicia is Mrs Potts's daughter,' Rosemary said breathlessly. 'They're hiding somewhere in the house. They almost killed me. But the wagon!' she wailed.

'It's only a tyre,' Laura snapped. 'Leave this to me. And yes, I know about them being mother and daughter.'

She marched past the conferring police officers, through the front door of the house, and straight to the room on the right, which she had found when searching for the loo, a week earlier. Without hesitation, she threw open the door and stepped inside. Shakily, Rosemary followed close behind her.

'Oh, gosh,' she said, as she slowly made sense of the sight before her.

'Come out!' Laura ordered, but the huddled tangle on the sagging old sofa made no move.

Alicia Kellaway, wealthy mistress of the grand Winterbourne Manor, was huddled on the lap of the woman everyone knew as her housekeeper, her thumb in her mouth. 'Mummy!' she whined, indistinctly.

'There, there,' soothed the old woman, still in her

impossible hat. 'It'll be all right.' She glared at Laura and Rosemary defiantly. 'Why did you two have to interfere? Coming here, and stirring up all this trouble.' She stroked her daughter's glossy black hair. 'Upsetting my poor girl like this.'

'You tried to kill me,' Rosemary accused, but with none of the rage or indignation of a few minutes earlier.

'Serves you right,' muttered Mrs Potts.

'Now then, Delia,' said Laura, sounding very like a police officer. 'It's all over now. Alicia's going to be taken care of, and my advice to you is to make a clean breast of it.'

A muffled chuckle behind her made her turn. Four policemen stood there. 'What?' Laura demanded.

'Nothing, madam,' said one of the officers. 'Except I've never heard anybody say that before, except in old movies. Making a clean breast of it, I mean. Sounds funny.' He dropped his gaze before her stern expression.

'Well, I suggest you stop sniggering and do your job,' she told him coldly.

Chapter Thirteen

'And you're sure you're all right, are you?' Laura asked Rosemary for the fourth time, as they sat with Doctor Whittaker on a seat in the garden. The police had finally driven off, with Alicia and Mrs Potts and assurances that they would be requiring statements from all concerned within a short time.

'Fine,' said Rosemary, with a faint smile. And then she turned an odd shade of green and leaned forward over her knees.

Doctor Whittaker, whose presence ought to have been useful, was taking absolutely no notice. His gaze was directed blindly at the treetops, as he worked through the sequence of events of the past hour.

'How could she?' he murmured brokenly. 'I still don't understand.'

'I think she's just a very damaged person,' Laura said. 'Probably completely under her mother's thumb. And now she's had some sort of breakdown, poor thing.'

'I should have gone with her,' he groaned. 'I'm a *doctor*. I should be helping her. What am I doing here?' He looked round in bewilderment. 'This used to be my family's home, you know.'

'Yes, we did know. We thought you wanted it back. I suppose we got all that part of it wrong.'

'What?'

Laura fiddled with an earring for a moment, before answering. 'The way we saw it, that was the final piece of evidence against you, when we discovered that your family used to own Winterbourne. We assumed you wanted it back in the family, and thought you could get it through Alicia. Makes perfectly good sense,' she added defensively.

The doctor's eyes widened. 'You must be joking!' he protested. 'Why would I want this great place? However would I maintain it on a GP's salary? The idea's insane. Besides, the honest truth is that I don't even *like* it. It might look lovely, but I could never dream of living in it. All those stairs, and rooms too big to heat properly. And I hope you'll believe me when I tell you I never reached the point of imagining myself and Alicia as a couple. What do you think that would have done to my standing as a doctor – taking up with the wife of one of my patients, who I'd allowed to die of a skin disorder?'

'Errghhh!' moaned Rosemary.

'Hey – are you going to be sick?' Laura drew back slightly.

'I don't think so. It's just starting to hit me, that's all. Shock.' She began to shiver violently. 'I thought she was going to kill me.'

'Leave this to me,' interrupted the doctor, in a drained voice. 'I'll make sure she's okay.' He put a hand firmly on the back of Rosemary's neck, and pushed her head right down to her knees. 'We'll make you some hot sweet tea in a minute,' he said.

'The wonders of modern medicine,' Laura muttered.

Twenty minutes later and very much her old self, Rosemary was examining the bare wheel rim of the Land Rover with an anguished expression. 'How could you?' she wailed. 'What a thing to do – driving her on this.'

'That's rich!' protested Laura. 'We were trying to save your skin, remember. As soon as Matthew dropped his bombshell about Alicia being Delia Kettle's daughter, I knew you were going to be in real danger. There wasn't time to go changing wheels.'

'Bombshell is right,' said Rosemary sombrely. 'You could have floored me with a feather.'

'We'll have to speak to Vickie as well,' Laura realised. 'After all, she's the person most affected by the whole business.'

'What a mess,' Rosemary sighed.

The doctor, whose recovery was proving to be much slower than Rosemary's, was beginning to realise that it was probably down to him to change the wheel.

'We can't just stay here,' he pointed out.

'No,' the women agreed, without moving.

'I can't help thinking how it must have looked,' he went on. 'One death, and two more narrow escapes – and every time, I'm involved. It makes me wonder whether I was guilty in some way, although I know I'm not. I haven't actually done anything wrong at all.'

'No, we know that,' Rosemary soothed him. 'You've just been very unlucky. And don't worry – You don't have to change the wheel all by yourself.'

'Oh?'

'No. Laura's nice and strong. She'll help you.'

Laura heaved a deep sigh and started to roll up her sleeves.

Rosemary seemed suddenly purposeful.

'I have two urgent tasks,' she announced. 'And I can't rest until I've done them.'

'Oh?' Laura raised her eyebrows.

'First, I still have to establish the precise problem with Daniel's trees. And second, I think I ought to go and explain everything to him. I mean, the way his wife and mother-in-law came close to murdering him – and me. I do feel I ought to talk that through with him. It's only common courtesy. And, poor chap, there isn't really anybody else now, is there. He's going to feel very bereft.'

Laura nodded. 'You're absolutely right,' she said. 'And while you're doing that, I'll go and see Vickie. The sooner the better, I suppose.'

Professor Hashim was in bed when Rosemary phoned him one last time, but he made no complaint. In fact, he had been waiting for her to get in touch, having received e-mailed reports from the laboratory at Bitterton, including images from their microscopic examinations.

'You know,' he said, 'you needn't actually have gone to all this trouble. Just knowing it was a fungus would have been enough to justify treatment.'

'You mean felling the trees and spraying the entire garden umpteen times.'

'Something like that.'

'You haven't seen the garden,' she told him. 'I want to limit the damage as far as I can.'

'Well, fortunately for you, your sentimentality might not be too misplaced.'

'It's not phytophthera then?'

'No.'

'Nor Indian Paintbrush fungus?'

'No.'

'Heart rot?'

'No.'

'So tell me. Please.'

'It's a relative of the echtomycorhizal fungus. We're still finding new variants, and it's been shown to affect temperate climate forests as well. That explains why it took hold when it somehow got transferred to you from Malaysia. Your slides show that it's mutated slightly already. But you can contain it, I think. The worst affected individuals will have to go, but if you spray with the usual fungicide, for six months or so, I think you'll conquer it. It isn't anywhere near so lethal in your latitude as it is here.'

'Thank you, Professor. Thanks a million. I owe you a favour. Fifty favours.'

He chuckled. 'I might just hold you to that,' he said.

With a feeling of relief, of a job completed and a solution arrived at, Rosemary sat back in her room at the White Hart. Her repose lasted all of two minutes, before she jumped up again. Now she had to go and see Daniel, to be by his side when the full impact of his wife's betrayal hit him.

The hospital tests had shown that Daniel's broken leg was healing quickly, that his skin was still capable of regenerating and all risk of septicaemia was past. His organs, many of which had been overloaded by the strain of his ravaged skin, were all performing normally. He long term outlook was excellent, with the only proviso that his face, hands, and other affected areas would always carry the scars of whatever had caused the skin disorder.

Nobody had yet supplied a credible answer to what this might have been. Samples were still being analysed in the hospital laboratory, but so far all remained mere speculation.

But for all these reassurances, he knew something else was going on. Something to do with Alicia and Sam's death and his own misery over the past year.

The sight of Rosemary peering tentatively around the door of his room initially boosted his spirits considerably. Then he took a proper look at her expression. She was not smiling. In fact her mouth was set in a tight line of anxiety.

'What's the matter?' he asked.

'Is it all right for me to come in?'

'Yes, yes.' He patted the edge of his bed impatiently. 'Come and tell me what in the world's been going on. I know it concerns Alicia. I can see the doctors have been told something, and nobody wants to break it to me.'

'I asked them to let me be the one,' she said gently. 'I came as soon as I could. Mind you, it isn't all bad news.'

He thumped the bed impatiently. 'Tell me the worst,' he said. 'And stop playing games.'

'I was afraid you'd say that. Look, I'm sure I'm not allowed to sit on the bed. The chair's fine.' She sat down, and shuffled slightly in a parody of somebody trying to get comfortable.

'Get on with it,' Daniel ordered her.

'Yes. Right. Um...I wish I'd brought Laura with me. She'd be much better at this than I am.'

'Rosemary!'

'Okay. Listen, Daniel. You know Alicia...'

'I ought to. She's my wife, isn't she?'

'I didn't mean that. At least, perhaps I did, in a Freudian sort of way. I mean, you obviously *don't* know her as well as you thought you did.'

Daniel thumped the bed again with a frustrated fist. 'Please! This is torture,' he begged.

'Sorry. Well, for a start, you might not have known that Mrs Potts is her mother. Alicia's. Your mother-in-law. Her real name is Delia Kettle.'

Daniel's eyes widened with shock and horror. 'No,' he whispered. 'She can't be.'

'It's true. And...well, you know Sam.' She bit her lip, with a nervous giggle. 'There I go again. This all involves Sam, you see, and how he died.'

Daniel nodded apprehensively. Rosemary gave a rapid description of what she and Laura had found in the barn, and the aggressive way Mrs Potts had driven them out at knife-point. 'The answers were all in there, as we quite soon realised,' she concluded.

'Explain,' begged Daniel.

'Dried foxgloves, hanging in bunches from the roof beams. There's only one thing foxgloves are useful for.'

'Digitalis,' supplied Daniel readily.

'Which is the source of Digoxin,' she said.

'The drug Sam was on?'

'Exactly. It seems obvious now that your house-keeper —'

'And mother-in-law,' he interrupted.

'Right. Well, she was putting digitalis in that herbal tea she kept giving him. He died because that, combined with his prescription drugs, was too much for his heart.'

'But she wasn't intending to kill him, surely? She probably thought she was helping, knowing he had a bad heart.'

Rosemary pulled a sceptical face. 'I think not, unfortunately. Not given her record. And not when you consider what she was also doing to you.'

Daniel's eyes widened. 'To me?'

'W also found large quantities of the hydrocortisone cream you were using. Laura took a bit and rubbed it on her hand. As soon as she got out into the sunlight, it came up in blisters. Then we made the connection with the giant hogweed that's growing at the end of your garden. She'd been mixing the sap with your cream – probably for months and months. That's what was wrong with you all this time.'

He closed his eyes, trying to absorb the implications. 'And that's it? That's what kept me in bed for most of the past year? And I had absolutely no idea. What a fool!'

Rosemary patted his arm consolingly, waiting for the rest of the story to fall into place for him. The worst was still to come, and she was in no rush to reveal it.

It didn't take very long. 'Alicia!' he gasped. 'What about Alicia? She couldn't possibly have realised, of course.'

Rosemary made a wry face. 'I'm so sorry, Daniel – but I'm afraid she did.'

He took a deep breath, as if bracing himself for a blow. 'The sunlamp,' he muttered. 'And the gloves she always wore. And the doctor's bewilderment at my lack of progress.'

Rosemary nodded. 'Mother and daughter were in it together.'

'But *why*? What had I ever done to them?'

'I think you were too rich for your own good,' she said. 'That sounds dreadful, I know. But there's a history, you see. They'd done it before and got away with it.'

'Done it before?' Daniel echoed, his voice choking.

'Allegedly Delia Kettle – Mrs Potts – poisoned her husband. She was acquitted at the trial, from lack of evidence, but there doesn't seem to be much real doubt about it.'

'I just thought she was obstinate, and possibly a bit loopy. Not a cold-blooded killer. And Alicia. Oh, *Alicia.*'

Over the next fifteen minutes, with Rosemary's help, he ran through the events of the past year. The bizarre course of his illness, acute one week, almost better the next, a dreadful seesaw that kept his nerves jangling and his spirits hovering agonisingly between hope and despair. Alicia's constant admonishments that they would win the fight, and emerge victorious from the struggle with whatever elusive virus or allergy was causing his ghastly symptoms. And always, hovering in the doorway with a tray of home-cooked food, or bringing up another giant tub of the everlasting hydrocortisone cream, was Mrs Potts in her ludicrous hat, smiling crazily at him.

And she had made those strange herbal concoctions for Sam, standing over him while he drank it, a manic gleam in her eye, which Daniel had always interpreted as motherly concern, or pride at her skill with therapeutic infusions. Was it really possible that she had deliberately poisoned him?

Wracked with emotion, he lay back on the pillows and let the feelings wash through him.

'You're going to be all right,' Rosemary urged him. 'You've still got that wonderful house and garden, and your business and your health restored to you. Please don't despair.'

'I need to think about Alicia. They had a plan. I see it now. Because Sam and I made reciprocal wills, each leaving our share of the house and business to the other, it made a big difference which of us died first. If it was me – and obviously that was looking more and more likely – then Sam and Vickie would benefit, and it would all go out of the hands of the Kellaways. Alicia would lose Winterbourne. How *stupid* of me to arrange it like that. I put all that temptation in her way. The poor girl. She really isn't very strong, you know, despite how it must appear.'

'No, that much is obvious now,' Rosemary nodded.

'What do you mean?'

'I'm afraid she's had some sort of collapse. A breakdown. They'll have taken her to a secure psychiatric unit, I think.'

'There! You see!' Daniel seemed almost triumphant. 'She was ill, carrying all that strain, dominated by that terrible old woman.'

Rosemary bit her tongue, badly wanting to remind Daniel of all those months of deception and betrayal. He would work it out soon enough for himself, she realised.

'Is she really insane, do you think?' he asked, after a few moments.

Rosemary spread her hands helplessly. 'I don't know,' she admitted.

'I do think she loved me at first.' He grimaced, self-mockingly. 'I have to believe that, don't I?'

'I think her mother is the real driving force. Alicia's had a lifetime of skewed upbringing, being taught that killing gets you what you want. It worked for them, you see, that first time.'

'Ah yes, the poisoned husband. Tell me about him.'

'It sounds as if he was a brute. It's only a guess, but I wouldn't be at all surprised if he was abusive to them both. So killing him was an obvious solution. His life was well insured, so they got some cash, as well as freedom from whatever he was doing to them.'

'Thanks, Rosemary,' he sighed. 'If I can hang onto that view of things, I might not feel quite so awful.'

They sat in silence for a while, each with their own thoughts about wickedness and blame and the ways of the world.

'So what's the good news?' Daniel asked suddenly, with a hint of his old self.

'Pardon?'

'You said there was good news.'

'Oh, so I did. Your trees. I've found out what's wrong with them.'

'And you can cure it?'

'Well, yes, eventually. I'll explain it all to you when I've taken you home. I think the best medicine for you now would be a summer in that fabulous garden, getting your leg mended, and ordering a whole team of menials around. You know, don't you, that bindweed can grow a centimetre a day at this time of year? If something's not done, you'll have a forest of it by midsummer.'

'You're taking me home?'

'Indeed I am. I spoke to one of your doctors before coming in, and she says you can leave tomorrow, if there's somebody on hand to look after you.'

'Oh, I've just remembered Doctor Whittaker! I have to tell him all is forgiven. Poor man! He must be feeling awful.'

Rosemary judged that this was not the moment to mention the full role that Doctor Whittaker had played in the story. The last thing Daniel needed was further proof of his wife's depravity.

Rosemary had dropped Laura at Vickie's house, on her way to the hospital, unable to give a firm time for collecting her again. 'I can stay all evening if necessary, I suppose,' said Laura, with little enthusiasm. 'Just come when you can.'

Vickie came to the door looking drawn and suspicious.

'You'll have to let me in,' Laura said. 'I'm stuck here until my lift comes back for me.'

'This is getting to be a habit,' said Vickie, with a tight smile. They both remembered the previous occasion, thinking it seemed a hundred years ago.

'Vickie, I've come to explain to you just what happened to Sam. The police will confirm it all, probably tomorrow. You can be sure they'll charge the person responsible. Justice is going to be done. I know it won't bring him back, but I think I can promise that it'll make you feel better.'

Vickie led the way into the living room, her arms wrapped tightly around herself as if cold. Laura could see that she was trembling. They sat down facing each other.

'It's Neville Grant, isn't it? He poisoned Sam.'

'Who?' Laura was utterly confused. 'Who's Neville Grant?'

'The manager of the garden centre. He wanted Sam's position in the business. He gave him some sort of pills or powders that reacted with his medication.'

Laura had to choke back the urge to laugh. She shook her head vigorously. 'No, no,' she said. 'You've got it completely wrong.'

'Have I?' Vickie scowled mutinously. 'I don't think so.'

'Honestly, Vick. Listen. The police have just left Winterbourne Manor, with the housekeeper and Alicia Kellaway in custody. It was them – don't you see? They were responsible for Sam's death.'

It took a long time to convince her friend. Nothing Laura said had ever once occurred to Vickie, and new ideas took root slowly. Eventually, light dawned. 'The bitches!' she shouted. 'They were robbing and cheating *me*, as well as murdering my darling Sam. They've left me with nothing, nobody. I thought Alicia was my *friend*.'

'They betrayed you,' Laura confirmed, holding Vickie's hand. 'It's a terrible feeling, I know.'

'Well, they won't get the better of me.'

'That's the spirit,' Laura encouraged.

The evening wore on, with Vickie see-sawing between despair and rage, panic and purposefulness. Laura made a lot of coffee, and listened patiently to the outpourings. When Rosemary finally returned to fetch her, she and Vickie were watching television, slumped exhaustedly in front of an American romance, cathartic tears running down both faces.

'Well, you two seem to be okay,' said Rosemary, with an appraising grin.

Laura and Rosemary took it in turns to push Daniel down the paths of his magnificent garden, pausing frequently to inspect the summer growth and to admire the effect. A gardener had been hired to oversee the treatment of the diseased trees, and Daniel's leg was mending well.

'I love it here,' he sighed. 'Despite everything, I find myself feeling at peace when I'm outside with all my plants. They have such a soothing effect.'

'That's the spirit,' said Rosemary. 'I can see you're going to be fine.'

'Such a shame about the avenue, though. It'll hurt to see those trees go.'

'I know,' she sympathised. 'But it won't be all of them, and you can have a think about making some changes. I was wondering whether you might like to keep a gap there – ' she pointed ' – and then if you turned that area *there* – ' she pointed again, in a new direction ' – into a sort of sunken lawn, you might find the whole things even better than before.'

Daniel followed her pointing finger, narrowing his eyes as he tried to visualise her suggestion. 'Good grief, I think you're right,' he said. 'But better than that – if we cut back some of those camellias a bit, and straightened the path...'

Laura smiled to herself and left them to it, drifting a little way down one of the side paths. The broad flights of fancy that garden design sometimes led to were beyond her expertise; she was more interested in the detail, in presenting the individual plants to their best effect and making them grow.

But Daniel was right. There was nothing so soothing as a good garden, with its scents and colours and humming vitality. There was nothing so worrying or sad that a garden couldn't do a lot to assuage.

Robin was gratifyingly sorry to see them go, when they finally packed their bags and loaded up the Land Rover. His grief made it all much harder than they'd anticipated.

The plan, originally, was for them to spend a few days with Rosemary's mother, while they decided what would happen next.

'But what *are* you going to do next?' Robin asked, more than once. By this time, he had almost their whole life stories out of them both, over some late night drinks. 'You can't just disappear over the horizon, you know.'

Laura and Rosemary looked at each other. 'We'll think of something,' said Laura.

'Yes, but *what*?' Rosemary frowned. 'I think Robin might be right. We ought to give it some thought now.'

'Come and have one last coffee,' Robin urged them. 'For old time's sake.'

They followed him back into the White Hart and sat in two of his big soft armchairs with a coffee table between them.

'So?' Rosemary prompted her friend. 'Any thoughts?'

Laura flushed slightly. 'Well, tell me if this sounds daft, but I did wonder about hiring myself out as a gardener. It's what I do best, after all. I thought perhaps somebody might give me a job, even at my age.'

'Hmmm.' Rosemary tapped her teeth. 'I think you could do a bit better than that. But I agree gardens are a good start. How about aiming a bit higher, though?'

'You mean become a tree surgeon? I'm not sure my physique is quite right for that.'

'No, you idiot.' Rosemary paused for another spell of teeth-tapping. 'How about this. The two of us could start up a business together, as garden trouble-shooters. Loads of people have problems with their gardens, after all. All sorts of things can go wrong, and I like to think I'm pretty good at solving most of them.'

'Okay,' Laura nodded slowly. 'So what's my role in this?'

'Come on!' Rosemary widened her eyes. 'Where would I have been without you? It's vital to have somebody to give a different viewpoint, to bounce ideas off – and to do at least half the donkey work.'

'I thought you might say that.'

Robin came in with a tray of coffee things, as well as his best chocolate biscuits. 'Any luck?' he asked.

They updated him on their thoughts so far.

'Brilliant!' he enthused. 'Perfect! All you need now is a name.'

'Pardon?' said Rosemary.

'You can't set up in business without a name. After all, your first step is to place some adverts in the county magazines, *Home and Country*, that sort of thing. Or do I mean *House and Garden*? Whatever, you've got to have a name.'

'Well, Thyme and Boxer,' I suppose, said Rosemary.

'Or how about The Plant Protectors?' suggested Robin, backing away as both women howled in derision. 'No, well. I never was any good as that sort of thing.'

'Maybe something a bit more friendly, like Laura and Rosemary,' said Laura. 'That's not bad.'

Rosemary regarded her with widening eyes. 'We're missing the obvious,' she said. 'Don't tell me you can't see it.'

Robin and Laura looked at her blankly. 'Tell us,' Laura invited. 'We're much too thick to guess.'

'There's only one possible answer,' Rosemary teased. 'Think about it.' She began to mouth her own name, pointing first to herself, then to Laura.

Laura's face relaxed into a wide smile. 'Oh yes,' she laughed. 'Now I see.'

Together they recited loudly: 'Rosemary and Thyme!'

07929387697